"My favorite Maggie Brendan book to date! Fun and fast-paced, *A Sweet Misfortune* will hold you captive with its colorful Western setting and cast of memorable characters. Rachel is no ordinary heroine—and John is much more than a handsome hero! Woven within this heartfelt story is a beautiful thread of faith and love that is timeless, sure to win readers of all ages. Well done!"

—**Laura Frantz**, author of *The Mistress of Tall Acre*

Praise for *The Trouble with Patience*

"The compelling first installment in bestselling inspirational author Brendan's new Virtues and Vices of the Old West series, this is a sweet love story with plenty of nods to the iconic Old West, complete with gunslingers, vigilante posses, and breathless shootouts . . . The perfect Christian romance blend."

—*Booklist*

"Brendan (Heart of the West series) delivers a charmingly quirky and endearing romance that reveals how love and faith can heal two damaged souls. Rendering skillfully depicted protagonists and an authentic Western sense of place, she provides plenty of pleasant escape reading."

—*Library Journal*

"Maggie Brendan pens an entertaining romance set in my home state of Montana. She takes the reader on a delightful tale of love, betrayal, and intrigue that will keep you turning the pages. If you're looking for a good book to curl up with, *The Trouble with Patience* will fit the bill nicely."

—**Tracie Peterson**, bestselling, award-winning author of over one hundred novels, including *A Moment in Time*

"Patience is the perfect protagonist for this story—spunky enough to hold her own against the cowboys and gold miners of 1866 Montana."

—*RT Book Reviews*, 4½ stars

A SWEET MISFORTUNE

Books by Maggie Brendan

Heart of the West

No Place for a Lady
The Jewel of His Heart
A Love of Her Own

The Blue Willow Brides

Deeply Devoted
Twice Promised
Perfectly Matched

Virtues and Vices of the Old West

The Trouble with Patience
A Sweet Misfortune

Virtues
AND **VICES**
OF THE
OLD WEST

BOOK 2

A SWEET

Misfortune

A NOVEL

MAGGIE BRENDAN

Revell

a division of Baker Publishing Group
Grand Rapids, Michigan

Published by Revell
a division of Baker Publishing Group
P.O. Box 6287, Grand Rapids, MI 49516-6287
www.revellbooks.com

Printed in the United States of America

Library of Congress Cataloging-in-Publication Data
Brendan, Maggie.
    A sweet misfortune : a novel / Maggie Brendan.
        pages ; cm. — (Virtues and vices of the old West ; book 2)
    ISBN 978-0-8007-2265-4 (pbk.)
    1. Frontier and pioneer life—Montana—Fiction. 2. Man-woman
relationships—Fiction. 3. Ranches—Montana—Fiction. I. Title.
PS3602.R4485S94 2015
813'.6—dc23   2015032723

16 17 18 19 20 21 22   7 6 5 4 3 2 1

For Bruce and his support,
but most of all for his love.

[Jesus] said to them, "Watch out!
Be on your guard against all kinds of greed;
life does not consist
in an abundance of possessions."

LUKE 12:15

1

Paradise Valley
Cottonwood, Montana Territory
September 1862

John McIntyre reined in his horse along the ridge above Cottonwood Creek overlooking Paradise Valley below. The vista before him never failed to impress him, and this perfect fall day with its cloudless sky was no exception. He fished inside his leather vest pocket for a piece of paper and read it for the third time.

> *I need your help, John. After I left Paradise Valley, I received a letter from my sister, Rachel, that has me very disturbed. She is now working in a saloon called the Wild Horse as a dance hall girl. You have to get her out of that situation until I can return. I'm begging you, do what needs to be done—horse-tie her if you have to. And knowing her fiery disposition, you might have to. Get her out of there before it's too late to save her*

reputation. With all your connections, maybe you can find her a decent job.

> *Your friend,*
> *Preston Matthews*

John sighed, wishing he didn't have to get tangled up in a situation not of his own doing, and he stuffed the letter back into his vest pocket. He'd known Preston a long time and didn't want to let his friend down. A saloon was no place for Preston's sister. John hadn't seen Rachel since she was a gangly adolescent and he'd already graduated from high school. Would he even recognize her now? He remembered a time when they'd argued at a church picnic after he didn't want to enter the potato sack race with a girl. She could never take no for an answer.

With a gentle tug of the reins, he turned Cutter in the direction of the trail into Cottonwood. He wanted to get this done and get back to his ranch on the outskirts of town as quickly as possible—and he only knew of one way to do it.

John made his way through dust-filled Main Street, hearing piano music coming from the saloon long before he reached the hitching post. He dismounted, then stepped aside to let two drunks stagger through the swinging café doors. They dissolved into laughter and slapped one another on the back. The odor of liquor was strong, and he wondered how on earth a man could derive any pleasure from imbibing and losing control. He preferred to stay in control . . . most of the time.

He strode into the Wild Horse, his senses assaulted with the buzz of activity and music. There were girls dancing on a small stage, twirling about in scanty satin outfits, their bare legs kicking high into the air while they kept time with the beat of the banged-out notes of the piano. He scanned the room quickly, noticing men oblivious to the dance hall girls while they concentrated on their cards. He was surprised it was crowded this early—it wasn't even dark yet.

John looked from left to right at the young dancers' faces until he spotted Rachel. He strode to the stage and in one leap was in the middle of them, ignoring someone who yelled for him to get down. After lifting a strawberry blonde off her feet, he moved down to the floor again.

"What the devil do you think you're doing?" The young girl thrashed about and pushed against his chest.

"Rachel, you need to come with me NOW!" he ordered.

"I'm not Rachel, you fool! Let go of me." She twisted away. "I doubt Rachel's gonna let you manhandle her either!" She giggled, covering her mouth in an attempt to hide the gap between her teeth.

"Beggin' your pardon, ma'am," he said, stepping back before swinging his line of vision across the stage floor to peer at each painted face.

Some of the ladies were still dancing, but one stopped—placing her hands on her hips and glaring at him. *That's Rachel!* In two strides he was up the steps on the stage and lifting her unceremoniously to his shoulder, despite the pounding of her fists on his back and unintelligible mutters under her breath. The music stopped and the piano player stood up. "Where do you think you're going with Rachel?"

"Move aside, man," he said, pushing his way through the crowd who stood by watching. "Don't get in the way of a lovers' quarrel."

"I ain't never seed you here 'afore," a snaggletoothed patron sputtered.

"Let me go, you brute!" the lady yelled, kicking her heels in the air.

John ignored her protest, continuing on past the café doors and straight to his horse. He straddled Cutter and, holding tightly to Rachel, settled her on his saddle. One swift kick in the side of his horse, and they galloped off—leaving bystanders in a cloud of thick dust.

Rachel had no choice but to hang on for dear life while she considered her options: jump off and risk a broken neck, or wait until the crazed cowboy came to his senses—which she hoped would be any moment now. He smelled of sunshine and the outdoors mixed with the peculiar smell of his worn leather vest, and despite her predicament, she found herself mystified by this man.

There was something vaguely familiar about his tall, dark looks and penetrating eyes that held hers briefly before he'd reached for her. Had she met him before? Perhaps he'd been to the saloon before. Why couldn't she remember? *Lord, help me get away!* Her heart thumped hard against her ribs.

The landscape rushed past, and she closed her eyes to keep from getting dizzy until the horse began slowing. She opened her eyes to see they were at someone's home. Before her sprawled a two-story Victorian ranch house, smoke curling from its chimney. Nearby were a large barn and corrals— some with horses and cattle being tended by ranch hands. A sheepdog rushed up to greet them as the cowboy slid off the horse's back. *Well, at least he didn't take me to a deserted hideout to be his slave!*

"Stay back, Winchester." The dog sat next to his master with his tail curled, and the cowboy turned to stare up at her briefly, holding out his hands to assist her down. Instead of accepting his help, Rachel abruptly slid forward onto the saddle, grabbed the reins, then slapped the horse's flanks and raced out of the front yard in the direction they'd come. She barely glanced back but saw the cowboy with his jaw dropped.

Teach him to snatch a lady! she thought with a chuckle. Suddenly there was a whistle from behind her and the horse came to a screeching halt. Despite her pull on the reins and another swift kick in his ribs, the horse wouldn't budge. She muttered under her breath when she observed two ranch hands on horseback approaching her. There was no way out—the horse obediently turned around, trotting straight back to his master, who stood with hands on his hips and a dark look directed right at her.

John sighed and looked up at Rachel's face, which was red with anger. He knew Cutter would listen to his commands, but he had to admire her—she had tried—and he supposed if it were him, he would've done the same thing. He walked over, taking the reins and giving Cutter an affectionate pat on his head. "Good boy."

"Why don't you let me help you down and then we'll talk."

"WE have *nothing* to talk about!" she spat out. When she turned her nose up in the air like she was the queen of England, he laughed out loud.

"Suit yourself, but you're going to get mighty tired sittin' up there, and I believe supper is being held for us." By now, more than a few of the ranch hands had sauntered over to see what was taking place, and stared at the pretty lady in her satin outfit.

"Meet Rachel Matthews, men. She'll be staying with us for a while—"

"I will not!" Rachel sputtered, sliding off the horse to confront him, feet apart, her thin arms akimbo. She looked rather ridiculous in the frilly purple satin can-can skirt, high-top heels, and messy hair. "You had no right to bring me here and I demand that you find a horse to take me back to Cottonwood." A snicker filtered out through the small bunch of hands, and she glared at them.

One bowlegged cowboy swept off his hat and bowed slightly. "Pardon me, ma'am, but I don't think you're gonna fit in with the bunch here lessin' you know how to rope a steer!" The others guffawed and slapped their thighs.

"No thanks to you loggerheads—none of you are even man enough to stop this brute from kidnapping me!"

"Never interfere with a man and his lady when they're in a spat, is my motto," another cowpuncher added.

The cowhand's comment seemed to infuriate her even more. "I'm *not* his lady!"

John watched as Rachel rolled her eyes, then folded her arms across her chest. He could tell she was not in the least bit flattered by their attention, and he hadn't wanted to embarrass her. His eyes flicked over her willowy form and the pretty face underneath all the paint and powder. It was hard to believe she'd grown into such a beautiful young woman. *Wonder why Preston never told me what a pretty young lady she's become?* He shifted his weight from one hip to the other. "You men go on about your business now." The punchers shuffled out of the yard leaving the two of them to battle it out.

He stepped forward to take Rachel's hand but she snatched it away. "Rachel, if you'll step inside, I'll explain everything to you."

"How do you know my name?" She tapped her foot in the dirt. "And what do you want from me?" Her eyes snapped in anger. "I demand to know your name and why you've kidnapped me!"

"I choose to call it a *rescue*. My name is John McIntyre, and I own this ranch. Your brother, Preston, wrote and asked me to rescue you from the Wild Horse to protect you from that unscrupulous lifestyle."

Her head thrust upward in surprise. "Preston? You've heard from Preston?" It was almost a whisper. For a moment her face softened and she seemed to forget her anger at him.

"Yes. Now, will you please come inside and we'll have supper and talk?" He was pleading with her, which was against his nature. What had he gotten himself mixed up with? On any ordinary evening he would have been long finished with supper and sitting by the fire with a good book, or planning the next day with Estelle, his grandmother, or discussing ranch work with Curtis, his foreman. He was beginning to get impatient with this painted lady from the Wild Horse.

Reluctantly, Rachel nodded. "I don't plan on being here for longer than I must, so you'd better explain what *you* have to do with my brother."

"Fair enough." John motioned for her to go ahead of him up the steps to the front door, then reached over and opened it for her. A light scent of rosewater tickled his nostrils as she walked past him, and he wondered how many men had held her in their arms . . . He shook himself, clearing away the thought. What she'd done in the past didn't involve him one bit!

2

Rachel stepped inside and knew immediately this was not an ordinary rancher's home. Large and spacious, it spoke of wealth and a woman's touch, from the fresh cut flowers on the hall table, to the chintz-covered chairs she glimpsed in the living room, to the delicious smells of food wafting from the dining room. So Mr. McIntyre was married? She breathed a sigh of relief and then realized he was speaking to her.

"While you're here, please make yourself comfortable—"

"I hardly see how that can happen when you have taken me captive!" Rachel held her fists to her side, though she'd rather take a slug at him instead.

"Believe me, if your brother hadn't written to me begging for help, I'd never even know you were alive."

"It might be better that way. There was no need for you to involve yourself." Rachel caught his steady gaze studying her.

"I'm sure I'm going to regret doing so." He shifted on one leg, arms folded across his chest.

"Then why on earth would you agree to help?"

"I paid the back taxes on his land for two years to keep

the bank from foreclosing on him. We had a bargain that if he could scrape up enough to pay me back after two years, the ranch would return to him."

Rachel took a deep breath and blew the air out from her bottom lip, sending her bangs fluttering. "You mean foreclosing on *us*. That ranch was half mine. He had no right to make that arrangement without my signature too." Her voice was loud even to her ears.

"Hold on now—I didn't see your name anywhere on that deed."

"I don't understand. I'm certain my father left it to both of us."

"Did you actually see that in writing?" He unfolded his arms, giving her a curious stare.

Rachel held a hand to her waist to still her fast breathing. "Well, no. There was no need. I trusted my father's word . . . and Preston."

"Then you can take that up with him when—*if*—he returns."

She glared at him. "I'm sure if Preston said he'd return, then he *will*—with most of the money to pay you back. And I can add my savings as well," Rachel confirmed with more conviction than she truly felt. Hadn't Preston made enough money to return by now? And why hadn't he come to rescue her if her job was so distasteful to him?

"We'll see about that. His time is running out." He made a move toward the hallway door. "Right through here." He pointed in the direction of the dining room and she went ahead. "Grams, we have a guest for dinner," he said softly to an older lady sitting at the head of the table.

The older lady with her gray, wavy hair cocked an eyebrow

as Rachel entered the room, her pale-blue eyes taking in Rachel's entire visage.

"Mmm, I can see that." Her wrinkled face softened suddenly. "Please, John, show her where she can freshen up. I'm sure she feels the need. Then I'll have Annabelle serve our plates. A few more minutes won't matter, will it?" she asked with a brief smile at her grandson. "And it wouldn't hurt you to wash up as well," she added as he bent to kiss her temple.

Rachel felt awkward but allowed John to lead the way. Fresh thick towels hung on brass rings next to the porcelain pedestal sink. She picked up a cake of lavender soap, breathing in the wonderful scent, and washed up. She peered at her reflection in the mirror, horrified. Land of Goshen! Her ruby lipstick was smeared across her cheek, and her wheat-colored hair looked as though it had seen a threshing machine. Quickly she tried to smooth the unruly curls into place, but with so many missing pins it was useless. The red rose in her hair looked ridiculous, so she yanked it out and then tried to pull the top of her sleeveless silk bodice up higher over her exposed bosom. Suddenly she felt embarrassed at the sight. What had become of her? How had she gotten to this point? *Lord, help me get away from this insane circumstance.*

Maybe this was the best time to sneak out the back door. But as soon as she turned the knob, John faced her from the hallway, tossing her a dress.

"Grams said for you to put this on for the time being—"

"But—"

"One thing I should warn you about—no one argues with Grams's common sense. Put it on, please," he said, then closed the door.

Rachel slipped off her thin, shiny garment and donned

the simple linsey-woolsey dress the color of dirt that did nothing for her complexion and hung on her like a sack. His wife must've been larger or with child. She sighed heavily. Anyway, it was better than what he dragged her here in. She slowly opened the door to face him.

"Ready now?" he asked. His steely dark eyes penetrated hers, and for a moment she could hardly breathe as an unsettling tangle of emotions struck her. He stood gun-barrel straight as if he'd already anticipated she might try to bolt.

3

Rachel straightened her shoulders and tried to look dignified, then nodded with acquiescence to the cowboy. She walked straight to the dining room, head held high. Her stomach growled noisily, and the food looked amazingly appetizing as the cook—who stared at her with large round eyes—laid plates on the table. She went on serving John's grandmother as if inviting a dance hall girl for dinner was an everyday occurrence.

John pulled out a chair for Rachel before taking his seat at the other end opposite his grandmother.

"John, please introduce your friend," his grandmother said with a smile directed at Rachel.

"Meet Rachel Matthews, Grams. Rachel, this is my grandmother, Estelle." He held Rachel's eyes then lifted his water glass.

Grams said, "Glad to make your acquaintance, Rachel—even if it is under rather unusual circumstances. However, I trust my grandson implicitly."

"He can't keep me here against my will." Rachel glared at him.

Estelle nodded. "And I shall see that he doesn't. Let's say grace, and then John, I expect you to tell us why you've dragged this very pretty girl here in the first place."

The older lady's kindness was not what Rachel expected. His grandmother seemed to be a woman of decency, she thought as she bowed her head. At the very least she decided she would stay and eat.

John cleaned his plate first, then began his explanation. "I've known your brother, Preston, for years. So when he received your letter saying that you worked at the Wild Horse, he wrote begging me to get you outta there." He ran his hand through his thick hair and continued. "I couldn't let a friend of mine down. Simple as that. That's also why I helped him out to keep the bank from foreclosing on him."

"And *I* told you that half the ranch belonged to me!" Rachel choked out. "It belonged to both of us. He never told me who the person was that bought the ranch from him to keep the bank from foreclosing on us, only that we had to move into the boardinghouse until he came back . . ." Her voice trailed off sadly while she looked down at her fork.

"As I mentioned, I don't recall seeing your name on the deed, just Preston's. Our agreement was that he could buy it back at any time within the first two years, but apparently he hasn't struck any gold mine, and his time is running out."

"What do you mean, John?" Grams asked with a concerned look shadowing her wrinkled face.

"I have plans to stock more cattle on that land eventually, since it's perfect grazing." He felt sorry for Rachel, but it was business and all legal. "Look, I'm really sorry, Rachel. I didn't even know you still lived in Cottonwood. I reckon I hadn't seen you since you were about eleven. I figured you'd married and moved away and had a passel of kids."

"I see. Well, you and Preston seem to have a lot of opinions about my life. You ripped me off the stage where I was performing, then expect me to be happy about it. Really! I do have a mind and can make my own decisions regardless of what Preston thinks is best for me!" Rachel shoved her chair back to leave, but Grams reached over to touch her on the arm.

"Please, do finish your dinner, Rachel. I'm sure my grandson doesn't mean to insult your intelligence. Let's all sort this out and see what can be done." She gave Rachel a reassuring look. "Your brother wants only the best for you, I'm sure." Her tone was low and comforting. "And we want to help in any way that we can."

John breathed a huge sigh of relief as Rachel took her seat again. Grams could talk the devil into doing her bidding. There was a way about Grams that couldn't be denied, and he loved her deeply for it.

He watched Rachel pick at her food. She finally started eating while Grams talked about the possibility of her staying for the time being just to be safe.

"I'm not sure what you mean by 'safe.' I *was* safe and earning enough money to save some, and with Preston's we might have enough to buy our land back. Fortunately, there was no harm done to me."

"I did you a big favor by getting you out of the Wild Horse." John shook his head briefly to clear it. Didn't she see what living with soiled doves and gamblers could do to damage her life? If they hadn't already. She was one determined lady, that was for sure. Pity the man that would have his heart broken by her. All they'd have to do is get lost in her golden eyes. It was the one thing he recalled about her growing up—those penetrating, pensive eyes. He decided he would try not to engage in much eye contact and save himself the trouble of falling for her.

"Isn't that right, John?"

"What? I'm sorry, Grams. Were you talking to me?" John jerked his attention to his grandmother.

"I said Rachel could have a few days to stay here then decide what she wants to do. Perhaps find a more lucrative job, such as work for my millinery shop in town."

"Not a bad idea—or she can stay here at the ranch and help out around here. Anything is better than working in a saloon."

Grams nodded. "I can use more help in my shop since more folks are flocking into Cottonwood every day."

"Do you think you can train her about millinery stuff? It's not as though she's the type of girl that'd know anything about that."

"Yes. I can teach her all she needs to know."

Rachel seemed to bristle. "Don't you have a wife to help you manage the ranch? Isn't this her dress?"

"No. That dress didn't belong to her—what I mean is no, I'm not married." John swallowed hard. Outside the dining room window, he heard the chimes singing in the wind and a bitter sweetness hit him in the chest as swift as a horse's hoof.

They continued to discuss the details as though Rachel wasn't present. Finally her nerves were stretched to the brink, and she found herself wondering what type of girl John *thought* she was.

"Could you please stop talking about me and the plans you're making as though I'm not even in the room," Rachel said, clenching her fork and knife.

John and Estelle stopped talking and openly stared at her.

"I beg your pardon, Rachel," Estelle said quickly. "I never meant to make you feel more uncomfortable than you already do. Some of what John says makes sense. Will you stay a day or two to think about it? Then if you feel you need to go back to Cottonwood, I'm sure he won't stand in your way. What do you say?"

She looked at Rachel with warmth in her aging eyes, but when Rachel glanced at John, a small twitch on the edge of his mouth gave away his amusement at the whole scene. Maybe she should stay just to prove to him what kind of girl she really was. Estelle's cajoling struck a chord in her heart. The old lady really seemed to care what happened to her.

"Okay." Rachel took a deep breath and agreed to the compromise—she'd take a few days to think over Estelle's offer to work at her shop in Cottonwood. The offer *did* pique her interest, not that she had much knowledge about fashion, but she could learn. And in her heart she knew it was better than working at the Wild Horse while fending off groping hands, slobbering drunks, and card sharks—not to mention dealing with the squabbling ladies working there.

She liked Estelle right away. The fact that she would give Rachel a chance to work for her really touched her heart, but she had no intention of staying here long. After all, Estelle didn't know her from Adam.

After dinner the housekeeper, who had been introduced to Rachel as Annabelle, directed her up the broad staircase and down the hallway, showing Rachel to her room. "If there's

anything you need, please let me know," she said at the doorway. "You'll find a fresh change of clothing and sundry items
in the wardrobe."

"Annabelle—there is one thing I'd like to ask you."

"Yes?" She paused with her hand on the doorknob.

"Whose dress am I wearing? Mr. McIntyre said he wasn't
married." It had been apparent that John was deeply sad
when she'd asked if he had a wife.

Annabelle took a deep breath before answering in a solemn
tone. "It was Miss Lura's . . . but she's gone now. I suggest
you ask Mr. John or Miss Estelle about that." And before
Rachel could say another word, Annabelle was gone. She
wondered what was the mystery surrounding Lura. She remembered Lura when they were in school but lost track of
her after graduation. Though they weren't close friends, she
was beautiful and popular and always treated everyone kindly.

Rachel clapped her hands with delight when she turned
around to see the spacious room with its four-poster bed and
large windows. It was too dark to see outside now, but the
room seemed to overlook a field or pasture. She would be able
to tell in the morning. The bed was covered in a luxurious
rose brocade coverlet with matching sheets and fluffy pillows
that beckoned to her weary body and soul.

She quickly undid the high button dress shoes and wiggled
her toes with relief, still surveying her temporary quarters.
The room had a fresh smell of beeswax and lemon and the
wood gleamed from a recent waxing. A small lady's desk sat
near the windows and she ran her hand over the scrollwork.
It was such a beautiful piece. Apparently either John or his
grandmother had spared no expense in decorating their home,
and Rachel felt like a princess about to wake up from a dream.

27

In a matter of moments she had donned the linen gown laid out for her on the bed and hurriedly sank into its comfort, happy to be off her feet.

She sighed contentedly before her heavy eyelids dropped, her thoughts about her dear brother's concern for her. She wished he'd been the one to rescue her instead of the cowboy with the brooding eyes. She could get lost in them if she wasn't careful.

4

Rachel had never felt more rested than she did the next morning. This was partly due to the fact she'd slept in a wonderful bed, but most of it came from feeling secure in a real home. Many nights after dancing she'd been waylaid by men who wanted more than to watch her dance, and more than once she'd slept with one eye open. She'd had some close calls with men, and somehow had been able to fend them off. But the game was wearing thin. Now she'd miraculously been given a choice, even though previously she hadn't been able to find employment in the small town of Cottonwood. John's offer was beginning to appeal to her—at least until Preston returned.

Hurrying to fasten the bodice of a sensible day dress that she found hanging in the wardrobe, she then clipped her hair into a neat chignon—a task made more difficult with her nervous fingers. She found a pair of boots that fit her almost perfectly. The house was very quiet, which told her she'd slept much later than normal. Perhaps later she could have a snack, as it was much too late for breakfast.

Rachel pulled the curtains back and peered out the window. She was correct in assuming it faced a lush pasture edged with large trees. One lone horse ran free, his mane flying with the wind before he abruptly stopped and eyed her with a snort. He was a beautiful stallion about seventeen hands high. She used to love riding horses on her father's ranch and missed it now.

She couldn't wait to take a walk outdoors, so she scooted down the stairs and, finding no one in sight, started for the pasture. The bright September sun glanced off the leaves swaying in the gentle morning breeze. Freedom at last! A couple of passing cowboys on horseback lifted their hats in greeting, and she nodded with a tight smile before looking away.

When she rounded the side of the house, she saw the beautiful horse peacefully grazing. She marched straight up to the wooden fence and the horse lifted his head high, shaking it in greeting. He was a fine specimen of horseflesh. Preston would have been impressed.

Rachel stepped onto the second fence rail, hoping that with her whispers the horse would walk over. He took a few steps in her direction, seeming unsure, and she called out softly, "Don't be afraid, boy." The stallion gave a low whinny and slowly approached the fence.

Rachel tucked her skirts between her legs and climbed onto the top rail in case the stallion made a move to come closer. To her delight, he did. She hoped the horse sensed there was nothing to fear from her and reached out to stroke his forelock gently. "You're a fine one, aren't you?"

"Yes, he is," a voice behind her said. Startled, she began to lose her balance in the tangle of her skirts. A strong arm reached out to steady her—John's, she discovered—and she held on to him, feeling the strength of his muscles beneath his chambray shirt. She could feel the warmth of his breath this close, so unlike that of the drunks every night who dared to whisper in her ear. His breath smelled of fresh mint—pleasant.

"I didn't mean to surprise you, but I'm glad to see that you're finally up," he said with a crooked smile.

Rachel jerked her hand away from his arm. "Of course I'm up. Why wouldn't I be?" She could feel her face burn with him standing so close, knowing full well that she'd overslept.

"Oh. Maybe because you were tired? There's nothing wrong with that."

They stood watching the horse trot away from them. "I'm rather surprised that he would even let you get near him. He's more of a one-owner horse and doesn't cotton to others."

"He's very beautiful, and I like horses. What's his name?"

"Midnight."

"Next time, I shall bring him a treat . . . if that's all right with you." She turned to look at him. His dark eyes looked into hers thoughtfully. Suddenly she was struck by his handsome, chiseled features and the tan, outdoorsy depth to his skin.

"Does that mean you're thinking of staying until we hear from Preston?" His gaze held hers for a moment before she looked back out to the pasture where the stallion romped.

"Maybe. I have to admit, last night was the first time in ages I've really slept all night." Rachel turned to face him. "What I'd like to know is how my brother talked you into this."

John looked out over the pasture, propping his arms up on the top rail. Rachel realized how tall he was, and slim. "It's wasn't that hard . . . a damsel in distress, or so he said."

"I see. Did Preston say when he would be returning?"

"Unfortunately, no, but I wired him back that I would watch

over you until he returned. He's hoping to have enough to buy the land back, but I'm not holding my breath on that one."

"You just might be surprised. With what I've saved and what he can add, we might have enough between us."

John dropped his arms and looked her square in the eye, his jaw twitching. "Not if he doesn't get here before our bargain expires."

"You'd do that?" Rachel's heart beat hard in her throat.

"It's just good business, missy—has nothing to do with you. After all, I paid the taxes fair and square so the bank wouldn't grab it."

"I'm supposed to be grateful that you rescued us? Why didn't Preston tell me about this 'bargain' between the two of you?"

John stood with his hands on his narrow hips. "How should I know? As I said, I wasn't aware that you were anywhere around. A beautiful woman like you would normally be married with a couple of kids clinging to her skirts and one on her hip. Why don't you write and ask him?"

"I did write—many times—but he didn't write back." Rachel stared down at the grass under her feet. It hurt her that Preston didn't write and she made up excuses for him, but her patience was wearing thin.

John cleared his throat and shot a glance at her. "Would you like to get a bite to eat since you missed breakfast? I could have Annabelle rustle up something."

His warm eyes on hers made Rachel's breathing shallow. What the devil was happening? *I barely know him! I don't need to know him.*

"I don't want to put Annabelle out. I'll be fine until dinnertime."

They turned around at the sound of a buggy coming up the lane to the house. Rachel shielded her eyes with her hand but couldn't tell who was in it.

"It's Grams. I think she wanted to take you for a ride around the place today while the weather is so nice."

Estelle drew the horse up sharply near them and called out, "Rachel, come along and take a ride with me. Annabelle has packed a lunch for us."

How could she say no to Estelle's cheery disposition? John followed her over to the smart black carriage and assisted her up on the seat next to Estelle.

"John, don't you have something better to do than stand about all day lollygagging with a pretty lady?" Estelle teased. "How about you go back to the Wild Horse and fetch the rest of Rachel's belongings?"

John grinned and pulled his gloves out of his back pocket, pausing a moment to put them on. "Matter of fact, I was just going to saddle up Cutter and ride out to check on the boys repairing the fence line, and then I'll take care of getting your things, Rachel. Enjoy your tour of the ranch, and maybe I'll see about you riding Midnight sometime."

"I'd appreciate that, John," Rachel said.

John's lingering gaze on Rachel, which she seemed oblivious to, wasn't lost on Estelle's keen eye. She tapped the reins lightly across the mare's back and with a jiggle of the harness, the two set off down the lane farther away from the ranch to enjoy the crisp fall air.

5

The ladies enjoyed the ride in comfortable silence for a few moments, neither wanting to break the serenity, but Estelle, being a no-nonsense woman, finally spoke. "Rachel, I want to get right to the point. We don't know each other, but I want to offer my assistance in any way I can. A young woman like yourself shouldn't be alone in a cow town like Cottonwood, and I shudder to think of you working in a saloon."

"It's not as bad as it could be, and I appreciate your kindness, but I really don't see why it matters at all to you. Did you know my parents?" Rachel's brow knit together in question.

"No, I didn't. But since your brother is a friend to my grandson and wrote to him for help, then naturally, I care what happens to you. I don't take that sort of thing lightly." Estelle steered the horse around uneven ground as they bumped along. Now that she'd driven off the dirt lane, she needed to pay close attention to the land ahead. She was too old to fall off a carriage now or it'd be the end of her for sure . . . just like Lura. She shook her head—it wouldn't do to start thinking about that now. Estelle sensed Rachel's gaze on her.

"If you've lived here for years, I'm baffled as to why you didn't know my parents before they died," Rachel said.

"I only came to live in Paradise Valley after my husband died. I was still in good health, and felt like John needed me and Wyoming didn't. John's father, Milton, was the apple of my eye. His wife, Charlotte, died not long after he did—from pneumonia or a broken heart, I'm not entirely sure which. Life can be really hard sometimes." She paused, then asked, "What happened to your parents, if you don't mind me asking, Rachel?"

Rachel fidgeted on the seat, and Estelle decided she should've waited until Rachel felt comfortable around her to ask such a personal question.

"They both died of cholera," Rachel said matter-of-factly, showing no emotion when Estelle sneaked a sideways glance at her.

"I'm sorry. I remember reading about how quickly people died from cholera. How were you and Preston able to escape it?"

Rachel glanced around at her. "Divine intervention, I guess you could say. Preston and I were both shipped off to stay with our aunt and uncle in North Dakota for the summer to help them on their potato farm." Rachel took a deep breath. "My aunt wouldn't let us return home until nearly fall to be sure we were safe and the outbreak was nearly eradicated. Preston and I pretty much took care of the ranch, but we got behind on everything, including the taxes."

"Oh, I see—"

"No, you don't see. You don't know what it's like to lose your parents, then your livelihood, and then your home!"

Estelle felt sorry for the young lady, and her outburst and accusation stung, but it wouldn't do any good to go into that now, so she merely replied, "Maybe I can relate more than you know. Try to remember, Rachel, I'm a friend and not your enemy."

Stopping the carriage, Estelle gestured with a wave of her hand. "This gives the best view of the ranch and surrounding land that John has acquired. You can't see your place from here, but I'm sure your brother will return to repay the taxes to John soon, and then you'll be back at your home place."

Cattle dotted the grasslands below with ranch hands scattered about tending them, along with the sheepdogs. The valley was still green enough for grazing, but a change in weather could happen at any time in Montana. Estelle enjoyed helping John oversee the large cattle ranch and was glad that she'd come to live here. Lately, she'd spent plenty of time praying for the right woman to come along for John. He needed a woman in his life—something to center his life around besides becoming one of the largest cattle barons in Montana—and she wouldn't mind having great-grandchildren too.

She looked over at Rachel still taking in the scene before her. Her profile allowed Estelle a chance to observe her fine bone structure with long lashes brushing the tops of her cheeks and a perfect small nose. Her wheat-colored hair had abundant curls, and she had deep-set golden-brown eyes underneath her naturally arching eyebrows. When she turned to face her, Rachel's full lips gave Estelle a friendly smile, which Estelle returned. *She could make any man's blood percolate, and maybe she did at the Wild Horse.* Estelle wondered . . .

"It's something, isn't it?" Without waiting for an answer, Estelle turned the buggy and trotted the horse to the nearest shade tree. "Ahh, the perfect place to have the lunch that Annabelle packed for us." She stopped the buggy underneath a large cottonwood tree, climbed down, then reached in the back for the basket of food and her gun. Rachel followed her and the two of them spread a woolen blanket on the grass to share.

"You open the basket and let's see what Annabelle packed for us. I'm ravenous," Estelle said, laying her gun within reach and catching Rachel's eyes grow large at the sight of it.

"It's always better to be armed out here in the wild country," she said to reassure her. "Varmints and thieves alike in these parts."

The older lady's affability made Rachel curious about Estelle and she wanted to know more about her. *But will I be here long enough to get to know her?* She wasn't sure of anything, but an unplanned picnic outdoors on a gorgeous day suited her just fine!

As Rachel dug into the basket, she could hear the cattle bawling and a distant cowpoke's whistle or an occasional hoot. It brought to mind the smaller herd her family used to own—long ago. Her stomach growled, reminding her she hadn't eaten.

"Looks like roast beef sandwiches and apple pie slices to me," Estelle confirmed after removing the cloth napkin. "And she packed some apple cider in a jar, too. Let's bless the food so we can eat. I'm hungry."

Once Estelle said grace, Rachel unwrapped her sandwich, taking a small bite. It was so delicious! "Either Annabelle is a good cook or I'm just starving." Estelle nodded in answer, her mouth full.

"I promise not to sleep late tomorrow. I was exhausted last night." She paused from eating a moment. "Estelle, were you serious when you said I could come to work for you in your millinery shop?" Although the possibility wouldn't leave Rachel's mind and the thought of going back to dance at the saloon held little appeal, she wasn't sure she wanted to rush into anything.

Estelle patted her mouth with a napkin before answering. "Of course I was or I wouldn't have mentioned it. I believe you'll catch on quickly. You can start tomorrow if you think you want to stay here. You could try working three days a week, which would give you time here on the ranch to help John—though I doubt he needs it. It could help you in ranching in the long run . . . when you're able to get your land back. You can stay in the same room you're currently using unless you decide otherwise."

"I'd like to give it a try. It beats what I was doing, even if I was being paid decently. There was nothing else available for me at the time. What sort of things could I possibly help John with on the ranch? He already has plenty of help with all the ranch hands, it seems."

Estelle gave a small laugh. "I'm sure he and I can find things to keep you busy. He could certainly use help with his bookkeeping if you are good at figures."

Rachel quirked an eyebrow at the older lady. "I am, but I can hardly see him allowing me to work on his books."

"Don't be too sure. My eyesight is not what it used to be nor do I have the slightest desire to keep his books in order. I shall ask him myself. Now we need to decide on your salary."

"Perhaps you should wait until you see if you are pleased with my work first—say, a few days."

Estelle shook her head. "Oh, I have no doubt that you're bright enough to learn the business quickly."

They agreed on an amount for salary that Rachel considered to be more than generous. Rachel wondered what it would be like being on the ranch daily with John. *Preston, please come back soon.*

"Where did you learn to dance for the saloon patrons?" Estelle asked.

Rachel folded her napkin and looked at Estelle, who was pressing her question but not in a patronizing way. "The other girls taught me. It wasn't hard."

"I see."

Rachel waited for the next question she knew would probably be coming—whether or not Rachel was one of the "soiled doves." But Estelle didn't ask, and Rachel breathed a sigh of relief—not that she had done anything of the kind, but there were a few times when it was nearly forced on her. Thank God, she was able to flee the clutches of some of the Wild Horse's more dubious patrons. Now, she owed John—whether she wanted to admit it—for rescuing her, even if it wasn't how she would've wanted it to happen.

"I'm glad you've decided to work at my shop. You'll get to meet many of the ladies, whether they live on a farm or in town." Estelle laughed. "Some of them are very interesting to observe." She leaned against the tree trunk for support and closed her eyes.

"You're getting me very curious now—" Rachel stopped when she heard Estelle's even, deep breathing. The sun's warmth, the outdoors, and the food made Rachel feel relaxed too. *No harm in that*, she thought as she leaned to her side, propping up on her elbow. She relaxed for a change, with the gentle breeze caressing her face, but just as her eyelids were getting heavy, she heard a movement in the brush. Rachel jerked up to see a fox step warily into the clearing and snarl with white stuff dripping from the side of his mouth.

6

Rachel held her breath, not moving a muscle as the fox slinked with his head down, edging closer to Estelle's side. *I must do something!* Rachel's heart froze, but just before the fox was ready to pounce on Estelle she suddenly remembered the gun. She reached for it, lifted the barrel, and fired once—hitting the animal dead center between the eyes. His body bounced upwards, then plopped to the ground.

Estelle startled and gave a yell, holding her hand to her chest. "What the devil—" Her eyes flew wide when she spied the fox lying next to her right leg. She quickly scrambled up as Rachel steadied her.

"Are you okay, Estelle?"

"Yes, dear, but land sakes—you saved me from being bitten by a rabid fox!" She drew in a few quick breaths as both of them moved off of the blanket.

"I don't know if he would've bitten you, but I wasn't planning on taking any chances, that's for sure."

"Thank you," Estelle managed to say with a trembling mouth as Rachel handed her the gun. "Now, let's fold this blanket over the dead animal. He'll need to be buried. I'll find one of the ranch hands to do it."

"Let me move the basket first," Rachel said. She reached for it, making sure not to get too near the fox.

※

Sounds of a distant gunshot immediately alerted John and his foreman, Curtis, that something was amiss, so they hightailed it in the direction of the sound with Winchester running alongside them. John was a little more than concerned since Grams and Rachel were out perusing the ranch land. Normally, he didn't worry—Grams could take care of herself—but anything could happen in the raw territory.

They came over the rise and surveyed the valley below sprinkled with cottonwoods. It wasn't long before he and Curtis spied both women. It appeared to him that they must have stopped for lunch, in a spot he would've chosen too.

Reining their horses in, they hurried to where the ladies stood.

"We heard a gunshot. What's going on—" John began, walking toward them. He stopped, spotting the blanket on the ground.

"Rachel stopped a fox from taking hold of my leg while I was dozing." Estelle turned to glance at their foreman. "Curtis, this is Rachel Matthews."

Curtis tipped his hat in greeting and with a broad smile said, "Mighty nice to meet you, Miss Matthews. I admire a woman that can handle a gun at a moment's notice."

"And you as well. My papa taught me how to use a gun, thankfully." Rachel smiled sweetly at him, swinging the basket, and John couldn't help but notice the appraising look

Curtis gave her. It grated on him—not that Rachel would pay him any mind, but the fact that he seemed to do that with every pretty girl he met. John chided himself, realizing he was being silly. Curtis was one of the best foremen that they'd ever had, and a good man who'd become a good friend as well. Besides, it'd be odd if he hadn't noticed what a pretty young lady Rachel was. He remembered when Curtis used to flirt with Lura—but so did all the hands.

"Then I'm glad he didn't eat your lunch," Curtis teased, tossing her a warm grin.

"Well, I'm mighty glad you saved my Grams from a possible attack, Rachel." John walked a little closer to the blanket. "Me and Curtis will take care of this. Why don't you two go on and finish your afternoon."

Rachel's gaze settled on him. "You're welcome—but it was a natural thing to do. I would do it for anyone."

"Including me?" John teased. But Rachel only stared at him, folding her arms.

"We'll do exactly that, John. Thank you," Grams replied. Turning to Rachel, she said, "Let's get back in the buggy and enjoy our ride back to the house."

"Let me help you, Miss Estelle." Curtis rushed over to assist Grams into the buggy and then turned to hand Rachel up, but John was already at her side.

John observed Rachel's pretty hands and neatly filed oval nails. But that wasn't all he noticed—like the way the sunlight played across her shiny head of curls and the light dusting of freckles across the bridge of her delicate nose—all very appealing.

Rachel bristled at his look, then took her seat next to Estelle, murmuring a thank-you. A light flush warmed her cheeks as she adjusted her dress. John pulled his eyes away from hers. It was hard to judge from her expression whether she was still fuming about the saloon incident or not. *She'll thank me for it in time.*

"Grams, you'll have to buy yourself another picnic blanket. You ladies be careful, now," John said, taking a step back and looking up at them. He turned back to Curtis, who was openly admiring Rachel now, and said, "Let's go bury this creature." John waved a glove in Grams's direction before turning his focus to removing the dead animal.

A gentle breeze followed the ladies along the trail home where the cinquefoil and thimbleberry grew profusely. Estelle smiled to herself, remembering the many times she and Lura had driven over the ranch and stopped to chew the fat with the cowpunchers. She wasn't sure what to make of Rachel, but she did want to give the young woman a chance. She pushed aside nagging thoughts that surfaced.

"Rachel, tell me something about your brother, Preston. Do you think he'll come back to Cottonwood?" She cast a quick glance at the pretty occupant next to her sitting stiffly with her hands folded in her lap. Rachel was silent and Estelle wasn't sure she would answer, but finally Rachel looked her way.

"I certainly hope so. It's like John said. After my parents died, we couldn't afford the taxes for the last two years, and the bank was foreclosing on us. Preston said a friend bought it and it would be a matter of time before he returned to buy it back." Rachel sighed and paused, staring at the distant land-scape. "'Course I had no idea the buyer was your grandson. Preston never told me and it didn't matter at the time since we had to vacate the property."

"But he's never returned."

"No, but he did write John about me. At least he hasn't forgotten about me."

"It sounds like you love your brother, and we should give him the benefit of the doubt that he'll be able to do exactly as he said. Try not to doubt him." Estelle felt pity for the young woman.

"I'm trying, but I must admit it's getting hard, and he's been gone a long time." Estelle watched as Rachel's face brightened a bit. "I do have a little saved, but not near enough to buy the land back from John, who seems to want to stick to their bargain."

Estelle gave her an encouraging smile, masking a knowing look. "Well, my dear, we'll just have to work on that, won't we?" Rachel shot her a surprised look, then nodded.

7

Despite the fact that she would have loved to spend her days outdoors riding, with the wind caressing her face, by her third day at work for the millinery shop—appropriately named Estelle's Millinery—Rachel was beginning to realize her good fortune. She still didn't like how the new job had come about, but regardless of the circumstances, she was finding value in her work and soon forgot the horrors of working at the Wild Horse.

Estelle was incredibly patient with her. And so was her assistant, Molly, a rather plain, shy young woman with straight brown hair. The first day, Molly had walked her around the small shop pointing out where everything was kept and explaining how it was categorized.

"Miss Estelle likes everything to stay tidy—and I do mean tidy, so don't take my advice lightly." Molly gave her a lopsided frown.

"I understand perfectly." Rachel nodded as she fingered the fine lace on a lawn nightgown. She'd never had anything as nice as that. Surely this selection was for a bridal set. "For the bride?" she asked Molly.

"Oh, yes. Isn't it lovely? We have mail-order brides who arrive straight off the stage with very little in their suitcase, and some like to make their wedding night special." She blushed to the roots of her mousey brown hair. "Maybe soon, I'll have a proposal myself."

"Oh? Is there someone special courting you?"

Molly bit her bottom lip. "Not exactly, but I'm trying to get a gentleman's attention."

Behind her, Rachel caught the look of pity on Estelle's face from where she stood straightening the counter by the register.

"I see. I wish you well then."

"I'd better show you the rest before Miss Estelle thinks I'm dawdling." Just then the bell above the door jangled, and Molly excused herself to wait on some customers. Turning back to Rachel, she said, "Go ahead and take a look around." She rushed off to greet the customers who strolled in.

Rachel had since discovered the shop sold many other things besides hats and nightgowns. There were numerous capes, gloves, and corsets, along with ribbons and the frippery of lace and trims galore. Not much occasion for one to wear them in Cottonwood, she thought. But then again, the town—like nearby Lewistown—seemed to be growing, and she supposed all ladies liked to look their best when they traveled. There were practical items as well—aprons, neckerchiefs, muffs, and cloaks.

She couldn't help but wonder what it would be like to be the mistress of a beautiful home with a loving husband and money enough to shop here. Incredibly, she thought of John. She shoved away the mental image, thinking it laughable and highly improbable. A rich bachelor like John, who could have any woman he wanted, was not looking for someone without a penny to her name and a questionable reputation. That kind of thinking jolted her right back to the present, just as Estelle came toward her with two customers in tow.

"I'd like to introduce you to Rachel Matthews, our new clerk, who will be working with you on your purchases." Estelle smiled at Rachel when the two ladies stood looking at her from head to toe. "This is Vera Spencer, one of my best customers, and Beatrice, her daughter."

Beatrice could have been attractive had it not been for the sharp way she stared with small eyes beneath heavy brows, her nostrils slightly flared, and thin lips pinched as if ready to accuse Rachel of wrongdoing. Vera smiled and said, "How do you do," to Rachel, and Beatrice nodded her stiff head slightly.

"So happy to meet you." Rachel extended her hand in greeting but neither of the ladies reached for it, so she pulled back her hand with obvious embarrassment.

"Yes, well, of course. Good to meet you too," Vera said, quickly turning her attention to Estelle. "I hope we'll still receive the highest quality service that we've come to expect, Estelle." Vera implied with a look directed at Rachel that she couldn't possibly be able to satisfy their shopping needs.

"Never fear, Vera. I'm never far away. However, you will be in capable hands, I'm certain. Rachel is a fast learner."

Beatrice humphed underneath her breath and said, "You look familiar, but I can't recall where I've seen you, Rachel."

Rachel cleared her throat. "I don't get to town often," she fibbed, and saw Estelle quirk an eyebrow with a smidgen of a smile crossing her face.

"Oh . . . you must resemble someone else then." Beatrice's eyes narrowed in thought.

"That must be it." Estelle smiled, then said, "I'll bet you're here to try on that new hat I ordered from Chicago, Vera." Turning to Molly, who was busy rolling ribbon onto spools, she asked, "Molly, would you go retrieve Vera's package from the storage room?"

"Yes, of course." Molly gave a slight bob at the knees, laid aside the spool of ribbon, and hurried past the ladies to the storage room in the back of the shop.

Vera and Beatrice moved away to a glass case to admire the jet and pearl drop earrings, giving Rachel a chance to stare openly at the mother and daughter. There was a strong resemblance, with Vera having a more comely face than her daughter. She couldn't help but notice that the two seemed to be disagreeable in just about every way, as they argued over which sets were the prettiest earrings that Estelle kept in the glass case.

Vera's clothing was very nicely tailored, appealing to her full, matronly figure, while her daughter was of average build with a long, graceful neck. Dark wavy curls peeked from underneath Beatrice's bonnet. Her lavender-print crinoline dress was made of beautiful voile with cutaway lace sleeves, and in her hand she carried a parasol that complemented her spoon bonnet's flowers and matched the tiny pansies in the gown's print. *A little dressy for Cottonwood. They must be wealthy.* Rachel suppressed a giggle and watched as they walked about the shop like royalty.

Molly returned with a large hatbox and placed it on the counter, then stood back to allow Estelle to untie the blue ribbon around it. "Oh, how lovely," Molly exclaimed when

Estelle held up the hat. Vera and Beatrice hurried over to add up the charges.

Vera beamed with pleasure at the sight. "I shall love wearing this to church and social outings." Instantly, Vera removed the hat she was wearing and donned the new one, whirling around to catch her reflection in the mirror.

"And perhaps a wedding too," her daughter said quietly but loud enough for everyone to hear.

Estelle turned from her desk and smiled at Beatrice. "Well now, that is wonderful news! Who is courting you, my dear?"

"No one exactly, but John is always flirting with me whenever he's around," she said as she turned to throw a smug look directly at Rachel and Molly.

"Speaking of John, he's just walked in," Molly whispered to Rachel. "Beatrice fancies herself as his personal love interest."

Rachel looked over to see John coming through the door, his masculine presence filling the small shop of twittering females. *So, he's taken . . .* Somehow she felt disappointed but wasn't sure why. She hardly knew him.

Estelle hurried over as he came inside. "John, what brings you to town?"

He handed her a notebook. "I saw that you left your notebook with your supply orders and thought I'd better bring it."

She took the notebook. "Goodness, yes. Thank you— seems I can't remember where I place things sometimes." She walked over to the counter and he followed. "I do need this list to place my orders."

"Hello, ladies." He tipped his hat.

The cluster of ladies greeted him with chipper hellos, and Beatrice simply walked over and put her arm in the crook of his. "Just the man I wanted to see. Can you stay and have lunch today?"

"Not today, Beatrice. Some other time maybe?"

Beatrice pretended a pout then withdrew her arm. "I'll take that as a definite yes, then." She batted her eyes, flirting with him.

John glanced at Rachel. "How's the new job going, Rachel?"

Beatrice swung her gaze to rest on Rachel but never left John's side—probably wondering how he knew her enough to be friendly.

"I think I'm doing all right, but you'll have to get Estelle's opinion."

Estelle laughed. "She's a quick learner. Rachel will work out fine with me and Molly."

Rachel felt John's steady gaze on her—no doubt comparing her to Beatrice—and she felt uncomfortable in her own skin. Beatrice was *everything* she was not.

Molly broke the silence. "Mrs. Spencer, would you like to wear your new hat or do you want me to box it up again?"

"I'll wear it, Molly. Thank you. If you could just put the one I wore in the hatbox—"

The shop door swung open as a man, unshaven, stumbled through the door reeking of alcohol. "Looks like I'm in the wrong place." Then he noticed Rachel. "Well, lookee here," he said, swaying toward her. "But I'm glad I am. It's good"— he hiccupped then wiped his nose on his coat sleeve—"to see you again. I've missed you at the Wild Horse." He tried to straighten. "Where in tarnation have you been?"

At that moment, Rachel prayed the floor would open up and swallow her whole.

8

Humiliation threatened to undo her as she dared to look at Molly, Vera, and Beatrice, who were staring with shock. Before Rachel could utter a word, John sprang into action. Grabbing the drunk by the collar of his coat, John nearly lifted the man off his feet and dragged him to the front.

"You dirty excuse of a man! Get out and don't come back in here, ever!" He shoved the man into the street. All the while not a word was said in the shop and the only sound seemed to be Rachel's heartbeat in her ears.

"*The Wild Horse Saloon?*" Vera yanked her head back against her thick shoulders with disdain. Beatrice stood next to her mother with her arms crossed, glaring at Rachel.

"I, well . . . ," Rachel stuttered, mortified. "There's been some mistake . . ."

"*Really*, Estelle. I thought you hired the good, hardworking people of this town."

Lord, please contain this lady's sharp tongue. I don't want others to suffer because of me. Rachel stared down at her shoe tops to calm her own tongue.

"And I do, Vera. And you do not endear yourself to anyone when you speak that way," Estelle answered sharply. "Molly, hand me Vera's old hat, please."

Molly awkwardly handed Estelle the old hat and hatbox without looking at Rachel. Rachel dared not give John's brooding eyes contact. *Now he'll believe his suspicions about me.*

Estelle quickly placed the hat in the box and handed it to Vera. "That'll be four dollars."

"Just put that on our account as usual," Beatrice said over her shoulder before the two of them started out the door.

After they were gone, Rachel took a deep breath without even realizing that she'd been holding it. "Thank you, John. I don't know what else to say," she said.

John had been leaning with his elbows against the work counter but straightened. "The less said the better, I should think." His voice was steady and calm. "I'm leaving now, Grams. See you at supper." He doffed his hat and bolted out of the shop.

Molly walked over and laid a hand on Rachel's shoulder. "Don't worry 'bout those two. But tell me—what's it like inside a saloon?" she whispered.

Rachel groaned. *Sweet heavens above.* "Molly, it's nothing glamorous, I can assure you."

※

It infuriated John that Rachel hadn't defended herself against Vera's implied questioning of her reputation. Why hadn't she said something? Where was that spunky girl he'd taken off the dance stage? John spurred Cutter on toward the ranch. The fact was Rachel had affected him from the moment they'd sparred in the front yard after he'd dragged her kicking and screaming to his place. Maybe it was the fiery spirit she exhibited or her enormous golden-brown eyes that penetrated clean to his soul.

He shook his head. Ridiculous to have such thoughts about someone he'd only recently met. Then there was Beatrice . . . not as pretty but wealthy, from a well-known family, and eager to marry. A little *too* eager. Try as he might, John could not see himself being tied down to a woman just yet. Problem was, she kept throwing herself at him and there weren't that many eligible ladies around. Suppose he had lunch with her? No harm in that, was there? *And maybe it would get my mind off Rachel.*

He turned his attention to the surrounding beauty of his land with the high rolling valley and tall timber. Taking in a deep breath of the pungent smell of spruce, cedar, and wildflowers blooming, John relaxed.

He was proud of all he owned because it meant he was in control, which created a good feeling in him. He'd been so busy accumulating stock for his ranch and enjoying the finer things in life—traveling to Europe a few times and taking riverboat excursions down South—that he hadn't realized that something was missing in his life until he met Rachel. He chuckled. They mixed about as well as chili pepper topping on a rhubarb pie. She was a woman with a past in a saloon, for goodness' sake, and he doubted she was simply a pure little dancer for lonely men. But he did feel sorry for her today when the drunk stumbled in and spouted off about the Wild Horse in front of the ladies. He could've heard a pin drop, but she'd recovered quickly.

It wasn't long before the ranch was in view with its familiar smoke rising from the chimney, signaling a fire burning and Annabelle busy cooking. It was always a welcoming sight to him. His home was the one constant in his life besides God, and of course, his grandmother. He was suddenly entertaining an idea he'd never really dwelt on before. It'd be nice to have a little lady at home waiting for him at the end of a long day. He knew his grandmother would be most happy.

Annabelle took his hat with a smile when he walked into the house, which was filled with wonderful smells. "What's cookin' for supper, Annabelle?"

"Tonight it's roast beef, roasted carrots, and potatoes. I just slid it into the oven. It will be ready when the missus gets back and that young woman . . . what's her name again?"

"Rachel."

Annabelle's large dark eyes narrowed in response, causing the crow's feet around them to crinkle, proof of her fifty years of living.

"What? Why are you staring at me? Did I do something wrong?" John continued on to the parlor, plopping down in his easy chair by the fire.

"Just wondering why you brought that pretty young girl in here if you have no intention of courtin' her."

John sat straight up. "Whatever do you mean? I brought her here for her own safety. You heard me say that."

"I see the devilish look in your eye, John," she said, shaking her finger at him. "I've been knowing you since you were just a young'un, so don't play games with me. You certainly recognize a good catch when you see one."

John rolled his eyes heavenward. "Annabelle, why do you say that? You know nothing about the woman."

"My eyes know the difference—that's how. Don't let those

satin, shiny clothes she wore in here fool you none. There's a good heart underneath all that folderol. Don't you break that young girl's heart!" Annabelle stood with her hands on her hips. "I've seen how you've been watchin' and lookin' too."

"All right, all right," he said wearily. "I think I've been fully warned now. I have no intention of breaking anyone's heart. I'm not the worst cowboy around, Annabelle." He reached to yank her apron strings and she harrumphed.

"Can you fetch me a cup of strong coffee? My head's hurting." John propped his feet up and leaned back while Annabelle left, muttering under her breath as she hurried off to the kitchen.

It wasn't the first time their housekeeper had unleashed on him. Grams had a softer way of doing so, but Annabelle didn't bite her tongue. John wasn't entertaining any moves on Rachel . . . not that she'd let him get that close in the first place. He caught himself chuckling out loud at Annabelle's ravings.

"You are working out just fine at the shop," Estelle said on the ride home. She meant it to be reassuring, but Rachel didn't seem to want to talk about the scene they'd had earlier at the shop. The young gal sitting next to her looked straight ahead.

Estelle tried again after a long silence. "A penny for your thoughts."

Rachel sighed but continued to stare down the dirt road that led to the ranch. "You may want to rethink having me work for you. Your customers didn't seem to like me even before the drunk strolled in. I'm not good for your business."

"If you mean Beatrice and her mother, don't worry about them. They are good-paying customers, but it's time they learned a few manners." Estelle gave her a sideways glance as she steered the buggy toward home. Had she known the drunk? He seemed to know Rachel, but not by name.

"Truly, I'd rather be on my own land working."

"Rachel, think of this job as a gift until you can own your ranch or until the good Lord sees fit to send something else better your way."

"Ha! I don't think He's thinking much about me these days after my working at the Wild Horse." Rachel's pretty brown eyes were sad when she looked over at her. "Besides, He didn't help me save my home."

"Maybe not—God's ways are not our ways, His thoughts are not our thoughts. And you now have a roof over your head, a job, and three new friends. And if they get a chance, a slew of ranch hands that are dying to get to know you." The ranch house was in view now, and Estelle was glad that it was only a few miles to town. She pulled up in front of the barn and turned to face Rachel in the seat.

"Give us a chance to help you and let us be your friends until your brother returns."

"I don't mean to sound ungrateful, but I hardly think John wants to be friends with a former saloon dancer, even if I am Preston's sister."

Estelle wanted to say something in response, but Levi, one of the ranch hands, walked toward them to put the buggy and horse away. She knew Rachel was hurting and silently said a brief prayer for her.

9

Days later, with autumn sun warming her back, Rachel hiked along Mill Creek, then up a steep slope not too far from the house. Wildflowers flourished, and she was tempted to pick them. Perhaps on her way back. Cumulus clouds streaked the cerulean blue sky, with a hint of a possible shower filling the air with larger clouds that hovered over the towering Emigrant Peak. Rachel needed to get away to gather her thoughts since working at the millinery and living with the McIntyres.

Her head spun with the details of hat making after watching Molly and Estelle press and steam hat shapes against wooden forms in the back of Estelle's shop. Fabric was layered and stretched over a rigid core of starched linen from a wire frame to help hold the shape. Later, the pieces were sewn together by hand or sewing machine, which seemed a bit tedious to her. The trims of lace, ribbon, or flowers gave the hats a final touch. *That* part she was good at—matching the colors and design.

Rachel was glad she was a clerk and not the hat maker. Plenty of hats could be ordered from a catalogue, but they could take weeks or a month to receive, and occasionally Molly's creativity spurred her to design one of her own with Estelle's encouragement. She could tell the responsibility boosted Molly's suffering ego.

Rachel had seen little of John. Sometimes he was at supper, and sometimes it was only Estelle and her. She didn't ask where he might be as it was really not a concern of hers—at least that's what she told herself.

Strong breezes caressed her cheeks, threatening to tangle her hair that she'd worn loose today, free from its ordinary pins. Up here, in the quiet but vastness of open space, she felt freedom from the everyday cares of the world. She loved Montana and the way the mountains made her feel empowered but at the same time in awe of God's creation and splendor. Even so, a feeling of aloneness surrounded her, leaving her with only a spiritual connection to the Almighty. His presence was everywhere and it suddenly astounded her.

Rachel closed her eyes, pulling her wrap tighter about her shoulders against the cool wind, letting His presence fill her as she turned over to Him all the concerns of her existence. Moments later, when she opened her eyes, her spirit was mightily lifted with anticipation of promises of her future. As she prepared to leave, she bent down to gather an array of wildflowers for the supper table.

When she straightened, Rachel saw a rider leaning low over his horse's back, galloping across the valley toward the house. A feeling of unease drifted over her momentarily. It was none of her concern, she reminded herself. The ranch wasn't hers to be worried about. Even so she started back as she felt the first raindrop on the back of her hand.

She ran, but by the time Rachel reached the yard in front of the house her wet hair dripped down the front of her creamy white blouse and the stamens of the flowers she'd held against her had left their yellow stain. Her brown broadcloth skirt was heavy and dragging in the dust. She halted some distance away in spite of the rain when she saw John's face. Next to him was the man on horseback. John was holding a piece of paper in his hand, as rivulets of rain fell from the brim of his hat. When he saw her he quickly folded it and said her name in a thick, heavy voice.

The rider doffed his hat then returned the way he'd come, leaving Rachel and John alone.

"Yes, John. What is it? Did you get bad news? You look like you've seen a ghost." Rachel wiped the droplets of rain from her eyes and looked at him. She reached down to pat Winchester, who whined.

He handed her the telegram, and her large luminous eyes searched his for answers. He wished he had something to say that could help her . . . anything. He watched while she read the telegram, her lips silently moving, then bursting into an anguished cry that ripped from deep within her.

"NO! Not my Preston!" she screamed. "Tell me this isn't so, John!" Her tears began to mix with the rain. He stepped closer, then drew her to him as she sobbed, clutching the paper. She didn't resist, but allowed him to fold his arms about her until he too was drenched. He felt her heart beat against his chest and breathed in the lingering smell of violets from her hair.

"Rachel, I'm sorry . . . truly, I am." He pushed aside the wet, clinging hair from her face. He could barely stand to look at her uplifted golden-brown eyes full of pain when she finally pulled away. A sharp crack of thunder rumbled. "Let's get inside now. The storm is over us," he said.

Starting up the steps, John saw his tiny grandmother at the door, her wrinkled face full of questions, motioning with a wave of her arm for them to hurry.

Once inside, Grams shouted for Annabelle to bring a blanket, and John led Rachel to the fire. Annabelle was back in a flash and Grams wrapped the blanket around Rachel and handed him a towel.

John gave his hat to Annabelle and toweled off while his grandmother and Annabelle waited anxiously for an explanation. Briefly, with a somber tone, he told them about the telegram. "I've had a wire from a clergyman who informed me that Preston died of diphtheria in the mining camps."

His grandmother gasped and Rachel began to weep again. John felt helpless as he watched the stricken look and heard her cries. Annabelle handed her a handkerchief and spoke soothingly to her as Estelle laid her arm around Rachel's shoulder.

"I'm very sorry, Rachel. Let me and Annabelle show you to your room so you can remove your wet clothing."

When they reached Rachel's room, Annabelle helped her remove the wet clothes and placed a warm robe about her while Estelle pulled back the bedcovers and fluffed up the pillows. Rachel felt somehow detached from the scene, as if she were watching the ladies care for someone else.

"My dear Rachel, I know there are no words that I can express to ease your pain," Estelle said. "Do you want me to sit with you?"

"No, I'd rather be alone now," Rachel mumbled.

"I can bring you some hot tea or coffee," Annabelle whispered.

"Not right now, but thank you both." Rachel couldn't bear to see the pity in their eyes and she rolled over to her side, propping her arm up on her pillows and softly crying.

Respectfully, the two ladies slipped out of the room, leaving her alone, and Rachel pressed her hands to her mouth to keep from wailing aloud. *Preston, did you suffer terribly? How could you leave me now? We had so many plans!*

A hard knot settled in her chest and Rachel felt utter, total despair—so different from only an hour ago when she'd poured her heart out to God. She cried as memories washed over her while the rain beat against the windowpane and thunder rolled.

Preston—the brother whom she'd looked up to.

Preston—who teased her and pulled her pigtails every chance he got.

Preston—who'd given her a new kitten when hers was killed by a bear.

Preston—who'd sworn he'd return and they'd have a working ranch again.

What now? She had no family to speak of. *I'm only here because of the kindness of strangers. Preston, I don't know if I can go on . . .*

10

John strode out of the house, oblivious to the lightning and slashing rain, to the tack room in the barn—kicking a bucket with force as he entered. Good, he was alone with his thoughts. He could still see an image of Preston's earnest face telling him he'd be back to reclaim his ranch the way they'd agreed on. Had he even wanted to believe Preston? If John were honest with himself, he'd hoped Preston wouldn't return with the money to buy back the place—but that was before he'd met Rachel. Somehow it didn't sit well with him that she'd now lost her brother, her home, and her parents. He slammed his fist with fury on the wooden workbench used to repair lariats or tools, muttering under his breath.

Now he felt compelled to be her protector or guardian. At least his grandmother and Annabelle had taken a liking to Rachel. He'd find a marriageable man for her. There were plenty of honest, hardworking cowboys right here on the ranch, and John had noticed the look in Curtis's eye when he'd first met Rachel. With his decision made, he already felt better. He'd see her through this, and then hopefully with a willing partner she'd have a better future and he could go on as before.

The barn door creaked open and Curtis and Levi, dressed in their slickers, hurried in, leading their horses to the stalls. "Curtis, you're just the man I need to see."

"Sure, boss." Curtis handed his reins to Levi and he led the horses away. "What's up?"

"I need to talk with you after supper when we're alone," John said. "Come up to the house after Slim has fed you and the boys."

Curtis squinted, questioning, but John said nothing further and went on back to the house in the rain to check on Rachel.

⁂

Estelle wanted to give Rachel time off from work after Preston's passing, but she protested. "It'll give me something to focus on, but thank you anyway. I can't thank you enough for talking to Pastor Thornton about a memorial service."

She patted Rachel's arm. "I believe it will give you some peace. He said he'd love to do this for you and Preston tomorrow." Estelle watched Rachel stare vacantly into space and knew how she felt. Nothing could remove the pain other than the passage of time. She should know. Hadn't she lost a granddaughter, a daughter, and a son-in-law, as well as her own dear husband? Rachel would get as much time as she needed from her.

Rachel gave her a forced smile and picked up the loose ribbon she was rewinding on a wooden spool while Molly straightened the shelves. She was pale with dark circles under her eyes and had barely eaten all week since the news of Preston had come. Estelle had a sudden idea.

"Molly, why don't you and Rachel go have lunch as my treat today? I can handle things here for now, and Rachel could use some fresh air."

Molly flashed a bright smile, "Marvelous idea! We can have a bite to eat down the street at Abbey's."

"I'm not really feeling hungry." Rachel sighed, still wrapping the purple ribbon.

Molly reached over and took the ribbon. "Nonsense. You have to eat at least a little something or you won't have any strength at all."

Estelle smiled with a nod to Molly and watched as Rachel gave in, allowing Molly to get their capes and usher her out the door.

I declare, those two will wind up dear friends. I feel it in my old bones.

Rachel reluctantly followed Molly, who held her hand and was practically dragging her out of Estelle's. She knew Molly meant well but she was in no mood to eat or be pleasant.

"Slow down, Molly. We are supposed to be acting like respectable ladies on an outing." Rachel gave a soft laugh.

Molly slowed her steps, keeping time with Rachel's. "Nice to hear you laugh. You're right. I know my manners could use some refining, as Mama used to tell me."

"Oh? Is your mother still alive?" Rachel lifted her skirt above her shoe tops to keep from dragging it on the dusty sidewalk.

"No, she died when I was twelve. I live with my aunt, who tells me I'm incorrigible." Molly tried to cover a giggle. "I suppose I might be, just a little."

"Well, don't believe it. Everyone can improve to some extent—not that I'm saying you need improvement."

As they neared the door of Abbey's Café, Molly paused. "Oh, you don't have to pretend that you don't see my flaws.

In fact, I'd consider it a favor if you'd teach me to be more ladylike. I've noticed that you walk so gracefully."

Rachel saw the seriousness on Molly's face and realized what a sweet young lady she was. So open . . . and one who could easily get her heart broken. "I can give you some pointers as I see it when needed, I suppose."

"Then it's settled!" Molly pulled open the door. "Let's go eat. I'm starving."

The café wasn't too crowded, and a young woman showed them to a table and seated them. Rachel felt a pang in her stomach. Maybe she would be able to eat a little.

Only moments had passed after they'd given the waitress their order when Rachel noticed two girls from the Wild Horse enter the restaurant—Sue and Fannie. Rachel motioned to them to come over, and Molly turned in her chair to see who she was waving to and gasped.

Though nicely dressed, Rachel knew that their dyed hair and makeup gave away their profession—saloon hall gals. She would have to explain later the difference between dance hall girls and soiled doves to Molly.

"I wondered whatever happened to you, Rachel, the night that cowboy whisked you away. I see you're doing well, all dressed up in fine, proper clothing," Fannie exclaimed and leaned down to give Rachel a squeeze. "But I must say I hardly recognized you out of those red satin ruffles!" She leaned her head back, laughing heartily.

Molly's face colored, and Rachel noticed her looking around to see who was watching. "Nice to see you again, Fannie and Sue." Flamboyant and a little loud, Fannie's friendly demeanor put off some folks, but Rachel knew the pain beneath the surface of her painted face.

"Honey, you look good, but your eyes tell me a different story. Somethin' the matter?" Sue bent down close to Rachel's face and looked her square in the eye.

Molly coughed as if to signal to Rachel her presence. "Ladies, please meet my co-worker and new friend, Molly. Molly this is Sue and Fannie."

Fannie bobbed her head. "Glad to make your acquaintance."

"How do." Sue smiled. "Now back to what's ailing you. Honestly, Rachel, I've never seen you look sadder. What is it?"

"She's just lost her brother, Preston." Molly had suddenly found her voice.

"You don't say? My goodness, sweetie. I'm so sorry to hear that." Fannie shook her head.

"Aw, what a doggone shame," Sue added.

"Yes, it is," Molly said through pursed lips, still staring at the two ladies as if they came from another part of the world.

Fannie touched Rachel's hand. "Is there anything we can do fer ya? Anything at all—you just name it, honey."

Rachel was touched by their warm friendship. "You can attend Preston's memorial service at the Wildwood church tomorrow at three."

"Sure . . . we'll be there. Won't we, Sue?"

Sue nodded in agreement. "We'll be going now so you two can have your lunch."

"Yes, we must get on with it. We are on our lunch break." Molly seemed put off by their presence.

"Do tell. So you got another job? I figured you'd be hitched to that cowboy by now. Where might that job be, Rachel?" Sue asked.

"I work at Estelle's Millinery. You should stop in sometime," Rachel said.

"We'll have to do that, won't we, Sue." Fannie grinned over at Sue.

"Absolutely. Well, good day to you both." Sue took Fannie's arm. "Let's go eat."

With a little wave they were gone, and Molly sat staring at Rachel.

"Are they who I think they are?" Molly's eyes widened.

Rachel picked up her napkin, unfolded it, and laid it in her lap. Molly watched her movements and did the same. "Something you need to know, Molly, is that dance hall gals are not soiled doves."

Molly squirmed. "I never said they were—"

"But you were thinking just that, correct?"

"I guess so. I was told if you worked in a saloon you were a prostitute."

"Well—to be truthful—Fannie and Sue are just what you thought. But in the nicer saloons, most of the women that dance work there because they had no means of viable support—their husbands died or left them. The pay is good and they sometimes get a commission on the drinks they sell." Rachel paused. "I used to work at the Wild Horse . . . as a dancer. I was no 'soiled dove.'"

Molly blanched. "I don't know what to say."

"If you'd like me to leave, Molly, now that you know about me, I'll understand."

Molly flinched. "Oh no. Please, don't do that! It's just that . . . well . . . I'm shocked, but if Estelle believes in your character, then who am I to say anything?"

"Thank you. Your friendship means a lot to me."

"What do you think Estelle will say when they show up at the shop, or better yet, the memorial service?"

Rachel thought a moment, then answered. "I believe her to be a God-fearing woman and I think she will show them hospitality."

"I sure hope you're right, Rachel."

11

With her stomach churning, Rachel stood before the mirror adjusting her heavy brocade bolero jacket, the color of butter with black trim. Her full dress mirrored the same thick trim down the center and along the hemline. She frowned. It was the best she had for a memorial service. She'd worn this dress to church many times, but since she had nothing black in her wardrobe to wear on such short notice, hopefully the black trim would indicate someone in mourning.

Estelle walked over to where Rachel stood with a black hat in her hand. "John is waiting with the carriage. I thought you might like to wear my black hat today to complete your outfit."

Rachel turned and with trembling hands took the hat, then fingered the black tulle and trailing ribbons. "Thank you . . . yes, I'd like to wear it. You've been so kind to me. I don't know if I ever took time to say thank you."

Estelle blinked. "There's no need for you to say anything. I'm glad that I could be here for you," she said, watching Rachel place the large hat on her head. "Ah, perfect. Shall we go now?"

"I'm ready as I'll ever be," Rachel answered.

❊

Afternoon sunlight shafted through the tall spruce and pines, bestowing a warm glow on the little wooden church for Preston's memorial service. The recent rains left a few puddles in the front yard as John drove the carriage with Grams and Rachel. John assisted them both from the carriage, and as he did so, noticed Rachel's face full of calm, though her eyes were swollen with dark smudges below them. She leaned on Grams's arm as they took the steps inside.

He wished he knew what he should say, but his tongue felt thick. There were no words of comfort to add to what he'd already said. Seemed strange to have a service without a body, but Preston had been buried before John received the wire. It wasn't uncommon that folks were buried where they died. But his grandmother was convinced a memorial service would help Rachel deal with her grief.

He followed them inside, taking his seat next to Grams, and noticed the candles on the tiny altar were lit and a member of the church was softly playing hymns on the organ. A look to his left made him grip the arm of the pew. Two "soiled doves" sat whispering. When they caught him staring, they both smiled through ruby-red lips, and he quickly jerked his head away. Were they ladies in Preston's past? John didn't think he was like that. In fact, he didn't ever recall Preston going to any saloon.

Molly scooted in moments later and a couple cowboys who must've been Preston's friends shuffled in behind her. John didn't know them.

❊

Pastor Thornton waited a few minutes before he walked up to the podium and motioned to the organist to cease playing. He caught Rachel's eye and held it for a long moment.

"It's with much sadness today that this small group of friends assemble here to support Rachel Matthews and to honor the loss of her brother, Preston. Thank you for coming this afternoon. This candle burns bright as a memorial to him. Although there's no body here to which we can pay our respects, Miss Rachel has assured me her brother believed in the good Lord, both of them having been raised in faith. Preston and Miss Rachel have endured the loss of their parents and their home in recent years. But if you didn't know, our loss and suffering while on earth produces a further weight of glory in heaven. Preston died in the pursuit of wealth, but his true wealth was in his relationship with the Lord, and with Rachel. She has told me of the many fond memories of growing up with an older brother who protected and shielded her—and picked on her too."

Quiet laughter filled the church, and the pastor smiled.

Rachel fought back tears and pressed the hanky against the corners of her eyes. The pastor was doing a good job. She tried to look at him in order to concentrate on what was being said.

"So today, I would like to close by reminding all of you to seek the kingdom of God first, and not the treasures of this earth, because in heaven neither moth nor rust destroy. All too soon we find that material possessions mean little. Let us instead turn our attention to the One who created us, and the people in our lives."

John thought about that for a minute. What did he mean about moth or rust? What was Pastor Thornton talking

71

about exactly? He had heard or read those Scriptures before but he didn't see how it had anything to do with him. He wasn't expecting either one to affect his livelihood, and he always gave a tithe to the church. Better that the pastor talked about those ladies who sat across the aisle from him, staring up at the pastor and hanging on to every word he had to say.

John swung his gaze over to Rachel, her shoulders slumped, staring at her hands clasped in her lap. His heart gave a pang of pity. He understood how she felt. The loss of his sister Lura came flooding in to his heart and tears stung his eyes. He took his white handkerchief out and pretended to mop his brow, quickly wiping away his tears before anyone could see.

The pastor turned to look directly at Rachel again. "I'm sorry for your loss. We'll pray that the memories of your beloved brother stay in your heart and the peace of the Lord will comfort you as no other can. God bless you. This concludes our service."

Grams stood before the pastor left the lectern. "There will be refreshments served at my home only a short piece down the road. We'd be pleased to have you all if you'll follow us to the ranch."

Everyone sat still, allowing the pastor and Rachel to leave first, then they followed them out of the church into the yard.

"Thank you, Pastor Thornton, for your kind words today," Rachel said, sniffing into her handkerchief. "I hope you'll come for refreshments."

"I'd be honored, Miss Rachel, but I'd consider it a pleasure if you would please call me Jeffrey."

"All right, Jeffrey it is, but you must call me Rachel. I'll see you at the house, then."

Jeffrey gave her a warm smile and she hurried to catch up with Estelle.

John waited until the rest of the folks walked to their respective horse or carriage so he could have a word with the pastor.

"Aren't you going, John?" Jeffrey asked.

"Of course . . . but first I wanted to ask you about something, if I may." John shifted his weight from one foot to the other.

"Certainly. What can I answer for you?"

John looked around, making certain no one was in earshot. "Well, as you noticed, there were a couple of . . . er . . ."

"Prostitutes?" Jeffrey supplied for him.

"Uh, yes. Don't you think it rather strange that my grandmother or Rachel would have these ladies at the funeral, and even more so, to the house?"

Jeffrey gave a discreet laugh. "Worried about your own reputation, John?"

"It's easy for you to go around being goody-goody. You're the pastor. You have to be."

"We are all the same in the sight of the Lord, and may I remind you that Jesus made it His business to be among sinners and prostitutes to preach the gospel. I think it's wonderful that they can enjoy your grandmother's hospitality."

John swallowed, feeling foolish but still doubtful. He wasn't even sure Rachel hadn't been one of them.

"Besides, how can you be sure they *are* prostitutes?"

"Well, for heaven's sake! Just look at them . . . all that foo-rah on their faces and gaudy clothes."

"Mmm. We're not to judge a book by its cover. After all, Rachel once worked at the saloon, but yet she's living under your roof."

"If it weren't for Preston being my friend, you can bet she wouldn't be. And now—well, now I feel responsible for her."

"Maybe you should talk to her. Just because she worked in a saloon doesn't make her a loose person." He turned to leave. "We should go."

"Yes, well . . . the ladies are waiting for me." John strode to the carriage, pondering what the pastor said. But he was far from convinced.

12

Rachel allowed Annabelle to usher her to a chair in the parlor while the rest of the small group from the party followed.

"Miss Rachel, what would you like me to get you? How about a sandwich and some hot tea?"

Rachel shook her head. "Thank you, Annabelle, for taking such good care of me these last couple of days, but only hot tea for me. I don't think I could swallow a bite." She looked up to see the sweet look of sympathy in Annabelle's eyes and studied her for a moment. Annabelle was a rather plain soul but was always dressed in a stiff navy dress with a starched apron so white that it was nearly blinding. The tips of her sturdy black shoes peeking out from beneath her skirt had such shine Rachel could almost see her reflection. It was a known fact in Paradise Valley that Annabelle lived to take care of others. She knew that John loved her too.

"All right, sweetie. I'll bring you some tea, but I have to say I'm surprised at some of the guests Miss Estelle has invited," she said, pursing her lips into a tight line.

"She didn't, Annabelle. I asked them."

"Ooh, I see. Well, it's altogether strange, if you ask me. I'll go fetch your tea. Here come the rest of them," Annabelle muttered, then scooted out in the direction of the kitchen while Rachel prepared to receive condolences. She would be so glad when this day was over.

Moments later, Sue and Fannie entered the parlor, gaping as they looked around until Rachel lifted her hand with a small wave. They made Rachel remember how she too had gawked the first time John brought her inside.

"You've certainly come up in the world, haven't you? A job and now an elegant home." Sue clucked like an old hen.

Fannie strutted over to Rachel. She leaned in close and with a low voice said, "Are you in *his* bed now?"

"Fannie!" Sue pinched her friend's arm. "Have some manners, will ya?"

"Ouch! Sue, for heaven's sake! Stop pinching me or you'll put another bruise on me," Fannie complained.

Rachel tried to hide her shock, but then decided she should've expected that from Fannie. "No, I'm not," she answered firmly under her breath. "This is not the place to discuss this." She wondered about Fannie's comment and bruises. The pastor and John stood at the doorway talking, and Rachel could only pray they hadn't heard the conversation.

Fannie's face colored pink. "I'm sorry. I guess I . . . What I mean is, I shouldn't've opened my mouth. I'm sorry about your brother, really I am. He was a fine gentleman. He never took up with the girls, and that was long before you showed up."

Rachel let her hand holding her handkerchief to her nose drop to her lap in shock. "You knew Preston?"

Annabelle chose that time to bring Rachel her tea. "Excuse me, please," she said, pushing her way between Sue and Fannie. "Here's your tea, but I wish you'd try a bite to eat. I brought you a tiny sliver of pound cake."

Annabelle handed Rachel tea from the tray she carried. Then she turned to face Fannie and Sue. "Humph!" she said surveying the two women. "I reckon if Miss Rachel wants you here, then that's good enough for me. You folks go help yourself in the dining room. There's plenty of food."

The two left, twittering behind their hands, no doubt wondering why Rachel had wound up at the McIntyres. "Thank you, Annabelle, for being nice to them. They could probably use some real friends." Rachel took a sip of the scalding tea and burnt her tongue.

"You're mighty welcome, but I don't believe they'll find any friends here other than you, Rachel."

The pastor strolled over, reached down to take her hand, and asked, "Can I get you something else to go with that tea, Rachel?" He gave her a genuine smile, his eyes resting on her longer than she felt comfortable with.

"Nothing for me, Jeffrey, but please help yourself to refreshments in the dining room. Follow those cowboys." Rachel slowly pulled her hand away from his.

Jeffrey snapped his tall, lean frame upright. "I believe I will. My own cooking is getting a bit old and tasteless. I'll be back."

Estelle walked over. "I'll go with you, Pastor," she said after a pat on Rachel's shoulder, and they walked away.

Rachel caught a glimpse of John adding wood to the fireplace, which suited her fine with the late afternoon's chill. But how her head ached and eyes burned from crying. Once he had a fire going, he pulled up a chair and sat down facing her.

"How are you doing?" His face was close enough that she could smell his aftershave lotion. That reminded her of Preston, and she started to cry again.

He gently took the cup and saucer from her shaking fingers, while she searched her lap for her handkerchief. "I'm sorry," he began.

"No, it's okay. It's only that your aftershave reminded me of Preston's," she said, sniffing.

John looked at her, sympathy reflected in his dark eyes. "I wanted to let you know that Grams and I have talked at length about the circumstances, and have decided you are welcome to stay here as long as you'd like or until you are on your feet."

Rachel straightened. "Meaning I won't be able to get the ranch back and have no home to go *home* to?" she asked pointedly.

"Not unless you have five thousand dollars." His voice, though quiet, was calm and steady.

Silence.

She stiffened.

He stared.

She shifted.

His eyes held hers for what seemed like a long time. She had no answer. *He knows full well that I don't have that kind of money.*

"We'll discuss this later when you're in a better frame of mind," John said firmly.

"I assure you, John, there's nothing wrong with my mind." Rachel returned his look with what she hoped was a firm one as well. "You can bet we shall talk . . . as I intend to get my land back." Rachel lowered her voice when she saw Estelle and Jeffrey return to the parlor. Moments later, Sue and Fannie took a seat on the settee, balancing plates of food on their knees and coffee in their hands.

John rose from his chair and Rachel watched him leave through the front door. Estelle took note of him leaving too, Rachel noticed.

Fannie patted her mouth with her napkin, trying her best to act like a lady, Rachel thought. "How about I play a tune for you on the piano to cheer you up? Sue can sing." Fannie nudged Sue, who shook her head.

"That won't be necessary," Rachel murmured.

"I say let them. Music can be soothing to the soul," Jeffrey added.

Fannie set her dishes on a side table and dragged a protesting Sue from the settee. Rachel hoped they knew some hymns but braced for the worst. Estelle gave her a worried look but took the chair John had sat in next to her. Jeffrey stood with the couple of cowboys who were still stuffing their faces.

"This here song is for Preston and Rachel," Fannie said as her fingers quickly ran over the piano keys.

> "O bury me not on the lone prairie."
> These words came low and mournfully,
> From the pallid lips of a youth who lay
> On his dying bed at the close of day.
>
> "I've always wished to be laid when I died
> In a little churchyard on the green hillside.
> By my father's grave, there let me be,
> O bury me not on the lone prairie.
>
> "O bury me not on the lone prairie
> Where the coyotes howl and the wind blows free.

In a narrow grave just six by three—
O bury me not on the lone prairie."

The piano tune sounded painfully sad as Rachel listened. Sue followed along, singing in a sweet, refreshing voice. Annabelle came and stood by the door to listen, a mixture of surprise and sadness showing on her face.

Fannie joined Sue on the refrain, and they sang with mournful voices as Rachel's heart squeezed tight. A truly fitting song for her cowboy brother. No one in the parlor moved a muscle as they sang. When they finished, Rachel got up and walked over to them. "A perfect song for my brother. Thank you," she managed to say through her tears, and gave the two women a small hug.

"We need to be going, Fannie, it's getting late," Sue said.

"Yes, we do. Rachel, take care of yourself, now. You need anything a'tall, please let me or Sue know, you hear?" Fannie and Sue thanked Estelle and the pastor on their way out.

Annabelle expelled a loud sigh of relief after she showed them to the door, and Jeffrey stifled a chuckle. Everyone took time to share their heartfelt condolences with Rachel and soon the guests were gone and the house was quiet.

Rachel began helping pick up the dishes and add them to a large tray despite Annabelle's protest. She heard John's voice from the porch, but she was too weary to even think about talking to him. It would take her a mighty long time working at the millinery shop to save enough to buy back her parents' ranch. *How can I continue to impose on their hospitality indefinitely?* Suddenly she felt lightheaded, everything overwhelmed her, and she crumpled against the settee. John dashed to her side before she completely passed out.

13

Warmth caressed her cheek but Rachel's eyes were heavy—too heavy to lift. But it didn't matter. She rather liked this peaceful realm she'd fallen into. No worries. No cares. Only beautiful peacefulness. In the distance, her brother smiled and he looked vibrant and healthy. *I should go to him . . . but I'm so tired.*

Rachel awakened and looked around for the warm sunshine, but it was dusk she saw at the window. She sat up quickly, and Estelle popped up from her chair.

"Feeling better?" Estelle asked, walking to her bedside.

"I guess so. How long have I been asleep?" She blinked, then swung her legs onto the floor.

"Not too long. You passed out after everyone left—I believe you'd gone too long without food. John carried you to your bedroom."

"He did? The last thing I remember was helping Annabelle in the parlor. I remember feeling lightheaded." How embarrassing that John had seen her that way, especially after having words with him. One more thing that she owed him for.

"You've been under a lot of stress lately, dear. You need something to eat and some fresh air tomorrow." Estelle took her arm. "Would you like me to have Annabelle send you up a light supper or do you want to dine with us?"

Rachel stood and wavered briefly. "If you don't mind, I'd rather eat alone tonight. Then I'll try to get some rest."

Estelle gave her a bright smile. "I agree—I think that's best. I'll go get Annabelle to bring something up. I'm sure tomorrow you'll feel quite a bit different with some food in your belly and some rest." She walked to the door.

"Estelle?"

"Yes? Is there something else you need?"

"No. I wanted to thank you for having the refreshments after the service and being kind enough to let Sue and Fannie attend. I'm very grateful. I believe they're truly good women . . . a bit different, but good at heart."

Estelle squared her shoulders and with a wry smile said, "You're welcome. Although I'm not accustomed to having *those kinds* of folks in my home, there was no harm in doing so, and I believe they thought they were truly helping you. Besides, the singing wasn't all that bad." Then she chuckled. "However, I'm not sure John cared for it."

"He left before they sang, but I don't think that was what was bothering him."

"Oh?" Estelle's hand paused over the doorknob with a frown on her wrinkled face. "What do you mean?"

But Rachel waved her hand, wishing she hadn't said a word. "Oh, nothing really. We exchanged a few words, but don't worry about it."

Estelle hesitated, then reluctantly opened the door. "If you say so."

82

"I do. You've done quite enough for me, and I'm on my own now."

"But you don't have to be—remember that." Estelle quietly slipped out the door, leaving Rachel to consider her words.

✻

After telling Annabelle to take a tray up to Rachel, Estelle decided to take a walk to enjoy the way the soft evening shadows touched the outbuildings and the surrounding pastures. It was a peaceful night, and she needed to think. As she strolled with Winchester as her companion, she tried to come up with ways she could help Rachel other than to let her know that she was welcome to stay. But that hardly helped, since John lived under the same roof and now owned Rachel's home. She knew that her grandson didn't need to acquire more land. What he needed was a good woman and a family. If her instincts were right, and they were rarely wrong, Rachel could be a good choice for him. But he didn't see that now. She was sure the good Lord had sent her into their lives for a purpose—it was not happenstance. Perhaps Rachel was sent to take the place of Lura for her—and much more for John?

Estelle had so many regrets when it came to her granddaughter, Lura. She'd been hard on her, wanting to protect her after Lura's parents passed. Regrets . . . how they continued to remind her. Secrets she'd pledged to keep. Maybe that was why she so desperately wanted to help Rachel?

She paused on Mill Creek to listen as the water flowed over the smooth rocks and the meadowlarks chirped. She was reminded of the surrounding beauty of the ranch. In this place, she was happier than she'd been before moving here. She clasped her bony hands together, her heart full of gratitude for the length of her days, and spent some time praying and talking to God. Later, as she walked the trail back to the house for supper, she knew that He would somehow remove the remaining sadness from her heart.

❧

"I sure was surprised when your friends started singing, Miss Rachel," Annabelle said when she placed a tray of soup and crusty bread on the desk for Rachel.

"I have to admit, that was quite a surprise, but so fitting for my brother—a true cowboy. It was a sweet thing for them to do, though a bit unconventional."

"I'll say. Everything about them is unconventional." Annabelle tsked, shaking her head. "You need to eat everything on this tray unless you want John to keep hauling you around like a sack of potatoes!" She stood with her hands on her hips.

"I'll do my best to keep that from happening, I assure you. Once was embarrassing enough."

"I'd better hurry and get down to the kitchen to serve dinner," she said, her mouth twitching at the corners.

"Annabelle, do you have family?"

"Yes, my husband is the cook for the ranch hands, and my two daughters got hitched and moved to Idaho. Why?"

"Then why don't you dine with Estelle and John?"

Annabelle laughed. "'Cause I eat with my man, Slim, in the kitchen after we get everyone else fed. He used to wrangle horses, but his age caught up with him and now he's the cookie instead. That's the way we like it. Gives us time to catch our breath, although retirement isn't in our vocabulary." She giggled. "We feel pretty blessed to work for the McIntyres all these years."

"I see. Then I'm glad. I was worried you had to eat all alone." She smiled.

"Hope you can find some peace and rest tonight."

"Thank you for the meal."

Rachel saw Annabelle's face soften. Then she nodded and scurried out. Only after she'd eaten was Rachel able to finally relax.

She sat by the window watching the lights from the bunkhouse and kitchen where she imagined Slim bustled about. It warmed her heart knowing that Annabelle had a husband. *Maybe someday I'll have one.* She propped her arm up on her elbow and cupped her chin in her hand, gazing out at twinkling stars.

Preston, I know you're with our parents now, and my heart sorely aches for you. But now I feel like an orphan with no family to care whether I come or go. I so wish you would have returned and settled down with a nice lady here in Paradise Valley. But mostly, I wish you'd never left.

14

A sudden, stiff wind tore at John's hat, but he was quick to grab hold of it before it sailed away. The ride over to visit with Beatrice wasn't far, and he was glad. As he guided Cutter in the buggy across the Spencer ranch land, he observed their superb piece of rolling pasture, plentiful with creeks and streams for livestock. John wondered how many head of cattle Vera handled since her husband, Will, had died last spring. *I could always make her an offer, but more than likely she'll refuse.* But he couldn't help but plan ahead. If he owned it, he might lease out the house to Vera and convince her to sell the herd to him. Worth considering, he thought.

His thoughts strayed to Rachel. While he did feel sorry for her, he knew it was a matter of time before she'd be receiving marriage offers. He was glad that Curtis intended to court her after their talk the other night.

John wasn't sure what to make of her. He felt he should be her guardian—or at least protect her—but he wasn't sure she needed protecting in the first place. A beautiful woman working at a saloon was used to looking out for herself. He knew that just from the scene she'd made when he'd brought her home to his ranch.

And my—she was beautiful. Beautiful could get him into trouble though. He'd caught her looking at him when she didn't think he was watching, and he had to admit something in her personality attracted him. He was used to courting ladies who were very agreeable, but she—well, she spoke her mind about things. Not that she was aggressive, but assertive enough to say what she felt, and it was obvious that she was still angry at him. But when those golden-brown eyes flashed at him, it stopped him in his tracks. He shook his head, chiding himself for such thoughts. Well, no worry there. She wasn't about to let him get close to her.

He could see the Spencer house up ahead and felt somewhat nervous. He'd never actually been alone with Beatrice, but he'd promised her a ride on a beautiful Saturday afternoon. She was a spunky young woman and he had no doubt she was very attracted to him by the way she flirted with him—and truthfully, he was flattered. She could make a man feel very masculine.

Moments later, a servant answered John's knock and led him into the parlor where Beatrice and her mother sat chatting.

"John," Beatrice said and quickly rose to meet him. "I'm so glad you're here." She smiled, her eyes softening when they landed on his. Her blue dress brought out the color of her eyes, he noted.

"Hello," he said, then nodded to Vera. "Oh, please don't get up," he pleaded when he saw her start to rise from her chair.

"Would you care for some tea or coffee?" Vera asked with a pleased smile.

Beatrice took his arm. "Oh, Mother, I don't think we'll be here long enough for that. I'm ready if you are, John." She seemed anxious to leave.

"Yes, but I think you'll need a cape. The wind today makes it feel quite chilly," John told her.

"Then I won't be but a moment. Have a seat." Beatrice scooted out of the room.

"I'm so glad you are courting Beatrice," Vera said, looking at him from the chair next to his.

He hesitated, not quite knowing how to reply, shifting uncomfortably in his chair. "I'm not sure I'd call it courting yet, Mrs. Spencer. It's only an afternoon outing in the countryside."

"But I'm sure it will be after you've had some time to spend with my lovely Beatrice. Her hand in marriage is being sought by several gentlemen, you know, but I must confess, she seems rather taken by you."

John felt his face burn. He coughed slightly. "I had no idea."

"Men are usually totally oblivious when it comes to matters of the heart." She grinned at him, then leaned in close, whispering, "I don't know if you're aware of it, but the ranch falls to Beatrice's possession once she marries. Her father wouldn't have it any other way." Vera winked at him with a knowing look.

For heaven's sake! Was the woman baiting him with her daughter's land? John was appalled, but thankfully he didn't have to reply as Beatrice slipped back into the room with her heavy cape and a matching bonnet. When he rose to help her with the cape, Beatrice smiled up at him, and he couldn't help but notice again how blue her eyes were.

"Fall is a wonderful time for a nice afternoon drive. I'll have refreshments waiting when you return," Vera said.

"That would be wonderful, Mother. See you in a while."

Outside, John took Beatrice's hand while she stepped into the buggy, being careful of her voluminous skirts. The last thing he wanted to do was to put a rip in her finery. He had to admit, she looked very fetching. Satisfied that she was settled in the buggy, John hopped in beside her, then picked up the reins, and with a flick of his wrist, they trotted out of the yard and down the lane.

"Such a beautiful day for a ride, wouldn't you say, John," Beatrice bubbled.

John gave her a nod. Was the flush on her cheeks from the wind or being with him? He'd give anything to know. "It is indeed. Later on, those tamarack trees"—he waved his hand in the direction of a stand of light green trees—"will burn a golden color against the conifers and spruce. And the huckleberry bushes will have a red hue. It's a pretty sight in the fall."

"Do you like huckleberry pie?" She glanced his way.

"I certainly do. Do you?"

"Oh, yes. We canned huckleberries from our own bushes. I'm quite good at pie making," she bragged.

"Then I look forward to sampling one sometime." He found himself smiling at her, and she smiled back, patting his arm.

"It would be my pleasure, John." Her smile widened with a tilt of her pink lips and it was hard not to stare.

"Uh . . . okay." He slowed the buggy until they came to a large cottonwood tree where he parked the buggy. He turned in his seat to face her. "Do you help run the ranch now that your father passed?"

Beatrice giggled. "Heavens no! That doesn't interest me in the least. That's what ranch foremen are for."

"Then what is it you like to do, Beatrice?"

She fingered the edging of her cape while she gazed at him, and John noticed her small but slender fingers, fine-boned facial features, and skin that was nearly alabaster. "I enjoy riding, social gatherings, and the like. I enjoy traveling, seeing new things, meeting new people—someday, hopefully, with my future husband."

John was beginning to see Beatrice as a delicate woman who would never want to settle down and have children, but he could be wrong. "I see. Then when did you have time to do canning?"

She blushed. "Oh, well, to be perfectly honest, I didn't mean that *I* did the canning. The cook did that, but I did help pick a few berries."

"I used to travel a little, but lately I've found myself sticking close to home—not sure why," he commented.

She reached over and placed her hand on his wrist. "Sounds like you're getting ready to settle down, maybe?"

He was surprised at her move, feeling her hand warm on his wrist through his sleeve. "I might be guilty of thinking more about that occasionally, but Grams is getting slower than she was even a few months ago and I find myself staying close by . . . after losing Lura." His voice cracked and he clenched his jaw.

Beatrice patted his hand. "Oh, John, I'm sure this is still very painful for you and your grandmother. Lura was a beautiful woman, and even though we weren't close, I considered her a friend."

He took the small hand that covered his and squeezed it.

"Yes, it still hurts, and I miss her and her laughter. But look, I didn't mean to get morbid on you." He released her hand. "How about a walk to the creek? I need to stretch my legs."

"Good idea."

He got out of the buggy, went around to her side, and lifted her down, briefly feeling her slender form against his before quickly releasing her. She slipped her hand into his larger one as they walked over the uneven terrain to the stream. The wind whipped Beatrice's skirts, pressing them against her as she hung on to his arm until they reached the creek's edge. The rushing water over the smooth rocks was so loud they found themselves nearly shouting to be heard when they talked.

Beatrice laughed and pointed to a large boulder near the edge of the stream. "Let's go sit on that rock there in the warm sun."

"I don't think that's a good idea. One wrong step and you could fall in—"

But she interrupted him with a wave. "Oh, pooh! Where's your sense of adventure?" she teased, running ahead. She began stepping along the bank to reach her goal, lifting her hem high enough to keep the mud at bay.

"Be careful, the bank is slippery," John called out as he tried to catch up with her. But she moved quickly, and he saw her teeter and lose her balance. Before he could reach out to her, she'd slipped into the cold moving water with a squeal.

"Beatrice!" John hurried and was at the rock to reach down to her as her arms flailed about.

"John! I can't swim!" The current of the creek pulled her away from him. She flopped around as her heavy skirts threatened to pull her farther downward.

"I've got you," he said, holding on to one of her thin arms.

91

"Give me your other hand and I'll pull you up," he yelled over the roar of the foamy water. He couldn't believe this. What would Vera say? *Probably blame me.* By the time he lifted her up out of the water, Beatrice was thoroughly wet from head to toe except for the very top of her fashionable bonnet, and the sight made the corners of his mouth twitch though he dared not laugh.

She gasped for a moment while he held her steady until she could catch her breath, then she started shivering. Her wet lashes stuck together while water dripped from her hair. John removed her wet cape, then threw his coat around her shoulders.

"I've got to get you back to the house and into some dry clothes." He picked her up with ease and carried her to the buggy while she laid against him for warmth and protection from the wind. After depositing her in the seat, John quickly untied Cutter and sped back down the lane.

15

Rachel could not believe what her eyes told her was true. She'd borrowed a horse from the stable for an afternoon ride at Estelle's urging, then headed in the direction of her parents' ranch. After meandering down the trail that was so familiar to her, she decided to tie the horse to a bush and walk to the creek where she and Preston had played as children. That's when she'd seen Beatrice fall into the creek and watched as John pulled her to his chest, gently cradling her in his arms. Rachel's heart thumped hard against her ribs. He was romantically involved with Beatrice! She wasn't sure why this disturbed her or why it surprised her either. Why wouldn't he be wooing someone? She was glad they hadn't seen her in their haste as they rode away in the buggy.

Rachel waited for a few moments, then walked back to her horse to continue on her way, her thoughts all a jumble. Beatrice was pretty and delicate like a china doll, and she could see how John would be attracted to her. Molly had told her that she and her mother were very wealthy.

In no hurry to return to the ranch, she let the horse take

the lead to enjoy the wonderful, fresh mountain air. The wind blew through the pines, its mournful sound bringing memories of a sweeter time. There was something about having lost both parents and her only brother that left her floundering—with no place to go and really no one to answer to. Of course she answered to Estelle while she still worked at the shop, but she considered that temporary until she planned her next move. Whatever that was.

Pushing onward through the high prairie grass, Rachel made out her family's farmhouse just ahead. She gave the gentle horse a tap on her sides, and they cantered the rest of the way until she drew the reins in to stand in front of the log cabin. She dismounted, savoring the eerie silence. The place was deserted. No horses in the corral and no cattle anywhere in sight. Weeds were taking over the yard and the flower beds. She sighed deeply. Before John forced her to leave the saloon, Rachel would ride out when she had use of a horse and do a little weeding. It was all hopeless now. She reminded herself that it was not *their* place anymore.

She walked up the porch steps, noticing the peeling paint, then pushed open the door and stepped inside. Cobwebs were everywhere, but she swept them aside and looked around the now-empty living room where furniture had once stood. The sound of joy and laughter echoed in her mind. She could almost hear her mother's voice calling, "Supper's ready!" She stifled a sob in her throat. How she missed them all. Would she ever get over losing them? The pain was still fresh, and without Preston, almost unbearable. She folded her knees and sat by the fireplace, sobbing her heart out while the wind blew through the cabin chinks.

After what seemed an eternity, Rachel wiped her eyes with

a handkerchief she found in her skirt pocket. She was thoroughly spent. She'd not had any time alone to grieve Preston's death. She rose and made her way back outside, recalling the promise of God's words written on her heart—she would see her family in heaven one day.

On the way back home, the warmth of the afternoon sun caressed her face like a lover's touch. Would she ever feel someone stroking her face with love? It certainly didn't seem so. The thought only reminded her of John with Beatrice. She nudged her mount to go faster and soon came to a fork in the road, nearly colliding with Pastor Jeffrey on horseback.

"Whoa! Watch out there!" Jeffrey pulled the reins sharply to avoid running smack-dab into her.

With a swift jerk of the reins, Rachel was able to hold her seat in the saddle. "I'm so sorry, Jeffrey. Please excuse me." She heaved a breath, reaching down to pat the horse's neck to calm her. "It's so desolate out here I wasn't expecting anyone on the trail."

He flashed her a grin. "You're forgiven." He chuckled. "In fact, I was on my way over to visit you."

Rachel blinked. "Oh. Well, in that case we can ride together and no harm shall come to either of us." She tried to smile, but of all days, with red-rimmed eyes and a blotchy face, she wasn't keen on the idea of entertaining anyone. She was sure she must look frightful.

"If this is a bad time, I can come again later." He scrutinized her face. From his intense gaze, he could apparently tell she'd been crying. "Is something wrong?"

"Yes and no," she said as Jeffrey guided his horse into step with hers. "I took a ride over to what used to be our ranch." She paused to take a deep breath, controlling the tears that threatened again. "It's just that the place looked so desolate and lonely . . . and abandoned. I guess you could say it's the same way I feel." She stared ahead so she wouldn't have to see the pity in his eyes.

"Estelle told me about you and Preston losing the ranch, and I'm sorry, Rachel. But you must go on and face the future. Your brother would've wanted that."

"What future? I have no home. I'm just a sojourner at the mercy of others. Same with my job. I don't know what I'm doing in a millinery shop. I'd rather be outdoors ranching," she blurted out in anger. Immediately, she was sorry she'd said anything. But as she glanced over at him, he didn't seem ruffled in the least.

"Rachel, I think I understand how you feel. You feel like your anchor is gone—your brother and your parents."

"Yes. I guess I do." The horses slowed to walk side by side. Rachel had no idea why she'd confided in Jeffrey—either the fact that he was a man of the cloth, or because of the kindness she found in his warm eyes.

"Try to remember that your *real* anchor in this world is the good Lord. Yes, our families do matter greatly, but we are never promised to have them forever. There's a verse I'd like to share with you, if you don't mind."

"Not at all. I need *something* to cling to."

He looked directly at her, speaking in rich baritone. "'Why don't you look at the birds of the air—they don't sow nor reap or gather into barns, but our heavenly Father feeds them.' Rachel, you are more valuable than they are." Jeffrey smiled, then continued. "'Are not two sparrows sold for a farthing? Not one of them will fall to the ground without the Father.' He tells us that the very hairs of our head are all numbered, and He told us to fear not because we are of more value than many sparrows. That's from the book of Matthew, if you're familiar with it."

"I am, and I do remember those verses now. My mother quoted them often."

"Do you see how it applies to you?" His kind brown eyes mirrored concern, and for a brief moment, something in his eyes made her sense that he liked her more than a little. Maybe their friendship could develop into something more, but for now she considered him only a friend, not a love interest.

"I believe I do. Thank you for the reminder, Jeffrey." Rachel gazed ahead of them at the rolling hills, with the sun barely grazing the treetops now. "We'd better get on back to the ranch. It'll be dark soon. Maybe we can have one of Annabelle's special cinnamon muffins."

"Sounds wonderful to me. I'm not the best cook in the world and *never* try my hand at baking. The result would be disastrous." He chuckled. "A cinnamon muffin could hit the spot."

"I'll race you the rest of the way." Rachel took off down the dirt lane and could hear the hoofbeats of Jeffrey's horse close behind.

16

Between the majestic mountain streams and hills where purple asters and pink thistles lent their charm, John had set out early looking for strays, with Winchester to keep him company. He knew he was blessed to be able to do what he liked best—checking for strays on his vast property. He and Curtis would meet up where the Yellowstone River separated Paradise Valley and Gallatin Valley from Bozeman.

Earlier he'd had a quick bite to eat, and now as he looked across the valley he could see the thick blue smoke rising from the rooftop of the ranch house, which meant his grandmother and Rachel were sitting down to hot biscuits and smoked bacon before they set off to the shop in town.

When he'd come back from visiting Beatrice, he was a little more than surprised to see Rachel, looking a little worse for wear, quietly entertaining the pastor in the parlor over coffee and muffins. He'd hastily retreated to his room, but was unable to get the vision of the haunted look in Rachel's golden eyes out of his head. Of course she was still grieving over her brother, as evidenced by her swollen and red-streaked eyes—unless she'd been crying about something else, and he highly doubted that. Still, he was glad that she was seeing the pastor—it'd give Curtis a reason to look lively if he wanted Rachel's attention.

John heard a movement in a thicket a few yards ahead, so he moved in a little closer to the sound. He took a moment to grab his rope in case he had need of it, then slid down the slope to where he found a baby calf who'd wandered from its mama. As he approached the chokeberry bush, the little calf eyed him in fear. He talked soothingly to it. The bush had lost its meaty fruit but its golden leaves could be toxic to cattle if much was eaten. The calf appeared listless—not a good sign.

John scrambled down on his knees and reached for the calf, dragging it out from under the thick bush. The calf didn't fight him but still had a frightened look in his eyes. John lifted the calf and headed back up the slope to Cutter, who stood waiting for his master. At that moment he spied Curtis.

"Hey!" Curtis yelled. "Looks like that calf needs help," he said, hopping off his horse to meet him.

"Maybe so. Found him in a chokeberry bush. I can only hope he hasn't been eating a lot of the leaves or bark."

"Yep. That'd mean the end of him." They both walked back to their horses. Curtis mounted. "Why don't you put the calf up here with me, and I'll trot him back to the herd and tell Billy to keep an eye on him?"

John lifted the calf onto the space between Curtis and the saddle horn. "You find any strays while you were out?"

"Naw, but I believe Levi and Nash did. They led them back to where the herd was grazing."

John pulled himself into the saddle, and with a nudge to Cutter, started back down to the valley.

"I hear you're courting that Miss Beatrice now." There was a slight tease in Curtis's voice.

"And what if I am?" John threw back at him.

"I hear she's pretty darn wealthy. Might be a good match for ya." Curtis spit a wad of tobacco juice to the ground.

"I don't know Beatrice's business." John was tight-lipped. "Say, I thought you were going to call on Rachel?"

"I plan to, but Saturday afternoon I saw the pastor ride over, so I stayed outta the way."

"Well, don't take too long asking her out. Rachel's a mighty pretty woman and high-spirited too. I figure her married before too long."

Curtis sat up tall and straight in his seat. "Married! I'm not planning on marrying her—maybe sparkin' her, but that's about as far as it goes, boss."

John laughed outright. "It's gonna happen to you someday."

Curtis wiped his damp brow with his handkerchief. "What about you? Don't you find her attractive? Why aren't you sparkin' her?"

John gave him a straightforward look. "I don't think the two of us can get along for more than five minutes. Besides, she thinks I'm the reason for her predicament."

❧

Estelle had spent a busy morning placing orders for hats or haberdashery and was grateful when the shop became quiet after lunch. She let out a sigh of relief and looked at Molly, then Molly looked at Rachel and they all laughed. Rachel enjoyed the warm camaraderie of their working relationship.

"Why don't I make us a delicious cup of coffee to settle our frayed nerves," suggested Molly.

"That would be lovely. I brought some tea cakes that I made myself for us to have today." Estelle grinned, then turned too fast to retrieve them, striking her hip on the sharp corner of her desk. She gripped the edge of the desk for support.

Rachel hurried over to her. "Are you all right?"

Estelle mustered a weak smile and answered, "Ooh, just a little bang on my boney old hip."

Rachel took Estelle's elbow. "Here, Estelle. Have a seat and tell me where the tea cakes are."

"Oh, you girls fuss too much over me. I'm fine, just a little clumsy some days." But Rachel noticed she didn't put up an argument and instead obediently sat down in her desk chair. "The tea cakes are in a tin, sitting on the second shelf next to the hatboxes."

"I'll get them while you make the coffee, Molly," Rachel suggested.

"Uh, there might be a delay . . ." Molly nodded at the store front. "Looks like we have the honor of visiting with *Miss Sneertrice* . . . oops!" Molly said with a hand over her mouth to cover her giggle. "I meant Beatrice." The three of them turned as Beatrice waltzed through the door, pushing it to the side so hard that the bell overhead clanged with a loud noise.

Rachel stepped forward. "Hello, Beatrice. Is there something I can help you with today?"

Beatrice hardly gave Rachel a glance as she made her way over to where umbrellas were shelved. "I'd like a new pretty parasol." Without waiting for assistance, Beatrice stood on tiptoe, reaching above her head to get the one on top of the shelf, and pulled three more to the floor with a loud crash and tangle of handles. "Oh dear, I've made a mess, haven't I? Oh well, that's what Estelle hired you for, Rachel. Be a dear and pick those up for me," she said while admiring the pink parasol in her hands.

Seething at the implication that she was little more than a servant, Rachel politely held her tongue, then bent to pick up the umbrellas. Estelle said the customer was always right. That's how you kept them coming back. Rachel couldn't care less if Beatrice ever stepped foot in the shop again—but this wasn't her shop. It was Estelle's, and she would champion the older lady even if she had to swallow her pride.

Beatrice walked to the customer counter and handed Molly the pink scalloped parasol. "Put this on our bill, please, Molly, and there's no need to wrap it. I'll be using it to protect my fair skin in this dry weather when I go for rides in the countryside with John." She smiled at Molly, and Rachel thought that was Beatrice's way of letting them all know that John was courting her.

"Yes, ma'am. Let me get the price tag first." Molly took the tag and marked down the price in the ledger.

Beatrice must have noticed Estelle at her desk and paused to give her a polite nod. "Good day, Miss Estelle. See y'all at church."

Molly walked her to the door, and as soon as Beatrice had popped up the umbrella she was rushing down the sidewalk. Molly closed the shop door in normal fashion, turning to Estelle and Rachel. "I do declare that is the rudest woman in Cottonwood!"

Estelle shook her gray head. "Don't mind anything Beatrice has to say. That's exactly what she's hoping for, but she especially seems to want to annoy you, Rachel."

"No need to worry about me. If your grandson wants her and can put up with her, then I say that's fine. Now let me go fetch the tea cakes before we get busy again."

Rachel saw the exchange of looks between the two ladies but she didn't care. She had no pony in this race.

※

Once John made sure all strays had been rounded up and accounted for, he sat at the desk in the parlor going over his ledgers before supper. He had too many scraps of paper to deal with and hated keeping track of entries. But so far, it looked like when they shipped the cattle to market this fall he'd have enough money to buy up more land and cattle for next year. And he needed to decide how best to use the Matthews place. He'd been so busy he hadn't spent any time worrying about it. Maybe get a tenant and then put some of his own cattle on it? He wasn't exactly sure what he wanted to do. *I can always sell it back to Rachel if she isn't married soon. If she can scrape up enough to buy it back.*

Grams came in and sat down in her favorite easy chair. "Working on the books?"

"Yep! You know I hate this part of ranching," he answered without looking up.

"You should ask Rachel to handle the paperwork for you on her days off. You did say you wanted her to work on the ranch, and I'm sure she could use the extra income," she suggested.

John twisted in his chair. "I might. You look a little tired." He got up, walked over to where she sat, and took a seat in the chair next to her, picking up her veiny-blue hand. "Don't you go working too hard at that shop. I suppose Molly and

Rachel are doing a good job for you." It wasn't a question but a statement to his grandmother encouraging her to slow down. As if he could get her to listen.

She squeezed his hand. "I am tired. Must be my age. I am getting older, you know," she said, then pushed a lock of John's curly hair that hung across his forehead off to the side of his temple. "You have enough to worry about besides me. How did your afternoon go with Beatrice? I meant to ask you but forgot."

He pulled back. "Okay."

"Just okay? Doesn't sound like it was." Grams quirked an eyebrow.

He shifted in his chair, then adjusted his jeans over his boots. "Grams, I'm not sure how to take her. She's pretty and all, but I'm not sure if there's any depth to her. Do you know what I'm talking about?"

"Yes, I think so. I've seen enough of her in my shop to know that. Seems she's only interested in how she looks to others and trying to rope a man—my grandson."

"You've got that right. But that doesn't make her a bad person."

"Of course it doesn't, John. But you need to have some spark between you or you're wasting your time. Sometimes I think I've glimpsed a certain spark between you and Rachel."

He sighed. She knew him too well. "I guess I hold every woman up to Lura as a standard, and so far, I haven't come across a woman with all her qualities. She was so perfect in every way. She was my sister, but she was my best friend too."

17

Estelle's heart quickened. She knew it was time she told John the truth about his sister—not that she wanted to. She took a deep breath and plunged headlong. "John, there's something that I have to tell you. Lura was no innocent."

"What are you trying to say?" John frowned at her.

"Lura was pregnant with Will's baby."

"Our Lura and Will?" John remembered the ranch hand who helped for a few months back in '61 and left suddenly. He wiped his hand across his face, now a paler shade of white. "I can't believe that."

"He was a smooth talker in all the ways that a young girl longs to hear." She waited for his reaction.

A look of incredulity and shock filled his handsome features.

"It's true, unfortunately, but there's more." She leaned forward. "You see, John, I feel partly responsible for Lura's death."

"How can that be, Grams?" He folded his arms and shifted again.

"I hope you can forgive me . . . Lura had just told me she was pregnant, and we argued. That's when she stormed out and went on that hellish ride on Midnight and died."

Estelle held her breath as silence engulfed the room. John suddenly stood, a stormy, dark cloud infusing his face and making her heart ache.

"So help me, I'll find Will and tear his arms off!" He stormed to the door, nearly snatching it off its hinges.

Estelle hurried after him. "John. Listen to me. You know Will left a long time ago, and you can't blame only him. Lura was in love with him. Young people do stupid things sometimes," she pleaded with her hand on his arm.

"Not Lura!" he said, his voice rising in pitch and volume.

"I'm sorry, but it's true. I'm trying to tell you that we all make mistakes—even Lura. I know that's not what you want to hear. It was a terrible day and two lives were lost then." Tears stung Estelle's eyes. It wrenched her heart to tell him the truth.

He removed her hand from his arm. "I'm going for a ride. Don't hold supper for me."

"Wait—"

But he stormed down the steps. Knowing that she'd caused his pain only made matters worse. She closed the door with sorrow and said a quick prayer for her grandson just as she saw Rachel coming down the stairs.

"What's all the noise? I heard loud voices and came to see what all the fuss was about." Rachel walked toward her, then stopped. "You look upset."

Estelle's legs nearly folded, but she garnered her inner strength. "I am. I shared something with John that was none too pleasant and was shocking for him, I'm afraid."

"Would you like to talk about it?" Rachel took her arm, and Estelle was grateful for the assistance.

"Let's go into the parlor," she answered, noticing Rachel's face reflected genuine concern.

By the time Annabelle called them to supper, Estelle had told Rachel about Lura. She felt sure Rachel would keep her confidence. "Please don't mention to John that I've shared this with you. I feel like I'm to blame for what happened to Lura. If I had accepted the fact that she didn't save herself for marriage instead of berating her for it, she might still be alive today."

Rachel patted her hand and Estelle knew in her heart that the girl was troubled for her. "Estelle, you of all people know that you are not to blame for Lura's death. She might've had the accident on that wild horse on any given day. Now I know why John didn't want me riding Midnight. I never knew. I'm so sorry."

"I know you're right"—Estelle shook her head—"but my heart won't listen to my head this time, and now I've made John angry with me." She sniffed into her hanky. "You know, you have a good head on your shoulders, Rachel. I admire that in you. You'll make a good partner and wife one day." Seeing Rachel's face flush from the compliment made Estelle's heart feel good. *Now if only John would open his eyes.*

Rachel smiled. "Why don't we go have a little supper before Annabelle throws a dishtowel at us? I'd say let him mull it over in his mind for a while. He'll come around."

But instead of getting to her feet, Estelle blinked at her slowly and her head fell to her chest. She barely heard Rachel yell for Annabelle.

John had hurriedly saddled Midnight and rode as if the hounds of hell were nipping his heels. The magnificent stallion galloped down the open road with a stride that even the best horse trainer in America would envy. The power beneath him exhilarated John and he realized this must have been the way Lura felt—wanting to get away from the judgmental words and anger of their grandmother. It was Lura's way of letting go of everything bottled up inside her.

A full yellow moon was rising above the pine and spruce treetops by the time John reined the stallion in. He rode along the ridge he frequented when he was troubled—where it was so quiet, the only sounds were the wind flittering through the pines and the distant cry of a hoot owl.

Midnight's sides heaved from exertion while his nostrils blew out air. John pushed his hat back, crossing his arms over the saddle horn and thinking. Hunger had all but left him now. The only thing remaining was confusion. Why had Grams held this news back from him till now? Why hadn't Lura told him? *Probably afraid I would condemn her like Grams did.* He'd looked up to his big sister and was so proud to be her younger brother.

A huge tear rolled down one cheek and he wiped it away with the back of his sleeve. His heart ached knowing that Lura had kept her secret until she finally confided in their grandmother. As John recalled, Will had already left to go work for a large outfit farther west. He said it was to be closer to his family, but John knew now that was a lie. Will had used his sister but didn't want any part of being a father.

He had a good mind to go look for Will. Lousy scoundrel. But then what would he do? Lura and her baby were gone now. And to think he would've been an uncle! But he had to face the fact that Lura had made the decision to be with Will despite what consequences she'd have to face.

Midnight's ears twitched and John heard a noise behind him. He turned and was surprised to see Rachel on Cutter. Her hair was half down from its pins and her coat was askew. By the moon's light he could see her brilliant eyes deep with concern. She stopped Cutter next to him. Breathlessly, she started to speak.

"John, I'm glad . . . I finally found you. You must come quickly . . . Estelle has had a spell of some kind." Rachel's chest heaved in ragged breaths. "Annabelle had Curtis send for the doctor."

He didn't need to hear another word but flicked the reins across Midnight's hindquarters, racing back to the ranch house. Once Rachel caught her breath, she'd be close behind him.

Clay was outside waiting for him. He took the reins and said, "The doc's in there with her now. I hope she'll be all right."

"Thanks, Clay." John took the front steps two at a time, noticing that behind him Rachel was riding into the yard. He was glad Rachel was there.

Annabelle met him in the hallway, nervously wiping her hands on her starched apron. "The doctor is with her now. Curtis and Levi carried her to the guest bedroom downstairs."

John moved right on past her to the bedroom, quietly pushing the door open and tiptoeing in. His grandmother was in the bed, propped up on two pillows. Thank God, she was conscious. She looked weak and tiny with the thick comforter pulled up to her chin. Her thin arms, ensconced in the long sleeves of her nightgown, lay on the top of the covers, and it struck him that even the skin of her blue-veined hands looked pale.

Doctor Wilson, a tall, thin, middle-aged man, looked around when he saw John, then motioned for him to come closer. "John, your grandmother has had a weak spell and needs to rest, but I'll allow you to say good night to her."

Taking his grandmother's small hand in his, John spoke in a low voice as she looked at him through half-closed eyes. "Grams, you're in good hands with the doc here. He knows what's best for you. I didn't mean to upset you earlier, but we can talk about that another time."

Her watery eyes looked into his and she sniffed. "Just tell me you forgive me, John." She took a deep breath, trying to sit up, but the doctor gently touched her shoulder and she relaxed. Doctor Wilson gave John a questioning look.

"There's nothing to forgive. I love you and we'll all be praying for you." He leaned down to stroke her wrinkled cheek, kissing her forehead before he backed out of the room with a worried, heavy heart.

Moments later, Doctor Wilson emerged from the bedroom. "John, let's go to the parlor so we can talk." As soon as they were out of earshot, the doctor asked, "Did you two have an argument earlier today? Estelle said something about forgiveness."

"Unfortunately, she told me something that I think upset her more than me." John ran his hands through his hair. "Did you know that Lura was pregnant when she died?"

The doctor cleared his throat. "Lura came to me when she was two months pregnant. I thought either she or Estelle would have told you. It wasn't my place to," he said, his lips compressing.

John clenched his jaw. "I wish I'd known. Grams feels responsible for Lura's death because they argued before Lura took off on Midnight."

"It was an accident, and no one is to blame." The doctor picked up his coat and bag. "What's important now is that your grandmother has had a mild heart attack and should rest for a few weeks. Another one might kill her. Do you understand?" The kindly doctor narrowed his gaze at him, and John finally understood how serious his grandmother's illness was.

"Absolutely. We'll take care of her."

"Good! She can try getting up in a couple of days, but she's not to exert herself in any way or get upset. I would like to see her in my office in a week, but only if she feels up to it." John handed the doctor his medicine bag as he turned to go.

John trudged to the kitchen where he could smell coffee brewing. He knew Annabelle would be worried. But when he entered the cozy kitchen where a fire crackled in the hearth, it wasn't Annabelle but Rachel who waited. He sat down at the worn table, resting his throbbing head between his hands and closing his eyes. After a moment he looked up to see Rachel gathering cups and steaming coffee at the stove. Her figure was tall and slender, her step light and firm, and her appearance the expression of health and animation. Her complexion was a clear brunette's tone—rich in color. Her smooth oval face and small, well-formed nose were cute but not delicate, and her hair formed natural, soft waves close to her face.

It dawned on him that in the last week some of her intense sadness since her brother's death had diminished, but he knew she most likely held it privately now and close to her heart.

Silently she placed the cups on the table and filled them, then quietly said, "I'm sorry."

"The doc told me she's suffered a mild heart attack, but if she has another one it could be bad."

Rachel sat down across from him, adding cream and sugar to her cup before giving it a quick swirl with her teaspoon. "I was afraid of that. But your grandmother is a determined woman, and I believe she'll get better as long as we make sure that she gets her rest."

"I hope you're right." John blew on the hot coffee, taking several big swallows. Maybe it would ease his headache. He shouldn't have stormed out of the house like he did. "I upset her and I shouldn't have."

"John, it's not your fault, you know. It's part of growing older."

He set his cup down, blinking back tears he hoped Rachel couldn't see. "I know you're right, but the thought of losing her . . ."

Rachel reached across the table, covering his hands in hers. "Don't think that way. We'll help her get through this and regain her strength. I'll be right here to see that she does."

18

Rachel knew by John's look that he had his doubts his grandmother would recover. She tried to remember that it hadn't been that long since he'd lost his sister, just as she had lost her brother—both of them too young to die.

John drained the rest of the coffee and gazed at her thoughtfully. His thick brows crunched together. "You don't know the whole story."

Rachel didn't respond but looked at him over the rim of her cup, vowing to keep Estelle's promise not to let on that she knew about Lura.

After a deep sigh, John told her about Lura's "delicate condition," as he called it, and the discussion he'd had with Estelle. "So there you have it. I think I brought on Grams's attack with my anger, which I think she thought was directed at her."

"I don't believe that, John. Things happen. Sometimes for a reason. Estelle is getting on up in age. Perhaps she shouldn't work so much. Molly and I can handle the shop—with her guidance, of course."

He gave her a weak smile, and she caught herself wanting to stroke his face to remove the sadness there. He looked different without his hat, and his hair was flattened.

"I appreciate it, Rachel, and I mean that."

The sound of her name from his lips gave her pause, and she wondered what was happening to her tonight. She knew he'd been watching her when he first came into the kitchen.

"You're welcome." Rachel felt her cheeks grow warm. John locked eyes with her until she looked away, feeling totally unsure of herself.

"And here I was about to ask you if you had any interest in helping me with my books. Grams suggested it and said you could use the money."

"I could use the money to get back on my feet. I don't want to be beholden to you indefinitely. Remember—I had a job before, and a good paying one at that. If you and Preston hadn't interfered, I'd still be there." Rachel sounded harsher than she meant to, but it still grated on her how he'd literally snatched her from the saloon, however it had changed her life for the better.

He gave her an exasperated look. "Surely, you don't really think you were better off there?" He quirked an eyebrow in disbelief.

She shifted in her chair. "I was my own boss *there*."

"Ha!" He laughed. "You only thought you were. You had a boss that told you when to dance and how high to kick your legs, I'll wager."

Hot resentment washed over her, and Rachel shoved her chair back. Leaning over the table at him she said angrily, "Maybe so, but it was where I chose to be—not with you here, telling me what to do!"

He stood suddenly, then leaned over to touch the tip of her nose with a tweak of his finger—close enough that the scent of his soap, mingled with an outdoorsy smell, invaded her space. "Fine—there's the door. Don't let it slam and hit you from behind!" He pointed toward the doorway, feet planted apart.

This wasn't going right at all. Rachel hadn't meant it that way—not tonight with everything going on with Estelle—and now she floundered to come up with what she should say.

John rammed his chair up under the table. "You're mad because your brother let me buy your place to keep from losing it!"

"That's not true." She clenched her hands to her sides. "I'm not mad at you! I'm mad at my brother for not telling me about your agreement, then leaving me! I'm mad because my parents died. I'm angry that I'm alone!" Her voice rose, and remembering that Estelle was just on the other side of the house, she lowered it. "I'm angry that my new, dear friend Estelle had a near brush with death!" Suddenly, she burst into tears, angry at everyone and everything but especially at herself for acting like a child.

John stiffened, with a look of disbelief on his rugged face. She couldn't look at him anymore and started for the door, but he took two strides and was at her side before she could put her hand on the knob, touching the sleeve of her blouse.

"I'm sorry, Rachel. Sorry for what you've gone through in such a short time. Guess I've only been thinking of myself." He reached over and turned her face to look straight into her eyes. "I know this is beginning to sound repetitive, but do you think we can put this behind us and start again? I only wanted to help you."

His eyes, the color of dark coal, softened, and Rachel nodded. "I'm the one that should be sorry. I'm afraid I've acted quite childish."

His finger brushed a tear from her cheek gently, much like a caress. "Not at all. Lura was somewhat like you—full of fire and her own notions, but still needing love." He gave a small cough, then said, "I'm rather lacking when it comes to sensitivity where women are concerned, but I want you to know, Rachel, that if you're that unhappy here, then it's best that you leave. I guess I took on the role of your guardian to protect you for Preston's sake." His hand dropped to his side and he shifted on his boot heel, waiting for an answer.

Rachel looked down at her hands, which she still clasped tightly. "I sound so ungrateful. I think I wanted to be the one who made the decision to leave the Wild Horse instead of you. I hate to admit it, but you're right. I'm beginning to feel at home here. Some of the things I saw at the saloon I'd like to erase from my mind." She raised her head to look up at him. "Besides, you've lost a loved one, too. So I'd like to stay, and I'll do your ledgers for the ranch and take care of Estelle. With the extra income I can keep saving until I can get the ranch back."

With a broad grin exposing a set of even teeth, he appeared about to answer when Annabelle came sashaying through the door.

"Why in tarnation are you both still in here?" she asked, eyeing them like a hawk. "All your chattering will disturb Estelle." She nodded her head in the direction of the stairs. "Off to bed, you two. I'll be keeping a close eye on Estelle, so don't be worrying."

"But what if—" John began.

Annabelle held up her hand. "I promise to wake you, John, if there's any change, but I think with the sedative Doctor Wilson gave her, she'll sleep the night through."

John gave Annabelle a hug as he passed through the doorway. "Thanks, Annabelle, and good night, ladies."

Rachel looked at the back of his lean figure, lithely moving toward the stairs and out of sight for a moment. "I'm going too, Annabelle. Please wake me if you'd like me to take a turn with Estelle. I'm a light sleeper."

Annabelle nodded, and Rachel could tell her eyes were tired like everyone else's.

Later, before climbing in bed, Rachel prayed for Estelle's health and could only hope that by morning, she'd be improved.

Sleep wouldn't come. Tired of tossing and turning, she walked over to the window and saw the pasture bathed in the moonlight's glow. It was a beautiful sight—peaceful and calm—the way her soul needed to feel. John, his back to her, was sitting on the fence rail feeding Midnight sugar cubes and stroking the horse's forelock. At the sight of the man's quiet communion with one of God's creatures, Rachel felt a sense of peace when she most needed it.

19

For the next several days, John stuck as close to home as he could, limiting his time outdoors with his ranch hands. He worried something might happen to his grandmother, but she seemed to be slowly improving and had more color in her cheeks.

Annabelle was taking good care of her, and Rachel and Molly were well suited to running the shop in her absence. He was so grateful for all of these wonderful ladies and wondered how bleak his life would be without them.

Today he'd carried his grandmother out to the veranda to enjoy the fresh fall air. Winchester loped over and curled up next to her chair in a patch of sunlight.

"Are you warm enough?" he asked as he securely tucked the blanket around her legs. She wore a woolen cape about her shoulders and smiled up at him.

"Son, if I get any warmer, you're going to have to get a line of water buckets to put out the fire!" She chuckled, waving her hand to swish him away.

He laughed as he took a seat next to her in one of the big

rocking chairs that filled the porch. "There's a nip in the air, but I know you love to be outside when the weather is this nice. Let me know if you start to get chilled. I told Annabelle to rustle up some fresh coffee."

"John, don't you have chores you need to get to?" Her watery eyes clamped on his in earnest.

"Everything is being handled by the ranch hands," he answered. "I think I can afford to spend the afternoon with you."

Annabelle appeared with a tray of steaming coffee and lemon cookies and placed them on the small round table between them. "You warm enough, Miss Estelle?"

"Yes, dear Annabelle. You and John need to quit fussing over me. I feel perfectly fine."

Annabelle stood with her hands on her hips, eyeing her. "That may be, but we don't want you to catch a cold. I made those cookies this morning, so enjoy them with your coffee." She looked over at John. "Don't keep her out here too long now. You hear?"

"Yes ma'am!" He gave Annabelle a mock salute, and she rolled her eyes and went on back inside.

They enjoyed the warm afternoon sun that diminished the day's chill while passing the time talking about matters pertaining to the ranch. After a while, John decided it was time to take her back inside. "You're looking tired, Grams. Why don't you go back inside and have a nap?"

"I can nap right here in this wonderful sun," she replied, lifting her face up to the sun's warmth. "Besides, I love listening to the sounds of nature all around me. I'll be fine." She set her cup down and crossed her arms across her lap.

"Suit yourself." John smiled over at her, but her eyes were

already closing. He needed to make himself useful and was about to get up when he saw Larry, the young man who delivered mail, coming up the lane on horseback. Strapped to the horse's back was a small package.

"How do, John." Larry greeted him with a tip of his hat, then slipped off his horse and began untying the box.

John walked out into the yard where Larry was. "What do you have there? A package for Estelle?" He watched as Larry's nimble fingers unwound the rope before he turned to hand John the package.

"Nope. It's for you, John. All the way from California."

"You don't say?" He took the small box, then fished inside his jeans pocket for two bits, which he handed to Larry. "Well, thanks for bringing it all the way out here. I could've stopped in the post office next time I was in town. But since you're here, thank you."

"No trouble at all." He mounted his horse. "I have others to deliver anyway." With a brief wave he cantered out of the yard.

Now who in the world was the package from? John looked at the return address in bold writing on the left side at the top. It read, "*Robert Wilkes, San Francisco, California.*" It was beginning to make sense. This was obviously a friend of Preston's. His grandmother stirred and then shifted in her rocker but kept her eyes closed.

He quietly sat back down in his chair, then pulled out his bowie knife and cut the box open. Inside was a brief letter on top of a fine wooden box, explaining that Preston had left his personal effects to be sent to John if anything ever happened to him. The sender stated that Preston felt certain John would make sure Rachel received the box, but he was afraid to send it to the Wild Horse for fear someone else might get their hands on it.

John folded the letter but didn't open the box—that was for Rachel to do, and if she wanted him to know what lay inside, then it was her privilege to share that. He'd give it to her right after supper.

His grandmother's eyes flew open and she turned to him. "Did I hear voices, or was I dreaming? What have you got there?"

"Yes, you did, and no, you weren't dreaming." He quickly told her about the letter. "I don't know what the contents are, so I'll give it to Rachel tonight." He thought about how she might feel receiving something from her brother—almost like he was still alive. John still missed his friend. Life could be hard at times, and he sure didn't want to lose his grandmother too.

"I'm sure this will be unsettling for Rachel. Poor girl. John, could you take me to my room before dinner?" Grams placed her hands on the chair's arms, trying to stand. When had her fingers become so twisted with arthritis? How had he missed that?

He sprang up, placing the box on the seat of the chair and assisting his grandmother to her feet. "Let me help."

"I *can* walk, you know. I don't want to be babied," she insisted, patting his arm.

Stubborn woman. "I'm sure you can, but lean on my arm in case you get tired, all right?" His grandmother was a strong woman, like Rachel had said. John had to smile. She didn't give in easily, and her determination would benefit her recovery.

"I'm hoping by Sunday I can attend church, and then maybe by next week I can take a ride into town."

"We'll see," he commented as he settled her into a wingback chair in her bedroom. "I'm going to go for a ride before dinner."

"Good! You can't be sitting here all day mollycoddling me." She gave a small laugh.

"Okay. I'm beginning to get your message, Grams. I won't be too long. I'm getting hungry anyway from the scents coming from the kitchen." He leaned down and kissed the side of her forehead. "Can I get you something to read?"

"Yes, if you don't mind. I left my Bible on the nightstand."

"I'll get it for you then."

She squeezed his hand affectionately. John knew the earlier things between them had been put to rest.

After he took Grams her Bible, John retrieved the box from the porch and placed it on his desk. He was curious about the contents.

※

John had no specific direction he wanted to ride but felt the need to get away from the house and be alone with his thoughts. He was antsy and couldn't put his finger on what was the matter, but riding Cutter always allowed him to free his mind. Receiving the unexpected package today had put him in a reflective state of mind. Normally, he was too busy to give much thought to anything but his work. But now, with Preston fresh on his mind and his grandmother sick, it made him realize how brief life really was. Why, Preston was a good five years younger than he. He knew this package would open up fresh wounds for Rachel, and John didn't like to see her upset. He argued with himself that it was all about being her protector. But was it?

He wasn't aware of how far he'd ridden until he came

upon the Matthews homestead—his homestead now. He reined Cutter in, dropped the reins, placed his arms across the saddle horn, and shoved his hat back to contemplate what he should do about the place. It made perfect sense to let his cattle graze here, and he'd tell Curtis to start herding some of them in that direction. Besides, he planned on adding more steers very soon.

It'd been awhile since he'd ridden over here. The surrounding property needed attention and the ranch house needed repairs too. A soft breeze whispered through the pines near the house, adding a forlorn atmosphere that felt like something between sadness and the memory of a place where a productive family once lived. In some ways, John wished Rachel could buy it back. But even if he lowered the price, she wouldn't be able to cover all the expenses now. Giving it back to Rachel when she didn't have enough to take care of it wouldn't make sense at all. It took money to buy the stock and feed them, and there was no way she could run cattle by herself.

John sighed deeply. All that could change if she married the preacher or another suitor. He'd wait to see how it all played out. He was glad they'd cleared the air between them, and it nagged him that he cared more than a little about how her well-being would be affected by receiving Preston's package. Maybe by having her brother's personal things she'd feel closer to him—either that or her improved attitude he'd seen lately might change to despair. He hoped not—he rather enjoyed the tilt to her full lips when she smiled at something Annabelle said or the twinkle in her beautiful eyes when she teased him. He picked up the reins, and with a clicking sound, signaled to Cutter to return home.

꧁

Rachel sat on the edge of Estelle's bed after supper relating the goings-on at the millinery shop. She was pleased to see Estelle was improving and very interested in life outside the ranch.

"I hope you don't mind, Estelle—Molly and I ordered some grosgrain ribbon to adorn some of the plainer hats for fall."

Estelle's thin-veined hand took Rachel's. "Oh, not at all. I just knew you'd have some great ideas and ways to improve sales."

Rachel chewed her bottom lip. "Thank you. We'll have to wait and see, but I must tell you that Molly has a good eye when it comes to hats."

"You know, Rachel, Molly is a treasure but *she* doesn't know it. I'm glad that you are working together because I believe you'll be good for her. I fear her confidence suffers. She didn't have the best childhood." Estelle's smile faded.

"I'll do all I can to be a friend to her. Now I'm going to let you rest. Is there anything I can get for you?"

"You're kind, but no. I have everything I need. Annabelle is taking such good care of me. Have you talked to John since supper?"

Rachel paused at the door. "No. Why?"

"I know he had a package today that he's going to give you."

"Mmm . . . I'll go find him. Good night," Rachel said and softly closed the door, wondering about the package. She hadn't ordered anything, but then again, Estelle said John was supposed to give it to her. Her heart lurched. It must be something to do with Preston. She hurried down the hallway to the parlor, looking for John.

John was hovering behind the newspaper, but when he heard her enter the parlor he put the paper aside. "I've been waiting for you. Thanks for keeping Grams informed about the shop. I know she hardly knows what to do with herself, but she knows it's in good hands." Brooding eyes gazed up at her, belying his forced smile.

"Estelle said you had something for me?" Rachel drew closer, feeling curious.

"Yes." He rose and strode over to his desk in two long strides, returning with a wooden box in his hands. "A friend of Preston's sent this for you but I didn't open it—only the accompanying letter which stated that Preston thought it would be safer if he sent it to me." He held the box out to her.

As she took it, her fingers brushed his and warmth shot through her. Looking down at the plain box instead of into John's eyes was easier. It was slightly heavy and she wondered what was in it.

"It's Preston's personal effects, or what he kept for you."

Tears sprang to her eyes and she murmured, "I'd like to open it alone in my room, if you don't mind."

"No, not at all. I certainly understand." He backed away, giving her some space.

Rachel nearly ran from the parlor to her room upstairs, slipping into a chair by the window to carefully open the box. Inside were Preston's Colt revolver, a neckerchief, and a locket with a daguerreotype of her parents, along with his pocket watch. She held the locket in her hand for a moment, her heart beating rapidly, feeling the coolness of the gold against her skin. When she went to town, she'd find a chain to hold it. But that was all that was in the box. No letter. Rachel's heart sank. She sat there for a long time, fresh tears blinding her while she thought about the loss of her family, wishing she'd had other siblings to share Preston's things with—which made her cry all the harder.

She rose to find a handkerchief to wipe her eyes and dab her nose, but in her haste the box slid off her lap, landing upside down on the floor with a thud. She bent to retrieve the contents, and as she righted the box, a small spring on the inside corner flipped up to reveal a secret compartment. She drew in a breath of surprise. *What in the world?* She sat down on the floor, her skirts billowing out around her, staring down at the contents of the previously hidden section.

A letter? A key? Her heart pounded with excitement as she opened the letter. It was from Preston.

> *Dear Sis,*
>
> *Please forgive me for not writing you as often as I should have, but if you are receiving this, then my demise is near. I had hoped to return sooner with enough to purchase our home and land, but alas, things didn't turn out the way I planned. I trust that John is looking out for you—he's a good man, Rachel, and will treat you well, unless you've married by now.*
>
> *The key you've found is to a safe-deposit box in Lewistown. Take this letter and the key to the bank. They won't give you any trouble. Our heritage is in that box. Hopefully, someday you'll have enough money saved to buy back the ranch from John. That has always been our agreement—so remind him of it. However, you may desire to start a business or whatever. It's up to you, dear Rachel.*
>
> *I was always proud to call you sister and knew that*

somehow you'd be resourceful enough to find the hidden spring inside this box. I had it especially made for me for safekeeping of the key.

I'm weak so must close, but rest assured that I'll carry your heart with me to heaven where I eagerly join our loving parents and our dear Savior.

Love, Preston

Rachel crushed the letter to her chest, and a sense of peace and belonging crept deep inside her heart . . . along with hope.

20

John slipped on his leather vest before heading out for the day. From his window he saw Wyatt Kimball ride into the yard on horseback. Why would Wyatt be here so early? He stomped down the stairs to get the door before Annabelle.

Wyatt greeted him at the door as John opened it. "Mornin', John."

"Hello yourself. Come on in." John held the door open for him to pass through. "Would you like some coffee?" Wyatt was another rancher in the area, and although he didn't know him very well, John had liked him from the first moment they shook hands at church. He was a real cowboy turned rancher, complete with bowed legs from years of herding along the Bozeman trail—and in a rugged way, a decent-looking fellow.

Wyatt removed his hat. "No thank you. Can we talk for a moment? I don't want to keep you if you were headed out."

"Aww, there's no rush. What brings you out here so early this morning?"

"I wanted to talk with you about breeding one of your stud bulls with my heifers. Everyone says you're the best breeder this side of the Yellowstone River. I'd be willing to pay you well—within reason, of course."

John considered what he said. "Mmm . . . Let's have coffee and talk about it."

Annabelle was on her way to the kitchen and paused when she saw him. John motioned her over with a finger to his lips. He didn't want to raise his voice with his grandmother in the bedroom down the hall.

"Yes, sir?" Turning to Wyatt, she said, "Hello, Mr. Kimball."

Wyatt returned her greeting. "Annabelle, would you mind brewing a couple fresh cups of coffee for Wyatt and me? We'll be in the parlor."

"Comin' right up, John." She hurried off to the kitchen.

"Let's go to the parlor where we can talk." As they turned around, Rachel came walking down the stairs. When she reached the bottom she greeted both of them.

"Good morning."

John stifled a desire to rush over to her. Rachel was like a sudden breath of fresh air that entered the dim hallway. "Mornin'! Rachel, I'd like you to meet Wyatt Kimball, a neighboring rancher."

———

Rachel's hand flew to the high-neck collar of her blouse as her heart caught in her throat. She froze. *Wyatt.* His long duster made him appear shorter than he was, but he conveyed the outdoors, with his rugged, weather-worn skin and thick beard that was pleasing to the eye.

Wyatt's jaw dropped. "Hello again, Rachel." She remembered that same twinkle in his eyes when he would tease her.

Wyatt was a rancher who frequented the saloon to play

cards and often would ask if he could take her away, but he never gave her an offer of marriage. Rachel couldn't find her voice.

"Do you two know each other?" John asked, looking at her with a furrowed brow.

After what seemed a long time, Wyatt moved to take her hand in his. "Let's say we've met before. What are you doing here with John?" His eyes narrowed to slits.

With her heart thudding, Rachel pulled her hand from his warm, masculine one. No telling what Wyatt was thinking. "I . . . uh . . ." She stumbled over her words.

"She works for my grandmother. You remember—Estelle."

"I see. How nice that she lives here." His look was skeptical.

"Yes, especially since Grams has been ill."

Rachel knew Wyatt wasn't convinced. She tried to act normal, but her mouth felt full of chalk. "Yes, it is. I must be off to the shop now, if you gentlemen will excuse me."

"Without breakfast? It's still early. The shop doesn't open for a while yet," John said.

Searching for an excuse, Rachel blurted out, "Maybe so, but I have some things to do before we open, and we're expecting a shipment today."

With raised eyebrows, John stared at her. What was he thinking? She hoped he didn't think there was anything between Wyatt and her. All she wanted to do was get out of the house. She moved to the hat rack by the door, feeling their eyes on her back, and plucked her cape from the hook. Throwing it across her shoulders with a brief smile, she scooted out the front door.

By the time Rachel reached the millinery shop, her stomach was rumbling with hunger. Perhaps Estelle had left tea cakes in the back. She hoped so. She kept her cape on for the time being and headed to the cupboard in the back of the shop where, thankfully, she found a tin of them. The shop was cold, so she made a fire in the stove first and then a cup of strong tea to go along with the cakes, carrying them to the small desk in the corner. From this vantage point, she had a full view of the busy street.

While she munched on her breakfast and waited for Molly, Rachel perused the new catalogue of winter fashions. She loved the cool snap of September changing the leaves to brilliant fall colors of orange, red, and yellow. Autumn clothing and the array of plaid material in the shop made her long for a new outfit. How nice it would be to own such a cape with ermine fur, pretty matching shoes, and a woven woolen dress. It'd been a long time since she'd had anything new to wear.

Soon she intended to tell Estelle that she needed some time off to go to Lewistown, providing Estelle was stronger. She could make the drive there and most likely return all in one day. Then she could find out how much Preston had in the safe-deposit box. It seemed odd that he hadn't told her in his letter, but then again, maybe he was worried someone could intercept the letter and the box and steal the key. She was sure she'd never know the answer for that.

The front door swung open and Molly breathlessly entered the shop, untying her bonnet as she talked. "You're here early." Then she stopped, staring down at the cookies and tea. "Is this your breakfast?" she asked, removing her coat.

"You could say that. I was in a rush to get out of the house this morning."

Molly paused, cocking an eyebrow in Rachel's direction. "Well? I'm waiting."

"Let me get my cape off and I'll tell you. It was chilly when I opened up, but I must say I rather like a morning chill. Don't you?"

"Don't try to change the subject. What was so bad that you had to leave in a hurry? And how's Miss Estelle?"

Rachel removed her cape and stood for a moment holding it in her hands. "She's doing well—that's the good news. The bad news—I ran into a former patron of the saloon who was talking business with John. I could tell John was displeased that we knew each other."

"What's so bad about that? I don't understand." Molly's innocence was refreshing and sweet.

"I fear that John believes I gave . . . uh . . ." Rachel coughed. "Gave favors to some of the men that frequented the Wild Horse." She proceeded to gather her cape and Molly's coat to take them to the back of the shop. She returned to continue their conversation.

"Mmm . . ." Molly poured herself a cup of tea. "But you and I know it's not true. So why are you so worried about what John thinks? Do you have romantic feelings toward him—or the gentleman?"

"The gentleman's name is Wyatt, and I don't know how I feel about anything right now."

Molly set her cup down. "Wyatt? Wyatt Kimball?"

"Yes. Do you know him?"

Molly shook her head with her curls dancing on her collar. "Shoot, all the eligible women know who he is. He's quite the catch. Don't you like him?"

Rachel laughed. "My, but you're full of questions, aren't you? I guess I do. He used to offer to sweep me away to his ranch and get me out of dancing at the saloon."

132

Molly's eyes widened. "Really? Why didn't you marry him? You'd have had your own servants."

Rachel gave her a level stare. "Because he didn't ask me to, Molly. So I guess he had the same assumption as John. I admit it was tempting to leave the saloon with him, but not without a marriage certificate."

Molly looked exasperated. "Didn't you tell him that you only danced for the money and tips and nothing else?"

"I did, but I'm not sure Wyatt believed me." Rachel sighed and her shoulders sagged. "Why should he? In hindsight, my working there was not a smart thing to do, but I had to survive somehow after Preston left and my parents died. I had few skills other than ranching. I don't know anyone willing to hire a woman for that job, do you?"

Molly walked over and gave her a quick hug. "I'm sorry. Things have been so hard for you, but trust me, I do understand. We both know God is watching over us, right? Things could always be much worse."

"Yes, that's true, but I'm human and can't help but wonder why things have worked out the way they have for me. I did receive a letter from Preston yesterday."

"What?" Molly drew back. "How can that be?"

Rachel took a few moments to explain about the box and the letter, and Molly clapped her hands together.

"How wonderful! It's like a gift from God! Don't you see?"

Rachel walked over to the front door, turned the sign over, then pivoted to smile at her friend. "I guess you're right. I'm looking at it the wrong way. I should be considering it as guidance for the next step in my life. Thank you, Molly, for helping me to see that."

"I'm glad I can encourage you for a change!" Molly smiled, and it hit Rachel that she was becoming more like the sister she'd always wanted.

"Looks like we have some customers." With a smile, Rachel turned to assist a lady as she entered the shop.

21

The week flew by with Rachel and Molly managing the shop while Estelle made great improvement with her health. On Saturday after the shop closed, Rachel returned to the ranch to find Curtis waiting for her on the porch, standing around talking with a couple of ranch hands.

Curtis clambered down the steps as she parked the buggy by the barn. "I hope I'm not imposing on you, Miss Rachel," he said as he approached the buggy then assisted her down. "Clay will take care of the horse and buggy for you."

Rachel wasn't sure what to make of his waiting for her. "Hello, Curtis. Is there something I can do for you?"

Curtis cleared his throat. "Could you spare some time? Or I can come back later. I'd like to talk to you."

He was clearly nervous and Rachel was definitely curious about his visit. She could smell his aftershave and he'd donned a fresh shirt. "All right, Curtis, but I must check on Estelle first."

Red-faced, Curtis nodded. "I can wait on the porch for you, is that okay?"

Rachel removed her driving gloves. "Why, yes, you can. I

won't be long." He followed her up the steps and took a seat on the swing at the end of the porch.

She went straight to Estelle, who was sitting in the parlor laboring over her needlepoint. When she heard Rachel enter, she looked up and laid her needlework in her lap. "You're a breath of fresh air, Rachel. It's getting a little lonely without you here, and I must confess I don't like being idle for long." Estelle gave her a bright smile, her eyes crinkling at the edges.

Rachel walked over to her and bent to give her a quick hug. "Honestly, I feel the same, but if you keep improving, you'll be back in the shop in no time giving me and Molly orders. Not sure if we want that," she teased.

"Everything good today at the shop?" Estelle cocked her head up to Rachel.

"Perfect! So don't give the shop another thought. How was your day?"

The older lady chuckled. "Not bad—Annabelle fusses over me and John stops his work to check on me constantly!" She tilted her head toward the porch. "I couldn't help but notice that Curtis was out in the yard talking to you."

"He wanted to talk to me, but I told him I wanted to check on you first. I'm not sure what he wants to talk about."

Estelle tapped her fingers against the arm of her chair. "I think I can guess."

Rachel drew back with a quick glance to her. "You can't mean—"

"Yes, I can, and it's not surprising," she said with a grin. "You're a very eligible woman, and there're not many of them in Paradise Valley."

Rachel blew out a deep breath through a slanted lip. "Then I suppose I need to go speak with him."

"You give him a chance, Rachel. He's a good man, and so is the preacher. It's nice to have several men vying for one's attention."

"I'll see, Estelle. I want to talk to you later about something. Perhaps after supper?"

"Of course, dear. Now you run along and see that young man who's waiting for you."

⁂

"Can I get you something to drink, Curtis?" Rachel asked.

"No, nothing for me, thank you." His smile seemed forced, making Rachel confident he *was* nervous. He gazed at her, and Rachel decided he was handsome in his own rugged way, with deeply tanned skin and crow's feet around the edges of his brown eyes.

She sat at the end of the swing, turning slightly to see him. She was glad she'd kept her wrap on. Though the sun was bright, a breeze rustled through the leaves, swirling them in the yard.

"Was there something you wanted to talk about, Curtis?" she asked when he didn't speak.

He shifted against the back of the swing and placed his arm on the top of its back. "Rachel, this may come as a surprise, but I've wanted to ask if I might court you," he blurted out, his Adam's apple bobbing.

Estelle had hit the nail on the head. "I don't know what to say . . ." She glanced down at the toes of her shoes.

"Say yes," he said. He dropped his arm to finger the brim of the hat he held on his knee. "Unless the preacher's your beau now?"

She gave a nervous laugh. "No, we hardly know each other."

137

"Tell you what—I'll come Sunday afternoon and take you for a ride in the country while the leaves are a'turnin'. What do you say?"

He wasn't wasting any time, Rachel thought. While she didn't have any interest in anyone currently, a ride would be a refreshing pastime.

Liar. You know you are interested in John.

Yes! But he's not interested in me! she countered back to her conscience. And an afternoon ride couldn't hurt either of them. "I think that would be a nice change, but let's don't call it courting, Curtis—at least not yet."

"I understand. Then Sunday it is." He stood to leave about the same time as John rode into the yard.

John had a curious smile on his face as he stepped onto the porch, and he paused to give Curtis a clap on the back. "Things are looking good for you when you can spend time with a pretty lady." He tipped his hat to Rachel.

Curtis chuckled, red-faced. "Yes, it sure is. I'll be on my way, now," he told Rachel as she rose. "See you Sunday afternoon, then."

She nodded her agreement, then watched as he lumbered off toward the bunkhouse before turning to John. "Hello, John."

"I'm glad to see you're getting out more. You can't work all the time." He folded his arms and leaned against the porch railing, hat slung low and steely eyes resting on her.

Rachel's tongue felt thick and dry. "Yes, well . . . I've found that I enjoy working at the millinery shop. I was about to go freshen up before supper. How about you?"

"Headin' right in." He leaned across her to open the door, brushing her arm momentarily. Rachel caught a scent of sunshine with a woodsy smell of pine that clung to him, and her breath caught in her throat. She drew back a step, suddenly wishing it was John taking her out for a Sunday ride instead of Curtis. *When did I suddenly start noticing things like this?*

"Sorry," he said, then swung the door wide, moving aside.

"Oh, John, I may be taking a day off with Estelle's approval to ride to Lewistown and wondered if I might have use of the buggy and horse."

He stood in the hallway and cocked a brow upward. "No problem at all. Just let me know what day. Not to be nosy, but why are you going to Lewistown?"

She drew her shoulders up and expelled a breath. "It has something to do with the letter Preston wrote me." She fingered the locket around her neck.

"I see. Was that locket in there as well?"

"It was." She snapped it open for him to see. "It has a daguerreotype of our parents."

He leaned in and looked, then surveyed her face closely. "Beautiful mother. I can see that's where you get your looks."

Rachel blushed and murmured, "Thank you. I only hope to be as lovely as she was—inside and out." She snapped the locket closed, the nearness of his face causing her hand to tremble.

He grinned openly. "Have no fear, Rachel. You're already like her." He left her standing in the living room and walked toward the direction of Estelle's voice in the parlor.

His grandmother was sitting in a chair by the window, half asleep, her Bible in her lap. The sun drenched her wrinkled face and made her skin glow. She opened her eyes and turned to smile at him when she heard him enter.

"You look mighty comfortable napping there, Grams. Who were you talking to?" John strode over to her side to give her a kiss on her brow. "And your color is much better, so you're improving."

"I must have been talking in my sleep. The sun is good for one's health as well as the soul. I have regained much of my energy, praise the good Lord!" She gave him a bright smile.

"Yes. An answer to prayers." He settled down in a chair opposite her with a loud sigh.

"What's the matter, dear? Something troubling you?" Her keen eyes didn't miss much, he thought.

"No, I'm just a little tired today. I completed the purchase of another thousand acres and more cattle west of our property line today. The land will be great open range for grazing."

"More property, John?" She gave him a skeptical gaze.

"Grams, land is the best investment a man can make, and I intend to invest as much as I can from the sale of cattle. 'Strike while the iron is hot' is the saying—your very own son taught me that."

"As long as you don't forget God looks at a man's heart and not his possessions. They are meaningless in the broader picture of life."

John squirmed in his chair. "Grams, you sound like the preacher. I see no problem with a man having land *or* possessions. I've worked hard to get where I am. In fact, I'm meeting with someone soon about buying their property. It'll be another good investment."

She leaned over and patted his arm. "I don't mean to sound like him, but it concerns me sometimes when I think of all the land you've acquired. I wonder when it will be enough for you. Make sure you leave time for matters of the heart."

"Which really means find a wife and have a passel of kids."

Estelle pulled back, clasping her hands. "Would that be so bad, John?"

He flattened his palms on both knees. "Maybe not, if the right one were to come along." He stood, suddenly feeling weary. "I'm going to go clean up. I'll see you at supper." He didn't like the way the conversation was headed. Plus he was tired. Early to bed seemed appealing tonight.

Estelle watched her beloved grandson go, quietly shutting the door behind him. That boy—or man, as he really was—gave her much to pray about. She'd hoped by now he would be settled with a family. But not with Beatrice! She shuddered. Something about that girl didn't sit well with her. He needed someone like Rachel who had a good head on her shoulders and wasn't afraid of work. Too bad they'd gotten off to a bad start. She wondered if the fact that both Curtis and Jeffrey were hanging around bothered him, or if it was the notion that he couldn't let go of her dealings with the Wild Horse. She'd pray God's blessing on his future and try to keep her opinions to herself.

❧

Sometime during the night, John woke to the sound of rain hitting his windowpane. Dampness had crept in, and he buried himself deep beneath the heavy quilts for warmth. Was he getting old? His usual energy was lagging and his legs felt heavy.

22

On Monday morning, Rachel slipped on an old traveling dress with fuzzy brown polka dots on a tan background of heavy cotton. The skirt was set in vertical panels with pink roses and vines, with an added darker shade of brown appliqué along all the edges and paneled cuffs in the same brown at the wrist. The bodice was set in a V-neck insert with delicate brown trim at the throat and shoulders. She looked at her reflection, thinking someone would have to look closely to notice the fraying at the cuffs and skirt edges. She hardly thought that would be an issue as she knew no one in Lewistown. To complete her outfit she wore her bonnet trimmed in wide brown ribbon tied under her chin.

Rachel waited in the yard for Levi to bring the buggy around after breakfast. The dark clouds and a few stray raindrops boasted a gloomy day, to be sure. She planned to be home before nightfall and was looking forward to a drive to Lewistown alone with her thoughts. She hoped the safe-deposit box would make the trip worth her while. But she had to trust that Preston had saved *something*. She tried not to get excited that it might be enough to buy back her place, but anything would help out along with what she had saved. Estelle had been generous with her salary, especially while she'd been under doctor's orders not to go near the shop until he gave the approval. Estelle had cheerfully given permission for her to take the day off last night when they'd talked after supper.

Levi walked the horse and buggy to where she stood in the yard. "I gave ya the best horse for your trip to Lewistown, Miz Rachel. The only time Sal can be ornery is when she takes a notion to stop for a nibble on her favorite plants. You'd do well to let her have her way —it won't last long," he said with a big grin as he helped her into the buggy. "The whip is next to you on the seat should you need it."

Rachel chuckled. "Thanks, but don't worry about me. I grew up on a ranch, remember?"

He nodded. "Right you are." He tipped his hat as she waved goodbye.

Once out of the yard, Sal took off at a nice steady trot down the dirt road. It felt nice for a change not to be at the shop. She was glad Molly was capable of handling things by herself for one day. It wouldn't be long before Estelle would be allowed to return to supervise. She'd be glad to have her back since she'd grown fond of the older lady.

It wasn't long before her thoughts turned to Curtis and their outing after church on Sunday. He'd been all spruced up, his hair slicked down with pomade and the heavy smell of aftershave lingering about him. His mustache had been waxed to smooth perfection and curled up at the ends.

He'd had Slim prepare a snack for them that they shared under a stand of brilliant gold aspen trees whose heart-shaped leaves trembled in the cool breeze along Mill Creek. A very nice setting for a picnic.

"Tell me about your days as a cowboy, Curtis," Rachel asked since she knew nothing about him.

"I've been a cowboy since I was fifteen. I've worked in places like Texas and Kansas," he said. "When I got older I drifted up here to Paradise Valley, and with my experience handling Longhorns, I quickly signed on to work for John as his foreman. I've never had a better man as my boss," Curtis told her. "So here I am." He talked as they strolled along the banks of Mill Creek.

"Do you have plans to have your own ranch like the other drovers?" Rachel had tried to sound interested, but she had her mind on the drive to Lewistown. When he gazed at her, his eyes filled with hopeful intentions while hers skittered away.

"I like working for John and I'm happy with what I do. 'Course, someday I wouldn't mind having a little cabin close by to call my own where I could have a wife and maybe a kid or two. And you?"

Rachel thought a moment before answering. Somehow she knew what he wanted to hear. "I haven't given it too much thought. You know I lost my brother recently and our ranch. I'm grateful for the job Estelle provided me, and that's enough for now." They'd paused by the creek, listening to the sounds of its water rushing over the smooth rocks.

Curtis boldly took her hand in his large calloused one. "Well, I hope we can spend more time together soon—maybe next Sunday?"

She pulled her hand away a little too hastily. "Let's just enjoy this glorious fall afternoon. Okay?"

He had seemed a little miffed and took a step back. "All

right, but I'm not giving up. I can be a little stubborn at times. So I'm giving you fair warning." He chuckled.

Rachel had forced a smile. "We'll see. I think I need to go now, if you don't mind." As soon as they returned to the ranch she hurried inside to check on Estelle. She could feel his eyes on her back as she left.

Now, as she and Sal continued rumbling down the road to Lewistown, her thoughts were all a jumble. What was she going to do about him? She'd have to think about it later. Right now her mind needed to focus on getting to the bank in Lewistown. The damp morning sent a chill up her back, but the blanket across her legs kept her warm. She encountered a stray shower or two, and for certain there'd be no sun today. It'd be so much better sitting by the fire with a good book, she mused with a sigh.

She thought of Molly, wondering how the morning at the shop was going. Rachel found herself looking after the girl like a big sister. She couldn't help but notice Molly had a deep affection for Estelle, and it warmed Rachel's heart. Molly could benefit from a little mothering, and Estelle liked nothing more than to think she was being helpful to folks. It was a virtue that Rachel admired in her. Some people had the gift of putting others before themselves.

The Bridger Mountains to the northeast were a formidable sight, the gray clouds hanging over them with the promise of more rain. The breathtaking beauty of the mountains and surrounding slopes of conifers and aspen trees reminded Rachel that God created this vast, unbelievable landscape. Up ahead, Lewistown was coming into view.

She maneuvered the horse and buggy through busy Main Street and managed to avoid the muddy potholes, stopping in front of the town's bank. Several gentlemen walking about greeted her or tipped their hats with obvious interest. But she only smiled back and tied Sal to a hitching post, whispering in her ear, "I won't be long, so here's a treat for you." She held out an apple and Sal snorted before swiping it from her hand, her soft muzzle tickling Rachel's palm. She gave Sal a pat on the neck, took the steps to the bank, then entered the busy place filled with midday customers.

"May I help you?" asked a middle-aged bank clerk when Rachel stepped up to the window.

"Yes, please. I have a safe-deposit box and would like to retrieve the contents." She pulled out the document signed by Preston and slid it under the opening behind the barred window.

The clerk looked it over and glanced back at her. "Do you have a key to your brother's box?"

"I do." She reached into her reticule for the key and showed it to him.

"I'll meet you at the door over there." He pointed in the direction of a side door a few feet away.

Rachel nodded. "Thank you." She marched past several desks where employees were helping other customers, ignoring their inquisitive glances. When she reached the door, she waited until she heard a key in the lock. The door swung open to show the bank clerk standing in the doorway.

"My name is Herbert, Miss Matthews. If you'll just follow me . . ."

After they passed through a short hallway, he unlocked another door and they stepped inside. A straight-backed chair and a small table stood in the center of the room.

"Just insert your key into box 285. When you're finished

146

I'll be right outside waiting to lock up. I'll give you a few moments alone." The gentleman left her and closed the door.

Hurriedly, Rachel found the metal box with brass number 285, then slid the key in the lock until she heard the latch click. With trembling fingers, she pulled the box out and carried it to the table. She took a deep breath and opened the metal lid to what she hoped was her future. But what she saw was the Matthews family Bible! She slammed the lid shut in her anger, her eyes tearing. *This is what Preston left me? This is our heritage? What did he mean by that?* She opened it again, lifting out the worn Bible. Underneath were her parents' wedding bands inside a used cotton tobacco pouch. Recalling the many times she'd seen the Bible in her father's capable hands brought fresh tears.

She dropped the pouch with the rings into her reticule, then held the Bible to her chest and hurried out the door—her jaw set and lips tight lest something untoward spill out of her mouth. She couldn't believe she'd come all the way to Lewistown for this!

23

When Rachel scurried out of the bank, heavy sheets of rain were coming down. The wind whipped her skirts about and threatened to remove her bonnet. She paused under the portico, hoping the deluge would slack up before she made a dash to the parked buggy. Her mood had gone from hopefulness to anger in a mere five minutes. She was not in the mood for a rainstorm, not in the mood for the dreaded drive back to the ranch, and not in the mood to smile at a passerby who offered to share his umbrella.

"Rachel, is that you?" She turned to see Wyatt coming out of the bank.

"Good grief! Just what I need at this moment," she mumbled under her breath. But she turned to him and pasted on a pleasant expression. "Yes, Wyatt."

"Here, you can share my umbrella," he offered, holding it over both of them. "Which direction are you going?"

She pointed to her horse and buggy. "I was hoping the rain would stop."

"No chance of that now. I know a little tea shop not far

down the street. Why don't we go have a cup of hot tea until the weather subsides?"

Rachel liked the thought of a cozy tea room on this gloomy afternoon, but she didn't know what to make of Wyatt or her terrible disappointment in Preston. She was definitely not in the mood for trivial talk. She chewed her lip in thought. "Well —"

"Oh, come on." He took her arm. "It's not fit for man or beast to be out. I promise to escort you back to your buggy."

Rachel looked at poor Sal with her head down in the slashing rain. Wyatt caught her glance. "Why don't I step back inside and have someone take your horse and buggy to the livery for shelter? It's not likely to stop for a while."

"I suppose you're right. Okay."

"Wait right here and I'll be back in a flash." He handed her his large black umbrella and left her wondering if she ought to have said yes or no.

Soon they were settled at a table close to the window at Mittie's Tea Room sipping delicious orange pekoe tea served with scones. Ladies and gentlemen of means were the common clientele, with the glow of gaslights burning against the shadowy late afternoon gloom and a crackling fire in the enormous brick fireplace to chase the chill away. Maybe the coziness would help improve her mood.

She found that she was indeed hungry, and the scones were delectable. Wyatt's handsome face gazed intently at her over the rim of his tea cup. "Rachel, if you don't mind my asking, were you at the bank for a loan? From the expression on your face earlier, I'd say they turned you down. I'd be more than happy to give you a personal loan."

Rachel stiffened at his personal question. "It was nothing

like that at all. I was not there for a loan. I was settling up some business."

He smacked his lips after a bite of scone then dabbed the napkin to his mouth. "You? A businesswoman?" He chuckled.

"Is that so hard for you to believe?"

"Maybe, because I know where you *used* to work." He gave her a lopsided smile.

Was he implying she didn't have enough sense to be a businesswoman? She tried to check her growing anger. "I've left that behind me now and you know it. You also know from the numerous times you frequented the Wild Horse that I wasn't like some of the girls there, so don't insinuate it," she responded coolly, meeting his gaze. "I danced to earn a living."

Wyatt smiled even broader at her. "And a good dancer you turned out to be, I might add." His eyes lingered on her. "I guess that's why I was surprised that John said you worked for his grandmother. Seems a very odd arrangement, you living with him at his ranch."

She eased back against her seat with a sigh as he poured them more tea without asking. "It's not what you think. There's nothing between us. It's merely a place to stay for a while until I can get on my feet. Estelle wanted to help me."

He twirled the sugar spoon in his cup. "Good! Then perhaps you'll allow me to—"

"Please don't offend me by asking me to come live with you again. I can't be bought," she said, making steady eye contact with him.

He leaned forward and whispered, "I know that now. But what about marriage?"

Did I hear him right? Did he just propose marriage? She was completely stunned.

150

He continued, "Rachel, you're a beautiful woman and exciting to talk to. I knew that a long time ago from my visits at the Wild Horse. I can give you a beautiful home, clothes, or anything else you desire. I own half of Montana in land and cattle. So this time, I'm offering marriage."

Rachel blinked. This was the last thing she'd expected today. "I don't know what to say except I plan to marry for love."

He settled back in his chair. "What is love? Maybe it's overrated. We could make a good partnership, and I'm not half bad to look at. Perhaps we could grow to really care for each other. Many marry for less than that. At least give it some thought."

"You know very little about me, Wyatt, and I of you."

"Then it'll be fun finding out, won't it?" he teased. "I'd like to spend more time with you if you'll let me."

Rachel was confounded. She knew Wyatt was very wealthy and considered a good catch. She should be jumping at the proposition, but yet . . . She looked out the window. Rain was still coming down in slanted sheets. The streets were fast becoming full of mud holes, and she watched as a horse and buggy became stuck on the busy street.

"My goodness! The weather is worsening. I should be leaving now or I'll have to contend with the rain and the dark." She pushed her chair back and in a moment he was beside her helping with her cloak. He laid some bills on the table and picked up his coat.

"Let's go see how bad it is outside." He ushered her out onto the boardwalk and popped the umbrella open to share. After observing the conditions, he said warily, "Rachel, I don't know if it's safe enough for you to return tonight. The going will be muddy and dark. I don't think it's good for you to be alone. What if your buggy gets stuck or breaks down?"

She clutched her cloak tighter about her, the dampness and cold chilling her to the bone. "I suppose you're right, but I wasn't prepared to spend the night."

"There's a nice hotel close by and I know the manager. I'm sure they could find you a room and you could leave in the morning depending on the conditions."

"Oh, I don't know . . ." She didn't want to tell him that she had only a few dollars on her. Not enough for a room for the night, much less the added livery fee.

"I know what you're thinking, Rachel. Let me help you out this one time as a favor. In return, all I ask is that you allow me to call on you sometime soon and consider my proposal. I promise."

She took a deep breath. "You promise?"

He placed a hand on his heart. "Promise."

Rachel allowed him to lead her in the direction of a hotel where he quickly got her registered for a room.

Turning back to her, he said, "I'm coming back to take you to dinner. The hotel has a good restaurant so you won't have to step another foot outside in this weather."

"I don't know. I doubt I'll be hungry, and I'm tired." She really wanted to go to her room and be alone.

"Aww, come on. You have to eat so you'll feel fresh for your drive in the morning," he begged.

She gave in, promising to meet him at the restaurant inside the hotel later, grateful not to have to go back out in the rain. When he left, she heard him whistling a tune. She shook her head and smiled at the oddity of it all.

A welcoming fire burned in the grate of her room. She

could hardly wait to slip off her skirt, which was damp at the bottom, and allow it to dry over the bedpost. Having done that, she slipped off her soggy shoes and set them in front of the fire to dry out. Moments later, with the events of the day still cluttering her mind, she curled beneath the thick rose-covered bedding and laid her head on the fluffy pillows to rest before supper.

24

Will this rain ever stop? John gazed out the kitchen window, coffee mug in hand, doubtful that much would be done today. The sky was filled with heavy clouds of murky gray. Rain steadily dripped from the cottonwood boughs bending against the driving wind. Many of their colorful leaves were gone now, reminding him of the cold winter yet to face.

His men were ready to start fall roundup but this weather might interfere. Normally coffee worked wonders for his headache, but not today as the dampness seeped into his bones. Annabelle was getting his grandmother settled after breakfast and Rachel was away in Lewistown. She had not told him what business she had there, only that it was connected to Preston. It wasn't any of his business anyway. But he had to admit he missed her. The ranch was livelier when she was around.

He set his cup down and reached for his slicker, then headed out to the bunkhouse to speak to his men. Winchester slogged with him through the standing puddles and muddy expanse of yard to the farthest side where the bunkhouse stood. John yanked the door open. The scene reminded him of the times when he'd gone to the bunkhouse with his father as a kid. It was filled with boots, bedding, and the odor of sweat and leather—and a wet dog now that Winchester had plopped down by the potbellied stove. Some drovers sat on their bunks, others were at the table playing cards and laughing. One was trying to read a novel, lounging against the wall of his bunk space that was filled with yellowed newspapers to keep the wind from blowing through the chinks. A common practice, John knew, against the Montana wind.

Curtis hopped up when he saw John, while the others paused and listened. "Boss, anything wrong?"

John waved his hand in Curtis's direction. "Naw, just thought I'd check on everyone and get squared away with the plans to move the cattle for roundup."

"We're ready whenever you give the word," Curtis said. "Hope this blasted rain will be outta here in the morning."

Clay pulled out a chair for him. "Here, you may as well sit a spell and have some of the coffee that Slim's brewing."

"No coffee for me, thanks. Were you able to get the rest of the cattle sheltered in the coulee, then?" John directed his gaze to Clay, then took the offered seat.

"Shore did. Leastways it gives them fellers a little protection against the elements," Clay answered.

Billy put his books aside and rose up on one elbow. "Tomorrow's gonna be a better day according to the almanac."

"Is that so, Mr. Know-it-all?" Clay teased, but Billy only grinned back at him.

"If you men know of anyone who wants to sign on for the trail drive, tell 'em I'm hiring and to come see me." John looked around at his ranch hands and silently thanked God for their loyalty. They were a good bunch and worked hard. He wanted to somehow reward them after the trail drive— with more than just their pay.

Levi scratched his chin and said, "I know a couple fellas needing work who just arrived here from Kansas. I'll have 'em come talk to ya."

"You do that, Levi. I suspect we need a crew of twelve men, not counting Slim," John said, nodding to Slim who grinned at him as he walked in holding a large spatterware coffee pot. "So we'll probably need six more men to drive the two thousand head of cattle to market."

Curtis shook his head in agreement. "Mighty right you are."

Slim reached into his apron pocket for a piece of paper he handed to John. "Here's my list for supplies for the grub, boss. You'll notice it's heavy on the coffee." He chuckled.

"For sure!" Nash agreed, clapping Slim on the back. "A man can't live without his early morning coffee."

John glanced over the list before shoving it into his vest pocket. "Whatever you need, Slim, it's yours."

"Hey, how 'bout a round of cards with us?" Levi asked.

For a brief moment John considered it. "Not now. I've been nursing a headache, and I'm afraid you guys will slip something over on me when I'm not able to give my hand my concentrated attention." He laughed.

They all chortled good-naturedly as John strode toward the door. "You feed my men well, Slim. They're going to need all the strength they can muster for the trail drive."

Slim wiped his hands on his apron. "You got it, boss."

John whistled and Winchester came running and followed him out. He stopped by the barn to give Midnight his breakfast of oats and plenty of water. The rest of the horses were tended by Levi. He stroked his thick neck, whispering into his twitching ear. "You're a fine horse. Strong and fast." John never blamed the horse for what happened to Lura. He decided things that happened to folks were meant to be by the Maker. No accidents. Still, tragedies were hard to accept.

He closed the barn door and headed indoors. He'd use the inclement weather as a day to sit near the fire, then see if he could make sense of his accounts or catch up on his reading. No sense in wasting the day away because of the rain, so he hurried on inside, hung his dripping slicker, and plopped into his easy chair.

It seemed only moments had passed when Annabelle touched his shoulder and he jerked up in surprise. He must have fallen asleep. He tried to focus on Annabelle's face and glanced at the clock on his desk. It was two o'clock. "Good heavens, Annabelle! Did I sleep through lunch?"

"Yes, honey, but I hated to wake you. Curtis is waiting on the porch and wants to talk to you. He says it's urgent."

John got up, running his fingers through his hair. "By all means. Please show him in." Winchester, who'd been sleeping by his feet, lifted his head as though perturbed that anyone would disturb their rest, but without even a blink, laid his head back down on his two outstretched paws and closed his eyes.

John sensed something amiss with one glance at Curtis's sober face. "Well, what's wrong?"

Curtis stood, feet planted apart and hands on his hips. "John, I need you to ride with me to the south pasture. I was out looking for strays and I don't like what I've found."

John snatched his slicker off the hook by the front door.

"Lead the way." At the sound of their voices, Winchester quickly popped up to follow them.

"I had Levi saddle up Cutter for ya," Curtis said as soon as they were out the door.

Twenty minutes later, Curtis dismounted and John pulled Cutter up behind him. He directed his gaze to where Curtis pointed a few yards away.

A calf lay stiff as a poker with outstretched legs, his carcass bloated. *What in the world?* John had never seen this in all his years as a rancher. He would've stepped closer, but Curtis held out his arm. Winchester walked closer, sniffing the air, but John called him back to his side where he obediently sat on his haunches, waiting for orders.

"What happened?" he asked Curtis. "Does he look injured or have a gunshot wound?"

"I'm not positive, but there're no marks on 'im as far as I can tell. I think he caught some sort of disease. Have you ever seen anything like this?"

"I can't say that I have, Curtis. We need to keep the rest of the cattle as far away as we can until we can find out the cause. That's for sure."

John stared down at the calf with concern, his mind racing with thoughts of other cattle getting sick. "Wonder if the town doc would know? I could ride over to Wyatt's place and see if he's had any problems. Are there any others?"

"Not that I know of. No need for you to go over to Wyatt's. I can go or send someone else to ask around."

"Good idea. It may be a fluke but it bears checking out. He could've eaten something poisonous." John pulled his collar up around his neck. "Let's get out of this rain for now."

"I'll let you know what I find out, boss."

Once they were back at the ranch, Curtis rode to the bunk-house and John to the barn with his dog. Levi was there and took the reins. "I'll take care of Cutter and get him dry. What'd ya find out there? Curtis was pretty worried."

"I'm not sure if a calf was poisoned or ate something poisonous, but he's dead now."

"You don't say!" Levi began to remove the saddle from Cutter's back, while Winchester shook the rain from his heavy coat, then plopped down in the straw.

"We'll have to be on the lookout for any others that may come down with something. Thanks for taking care of Cutter." John turned to Winchester. "You stay right here in the barn, ole boy, and dry off," he said. John gave him a piece of beef jerky, then patted his wet head. Winchester whined, wagging his tail and looking up at John lovingly. He loved his dog, but with his wet hair and smell John couldn't allow him back inside tonight or Annabelle would have a fit.

His grandmother heard John when he returned and called out to him. "John, is everything all right? Annabelle told me Curtis seemed troubled about something."

John strode into the parlor, aware his stomach was growling. "There might be a problem or it could just be a sick calf that died. I'm not sure. Curtis is going to ask around, but I told the hands to move the cattle just in case."

"Oh dear. I hope it's not serious." She narrowed her eyes. "You look tired. Go get out of those wet things before supper. I think Annabelle is cooking shepherd's pie tonight."

"Mmm, that's what I smell." She laughed as he twitched his nose in the air. "I think I will get some dry clothes on and wash up then."

159

Estelle watched him trudge up the stairs—not with his usual lively steps. There seemed to be a big void without Rachel around. She was like a daughter to her. She secretly hoped that John would see Rachel's value as a good woman and perhaps develop feelings for her, but she knew those kinds of things could never be forced. *Let things take their course,* she reminded herself. God knew who was best for him.

Estelle was gaining strength daily and felt fit as a fiddle. Next week, she'd see the doctor and ask for permission to get on with her life. How fortunate she'd improved instead of having a major heart attack. She would count as a blessing every day that she was still around to be involved in her grandson's life.

※

Rachel had been late for supper, but the evening was turning out better than she'd expected with Wyatt. He didn't pressure her but was very attentive. The hotel restaurant had decent food, so they ate their meal to the sound of rain slashing against the windows again. There had been a few breaks between rain showers before supper, but heavier rain was coming down now. She was glad she'd decided to spend the night. Few patrons sat at tables, and the fire in the grate did little to warm the room.

"I'll pay you for the hotel room when I get back home," she said.

He looked up between forkfuls of chicken and rice. "There's no need to do that. You can repay me by allowing me to court you."

"No, I insist. I always pay my debts—or at least I try to."

"Have it your way, but I won't take no for an answer."

He smiled at her, allowing his eyes to linger on hers before glancing toward her mouth. "You know I could follow you home in the morning if you'd like—make sure you get home safely."

"I don't think that's necessary. Besides, that's out of your way."

"It's never a bother to escort a pretty lady home," he said.

"I rode here alone and I can find my way back, but thanks all the same. In fact, I'll be stopping off in town to help Molly. She will be expecting me."

Rachel squirmed in her chair. Wyatt was very handsome in a dashing way, with his black string tie, crisp white shirt, and black coat. His light blue eyes held hers longer than she was comfortable with, so she looked down for her knife to butter a roll.

"You know if you married me, you'd never have to work another day in your life," he whispered. "I know you were never like those other gals at the saloon too."

She looked up in surprise. "I thought we weren't going to talk about marriage. And I like my job at the millinery."

"Until you have children," he said.

Rachel felt her face grow warm. That was personal, and she didn't want to discuss it with him. *Why, we aren't even courting!*

He continued, "I heard from John that Jeffrey has called on you too. Are you thinking you want to marry a preacher?"

"I'm not sure what I want, Wyatt, but Jeffrey is a nice man. Why don't we finish our meal? It's been a long day and I want to get an early start tomorrow."

"Certainly. I hope I wasn't being too forward. I really didn't mean to be," he replied.

They continued to eat in silence until Rachel said, "Thank you for dinner. I believe I was quite ravenous after all."

"The pleasure was all mine." He paid the bill after the waiter removed the remnants of their meal. "I'll walk you to your room."

"Oh, no." Rachel shook her head as they walked toward the staircase. "I wouldn't want anyone to start something. See you back in Cottonwood?"

He tipped his hat. "To be sure, ma'am. Sleep well." He lifted her hand and leaned down to brush his lips against it.

She watched him a moment, wondering what it was that intrigued him about her. She had little money and no dowry, but he was wealthy. Purely physical attraction? Rachel wasn't sure, but if that was the case, a marriage couldn't be built on attraction alone.

25

The rain had diminished in the morning, and Rachel avoided the potholes in places where the road was washing out. She was careful in her maneuverings with the horse and buggy, and arrived at Estelle's Millinery a couple of hours after leaving Lewistown. Molly was happy to see Rachel but was assisting a customer when she arrived. As soon as she was through, she asked about Rachel's trip.

"I'll tell you later when we have no customers." Rachel indicated in the direction of a customer who was perusing the lingerie, and made her way over to assist the young woman. The pretty lady smiled at her shyly and said, "I was looking for something special to wear on my wedding night."

"I'll be glad to help you. We have a beautiful nightgown with a dressing gown that I'm sure you'll like. Let me show it to you." Rachel pulled out a delicate white lawn gown trimmed in baby-blue ribbons at the neck and cuff. The matching dressing gown was made of the same fine lawn. She watched as the young woman fingered the delicate material.

"Oh my . . . it's lovely. I'll take it. Please do wrap it up for me."

"Absolutely. I'm glad I could help on such a wonderful occasion." Rachel took the outfit over to the counter and wrapped it up after the purchase was made.

It was nearly closing time when everyone had left. "So? Are you going to tell me what happened in Lewistown or not?" Molly crossed her arms, waiting.

Rachel was straightening the shelves but paused with a sigh. "Well, it wasn't why I went, but I had a proposal last night from Wyatt."

"What? You can't be serious. He hasn't even courted you!" Her eyes grew large.

"That's true, but when I worked at the saloon, he was always making offers for me to come live with him."

"And of course you turned him down?" Molly cocked her head, making her curls bounce.

"Do you mean last night or then?"

Molly rolled her eyes. "You know perfectly well what I'm asking."

"I told him I barely knew him and would have to think about it, that's all."

Molly shook her head. "I must say you have men swarming around you like flies in the buttermilk."

Rachel drew back. "I do not!" she said.

"'Course you do—Pastor Jeffrey and Wyatt and Curtis. I wish *I* had your problem," Molly said with a deep sigh.

"Why don't you come over to supper after work this Saturday? I'm sure Annabelle won't mind another person."

"Really? I'd love to come, but only if you're sure it's all right. Rachel, you still haven't told me what happened at the bank." Molly stood next to her and propped an elbow on the counter, cupping her chin in her hand and waiting.

"Oh, Molly . . . there was no money—"

"Are you sure?" Molly gave her a pitying look and frowned.

Rachel sighed. "I'm sure. Only our family Bible and our parents' wedding rings were inside the box. I should never have expected Preston to save a lot of money in the first place. He was a young man looking for adventure."

"Oh dear. I'm truly sorry. At least Preston saved a family heirloom for you. Not everyone has one."

Rachel squeezed her friend's hand. "Always the encourager, Molly. I'm almost ashamed to admit that I was expecting a whole lot more—enough to buy our ranch back."

"If you ever do, can I come live with you? I can help out with the chores."

Rachel laughed, her mood brightening. "Silly girl, by the time I can afford the ranch or any property, you'll have a husband with three children racing around your ankles, and I'll be walking with a cane."

Molly giggled. "If only that were true," she said, peering out the large shop window with a dreamy look. "Not you walking with a cane, though," she quickly added.

"Don't be in such a rush. It will happen." Rachel felt certain it would if she had anything to do with it.

⚜

Before supper John heard pounding at the front door. "I'll get it, Annabelle," he said loud enough for her to hear. He swung the door open to see Clay anxiously twisting his hat in his hands.

"Boss, we got trouble! Billy and I think a couple more calves have come down with something."

John reached for his slicker, quickly saddled Cutter, and

followed the jawing cowboy down a hilly slope where Billy stood looking down. Sure enough, one calf was having trouble walking and another had a swollen leg. When John felt the calf's shoulder, it made a crackling sound.

"Clay, you're right. I don't know what this is but it looks serious. They both have a high fever too. That makes three calves now. I hope no more come down with this. Is Curtis back yet?"

"He is now," Clay said, pointing up the hill toward a man riding fast, jacket flapping in the wind. Curtis galloped up, quickly reining in his horse before jumping down.

"John." Curtis was breathing hard and so was his horse. "Wyatt said it sounds like blackleg to him. He'd just returned from Lewistown and heard another rancher talking about it. It is deadly to calves, but it's not contagious."

"Thank God for that. But what do we do? How'd they get it?" John was worried about his herd. If other calves came down with this illness, it could spell disaster. The thought made his head hurt even more.

"Well, he said the steers die within forty-eight hours. It affects calves aged six months to two years."

John tried to take it all in. "Where did the blackleg come from in the first place?"

"More'n likely from the spores in the ground that enter a small cut or crack on the steer. The spores are from ground that's been saturated with heavy rains."

Billy snorted. "Well, we shore 'nuff had that," he said with a glance to the sky.

"He said we have to burn their carcasses where they drop, but the rest of the calves up to the age of two is gonna have to have something called nitre in their food once a week. I sent

Levi on into town to see if the general store had the medicine we needed. Wyatt seemed to think they would."

"All right. Let me know as soon as he returns, and rain or no rain, we have to corral the cattle and give them a treatment or it sounds like we could lose the entire herd. I can't afford to let that happen. You hear?" John snapped louder than he intended. But his nerves were frayed.

Rachel was more than a little weary when she arrived back at the ranch but glad she'd worked part of the day with cheerful Molly. No one was around to handle the horse and buggy for her, which she thought was odd. Perhaps everyone was busy preparing for the trail drive. She unhitched Sal and led her to a stall, making sure she had plenty of fresh water and oats.

As soon as she entered the house and hooked her coat on the coat rack, she heard Estelle call out to her. Rachel smiled at the sound of Estelle's voice and greeting.

"I'm so glad you're back. I had no idea you'd spend the night. Was it because of the weather?" Estelle's eyes were filled with concern.

"I'm sorry. There was no way to let you know, but yes, the weather was atrocious, so I spent the night then drove on to work this morning. I hope I didn't cause you to worry." Rachel pulled up a chair across from Estelle.

"I'll admit I was concerned, but I reminded myself that you're a grown woman who's used to being on her own." Estelle smiled, wrinkles folding into one another. "I'd ring for some tea or coffee, but it's nearly time for supper. Where did you spend the night?"

"At the hotel in Lewistown, at the insistence of Wyatt." The older lady's eyes narrowed as she searched Rachel's.

"You must tell me all about your trip, then. I hope the safe-deposit box held something of value for you."

"It was a big disappointment," Rachel murmured. She related the trip to the bank and her dinner with Wyatt—as well as his proposal—as Estelle listened with rapt attention. She was glad she had Estelle to talk to.

"I detect some anger in your voice. Were you hoping Preston had saved a lot of money?"

Estelle could see right through her. "Honestly, yes. I did. I guess I got my hopes up that I could buy back my family's ranch." She inhaled deeply, sighing as her shoulders dropped. "Now I feel foolish *and* angry."

Estelle reached over to pat her knee. "I know. Try to remember all the blessings even through life's greatest trials. It'll help your heart heal the bitterness."

"You're probably right, but tell my heart that." Rachel rose. "I need to go freshen up. I feel as soggy as the road Sal and I traveled."

26

At supper, John seemed distracted and barely touched his food. Rachel tried to engage him in conversation but it was an effort. She noticed Estelle observing her grandson as well.

Annabelle sashayed into the dining room, hands on her hips, and stared down at John's plate. "You stopped liking my cooking?" she demanded.

He looked up at her without smiling and answered, "Now, you know you're the best cook in these parts—well, except for Slim."

"Then why aren't you eating like you love it?"

Rachel suppressed a giggle, watching the two of them.

"I've got a lot on my mind and my appetite's a little off. That's all."

Annabelle harrumphed, leaving the room while shaking her head.

John glanced down the table at Rachel, his eyes deep and searching hers. "Curtis told me this afternoon that Wyatt saw you in Lewistown. Did you have a good trip, in spite of the rain?"

"My, but word gets around fast, doesn't it? I did have a nice dinner with Wyatt. As to my trip—let's just say it didn't turn out the way I hoped." Rachel didn't want to say more. He gazed at her but said nothing further. However, Estelle did.

"She *did* receive an offer of marriage from Wyatt, which she is considering," Estelle said with a smile.

Rachel cringed, her cheeks flaming. She hadn't thought Estelle would say anything.

John took a long swallow of his water then asked, "Is that so?"

Rachel looked him in the eye. "Yes, he did offer, but I never said I was considering it." She was hoping his reaction might indicate that he was the tiniest bit jealous, but if he felt that way, it didn't show in his countenance.

"A little soon, don't you think? Oh, that's right—you knew him before from the saloon. Should I congratulate you then?"

Rachel's mouth twitched. "No, because I haven't accepted, and no, I didn't *know* him exactly—"

"Either way, it's clearly an honor to be asked by one of the richest men in the valley," Estelle interjected.

John turned to his grandmother. "You forget that I just purchased another thousand acres of land, Grams? Wyatt's a good man, but he may no longer be the richest."

"No, I haven't forgotten, but *you* aren't the one asking for her hand in marriage either," Estelle reminded him.

He coughed into his napkin and absentmindedly rubbed his fingers across his forehead. "I'm too busy to be concerned with who's eligible and who isn't at the present time."

"Oh? So does that include Beatrice?" Rachel asked.

170

Before he could give her a reply, Annabelle rushed back in with Curtis, hat in hand. "Sorry to interrupt"—Curtis paused to nod at Rachel—"but I wanted to let you know what Levi found out."

"Excuse me," John said to the ladies as he pushed his chair back. "Let's go talk, Curtis."

"Yes, sir," Curtis responded before turning to Rachel. "You look mighty pretty tonight, Miss Rachel." John gave him a nudge toward the door with an aggravated look on his face. Curtis gave a slight bow and shuffled to the parlor to talk.

Estelle thumped her fingers on the table. "It appears to me that my grandson is troubled by all the attention you're receiving lately."

"I doubt that. If that were true he wouldn't be courting Beatrice, would he?"

"All I can say is, he hasn't been that attentive to her. However, I know he has the roundup on his mind, which will be delayed because of the weather, and now this disease called blackleg that some of the calves have come down with."

"Oh my. I can see why he was preoccupied tonight."

Estelle added, "Apparently it's deadly and they're trying to come up with a treatment. I hope they can or he'll lose all the calves."

"Then we'll have to pray about that, won't we?" Rachel laid her napkin down. "Estelle, it's been a rather long day, and if you don't mind, I think I'll go on up to my room. Can I help you back to yours?"

Estelle waved a hand. "Oh, pish-posh. I can walk on my own now—slowly, but nonetheless it's still walking. But thank you, dear. Run along now and get your rest."

Rachel didn't need to be told more than once, and gave the older lady a quick hug.

※

John huffed out a loud breath. He was agitated at the interaction between Curtis and Rachel. Why, he wasn't sure, since *he'd* been the one who suggested this whole courting thing. He led Curtis to the parlor, and they both stood by the fireplace to talk. John stuck his thumbs in his jeans pockets, anxious to hear the latest.

Curtis removed his gloves, stretching his hands toward the fire. "Levi is back with the nitre—by the way, that's short for nitrogen. Anyway, the instructions say to add it to the feed once a week. I suggest we round up all the calves and get started early."

"I agree. If any of them looks sick or gives you the slightest indication that something is wrong, leave them. I'll be out there once you bring them to the corral." John rubbed his chin, thinking.

"I'll bid you a good night then," Curtis said. He turned to leave, then looked back. "Oh, I meant to thank you for encouraging me to speak with Rachel about seeing her. She's a fine woman and intelligent too."

John nodded and walked Curtis to the door. "See ya first thing in the morning then." John stood still for a moment, noticing the rain had nearly stopped but the wind was still blowing. He shuddered, wearily climbing the stairs to his bedroom. He'd deal with the accounts later when Rachel could look them over.

On the landing he paused, staring at Rachel's door. No light filtered from beneath it. Apparently, she'd gone to bed early as well. *It won't be long before my role as her protec-*

tor will no longer be needed. Not if Wyatt or the pastor had anything to do with it. Or Curtis. He sighed deeply and walked on past her door.

※

At breakfast, Estelle inquired of Annabelle as to John's whereabouts. "He didn't come down for breakfast. Maybe he left without eating, because he sure wasn't hungry last night. Is he lovesick over Beatrice?" Annabelle teased.

Rachel stifled a giggle. The thought of him being lovesick over anyone amused her.

Estelle politely answered, "No, Annabelle, he isn't lovesick over Beatrice, but maybe someone else. He seemed worn out last night. Would you please check on him and make sure he's already left?"

"Yes, ma'am. I'll go right now." Annabelle lumbered off.

"Estelle, if he's not lovesick over Beatrice, then who?" Rachel set down her coffee cup.

"There are times, Rachel, I declare it's over his land or the prestige of being a cattle baron, then other times I think he's lovesick over you."

"Me?" she said with surprise.

"I've seen the way he watches you whenever you're around. The problem is he's thinking that it's too late with all the recent competition."

Rachel could hardly believe her ears. "Are you sure you're not seeing what you hope for?"

Estelle took a sip of her water before answering. "Let's just say I know my grandson."

※

A pounding headache and a nagging cough woke John before the cock crowed. He had to get up and take care of the calves but somehow his legs didn't want to work when he tried to get out of bed. They felt like he'd run a leg race at the fair, so he stumbled back to the bed, shivering, then pulled the quilts up high around his neck.

He dreamed of sick cows, heavy rain, and his land slipping down the mountainside as he called out for Lura—or was it Rachel? It was too hard to focus as he slid into a dark space inside his head.

❧

Annabelle tore into the dining room. "Miss Estelle, somethin's bad wrong with John. He's in the bed and looks mighty sick with a fever. You don't suppose he caught something from those sick cows, do you?"

Estelle sucked in a deep breath and started to get up. Annabelle and Rachel were at her side.

"I'll go check on him. You can't be climbing the stairs until the doctor gives you the okay, Estelle." Rachel's hand pressed down on Estelle's shoulder, and Estelle looked up at her in fear.

"Okay, but I think Annabelle should send for the doctor. John is never sick," Estelle responded.

"I'll come right back after I check on him," Rachel promised. Then she rushed off.

27

Rachel pushed open the door to John's room and tiptoed over to the bed. "John," she whispered. His answer came in the form of a mutter—something about the rain. She bent down and put her hand to his forehead. He was burning up with fever and shaking with chills.

He slowly opened his eyes, which were bloodshot and glassy, but when he started to speak, he couldn't stop coughing.

"John, I'll be back in a few moments—"

He lifted his hand out of the cover to reach for her hand. "Don't leave," he whispered.

Her heart twisted in sympathy. "I'll be right back, I promise." She pulled her hand from his and he fell back to sleep. She took that moment to dash back downstairs. Estelle was waiting for her in the parlor, her face lined with concern.

"I'm afraid Annabelle is right. John's very sick. He has a fever and bad cough. I'm going back upstairs to sponge his face and neck. His fever seems quite high."

Estelle rose from her chair and teetered on her feet. "Maybe I should go to him."

Rachel grasped her boney hand. "I don't think it's a good idea for you to climb stairs until you talk to your doctor. Besides, we don't need you to catch something and get sick as well."

Estelle's lips tightened. "I suppose you're right. It'll be awhile before the doctor can arrive, but Levi has gone after him."

"I'll try to take care of him the best that I can until the doctor tells us what we are dealing with. But if I had to guess I'd say influenza."

"Oh dear, I hope not. He was out in that damp cold rain for days, but that would explain the headaches he's had."

"All the more reason for you to keep your distance."

Estelle nodded her agreement.

"I told him I'd be right back. He didn't want me to leave."

"I'll sit here and pray, Rachel," Estelle said with a worried look.

Rachel gave her hand a squeeze, then hurried back up to John's room. He appeared to be sleeping. Taking the water pitcher and basin over to his bedside, she laid the cool wash cloth against his forehead and neck and in moments the rag felt hot too. She repeated the process a few times, then lifted one arm from underneath the quilt, rolled up the sleeves of his longhandles, and sponged his arms. Once he looked at her through heavy eyes and blinked, giving her a weak smile before drifting off to an unrestful sleep again.

Rachel hoped Levi would get the doctor here soon to keep Estelle from worrying. She prayed John would be okay and for protection for Estelle.

Rachel must have drifted off to sleep, as she was suddenly startled by the voices of Annabelle and Doctor Wilson. She rose to meet them, realizing it was now late afternoon.

The doctor entered and walked straight to John's bedside,

placing his black bag on the bed. "I came as quickly as I could. If you ladies will step outside, I'll let you know what I find after I've finished my examination."

They left, pulling the door shut behind them. "Annabelle, you were right, John's a very sick man. I suspect influenza with the cough and fever, but we'll see what the doctor has to say."

"I'll build a fire in the fireplace when the doctor is finished. Slim's in the kitchen helping me out by cleaning up," Annabelle said.

A few minutes passed before Doc Wilson opened the door and pulled it closed behind him.

"He's pretty sick with pneumonia and I'm worried about that bad cough. I'll come back tomorrow, unless he worsens and you send for me."

"What do we need to do in the meantime?" Rachel asked.

"Same as you're doing. Keep him comfortable, and when he feels up to it give him fluids—warm soup, hot tea. That may not be for a few days, so don't be alarmed if he refuses to eat. Sponge bathing may help bring down the fever."

"What about the cough?" Annabelle asked anxiously.

"I left a bottle of syrup next to the bed for him, and I gave him a dose. Give it to him every six hours. Keep washing your hands and keep him in his room. I don't think he'll feel like leaving it anyway."

"Yes, sir. We will," Annabelle said.

"Oh, and keep Estelle from coming near him. I'd planned to release her this week if she's doing well, and she appears to look better. However, she shouldn't be exposed to pneumonia after her spell and at her age."

"I'll personally see to it that she goes nowhere near him, Doctor Wilson."

"Then I'll be on my way. Please send someone to get me if there's any big change for the worse."

"I'll show you to the door." Annabelle left with him and Rachel went back to where John lay helplessly in the bed. He was coughing and looked miserable.

Rachel pulled a chair next to his bed and put a cool compress on his head. She must tell Annabelle to bring fresh water when she came back to make the fire. And she'd have to get her cape if she intended to stay in this chilly room.

She had never stepped foot in John's room before today, and to do so now felt oddly intimate. Rachel settled in her chair, this time looking around the bedroom with interest. Heavy, expensive drapes framed the expansive window casings, and his cherrywood furniture suited his masculinity. A belt and jeans were draped on the back of a sturdy chair, boots were flung nearby, and his dark hat hung from a porcelain hook near the washstand. A white shaving mug with soap and razor waited for his next shave.

John moved around in the bed. "I'm not feelin' . . . too hot," he whispered, barely opening his eyes.

"Oh, you're hot, all right," Rachel gently teased before feeling his head again. His lips formed a limp smile.

Rachel and Annabelle took turns checking on John throughout the rest of the day and reported back to Estelle. After supper, Annabelle entered the room to relieve Rachel and made a nice fire to make the room more comfortable. "I'll sit with him awhile but there's really not much we can do, is there?" Annabelle asked.

"No, I guess not. Why don't you go on home and I'll check on him during the night."

"Are you sure?"

"Yes. My room is just down the hall," Rachel assured her.

"Now, don't you go staying up too late, or you might get sick yourself."

"I won't, but make sure Estelle is settled for the night and tell her not to worry."

Annabelle walked to the door. "As if that'll do any good." She chuckled.

Rachel found herself nodding off in the warmth of the comfortable chair, but once John was resting better, she slipped away quietly to her room. Sometime during the night, she was awakened by John's hacking cough. She listened a few minutes, but it continued and sounded worse so she decided she'd better give him another dose of the thick syrup the doctor had left.

Donning her robe, she padded down the hall to his room. The fire had all but burned down, so she laid a couple logs in the fireplace, stoked the dying embers, and soon had it going again. All the while, John continued to cough, which made her think it was deep in his chest. He still had a fever and was listless. Uncorking the elixir first, she tried to rouse him by lifting his head up in order to give him the medicine.

"Rachel?" he murmured. He lifted his arm out of the cover and attempted to reach out to her. She'd never before noticed his masculine hands and long fingers.

"Yes, John. Can you help me hold your head up? I need you to drink this." She reached for the spoon and filled it. She placed a hand beneath his shoulder, lifting him forward with his help.

"Mmm . . . you look different." He struggled to hold his head up but she got the syrup in his mouth and he swallowed, frowning at the taste.

"Pretty with your hair down," he whispered.

She pushed a lock of his hair away from his eyes. "That's only because you can't see well. Now, look again." His face was close to hers, and she resisted the desire to stroke his cheek.

"Nope. Still pretty." Another fit of coughing returned so he lay back against the pillows, closing his eyes. When she thought he was asleep, she turned to leave and heard him mumble, "Thank you."

"You're very welcome," Rachel answered. "Rest now or Estelle will be trying to barge her way up here."

Back in her bed, Rachel found it difficult to sleep. Occasionally, she would hear John coughing, but not as badly as before. She prayed he would get better quickly and was glad that she could help. She wouldn't want Estelle attending to him by herself. Annabelle couldn't stay with him the entire time with all her chores.

How much life had changed for her since coming here. She'd lost her brother, gained new friends, got a good job, and had three suitors! It all made her head swim. Although they were all good men, none of them made her heart skip a beat when they entered the room. Only one man did that . . . John. But as far as she knew, her feelings weren't reciprocated. *He did tell me I was pretty! Probably only the fever talking.*

She spied the worn family Bible right where she'd left it when she returned from Lewistown but felt no desire to pick it up tonight. Another day maybe. Finally, her eyelids grew heavy, succumbing to sleep.

A light rapping on her bedroom door awoke her, which seemed to Rachel to come only a few minutes after she'd gone to sleep. Glancing over at the clock on her nightstand, she realized that it was six o'clock. She rose up on her elbows and answered, "Who is it?"

"It's me, Annabelle. Can I come in?"

"Yes, of course." She threw her legs to the side of the bed, pulling on her robe.

"I think John is much sicker this morning and his cough sounds very congested, so I'm sending Billy after the doctor."

"I was worried about that last night, but I gave him more syrup. How about the fever?"

"He still has it. I'm real worried. Maybe after you're dressed you can let Estelle know. I didn't want to disturb her so early, but Curtis has already showed up asking about him. They were to handle the sick calves today." She just shook her gray head. "I don't know what to tell him."

"It's okay. I'll go speak with Estelle as soon as I'm dressed and can assess the situation."

"Yes, ma'am." Annabelle turned to leave, then paused to look at her. "I'm mighty glad you're here—you've become part of this family."

Rachel knew she was being sincere. "Thank you. I don't know how much help I am, but I'm glad I'm here."

"I hope you continue to stay. It'd be nice if you were Mrs. McIntyre and not Beatrice," Annabelle said with a smirk. "I don't think Estelle likes her much, and I sure don't!"

"I'm afraid that I have nothing to do with who John marries."

"Maybe. Maybe not. But don't let her get in the way if you do care for him." Annabelle walked on toward the door. "I'll let you go ahead and get dressed. Breakfast is a-waitin'. I don't believe John is going to want a thing but water, but I'll try to get some broth down him."

181

"Annabelle, if he's worse, then I think I should stay home today. Do you think you could have Billy run over to the shop to let Molly know since he's going after the doctor? Then she won't be worried."

"I surely will." She hurried out. Rachel quickly washed her face, searching for a clean dress to wear while she pondered what Annabelle had said.

28

Estelle waited with Rachel and Annabelle for Doctor Wilson to come talk to them about John's condition. Estelle was deeply concerned. *If something happens to him . . .* She squeezed her eyes closed, shutting out the very thought, and heard footsteps on the stairs.

Doctor Wilson walked over to them. "I'm afraid John is gravely ill. He has pneumonia in both lungs."

Estelle's legs nearly gave way, but Annabelle steadied her.

The doctor continued. "I didn't want to have to tell you, Estelle, since you're only now beginning to feel stronger. I don't want you to fret."

Estelle finally found her voice. "What do you need us to do?"

"Listen to me carefully and I'll tell you. Please sit down, Estelle."

Her legs found the chair touching the back of her knees and she took a seat, then listened with rapt attention as he explained to them there was nothing he could give John for the infection. "I wish there was, truly I do. If he can cough, all the better. He will be left with little energy, if he survives."

Estelle drew in a sharp breath. "You mean—"

"I don't want to alarm you but his condition is very serious. He is young and strong, which gives him the advantage. Keep him as comfortable as you can." The doctor's tone was sober. "Ladies, I must be on my way now, but I'll be back later on. And Estelle, please take it easy. I know you want to see him, but it's best you wait until his fever breaks."

Estelle's heart sank, but she nodded her head in agreement as she clasped her hands tightly.

"I'll show you out, Doctor," Annabelle said. "Thank you for coming all the way out here."

As soon as they were out of sight, Estelle burst into tears. "Rachel, I can't lose my grandson. I feel so helpless." As Rachel put an arm around her shoulders, Estelle felt comforted. "I'm so glad you're here, especially now that I can't take care of him."

"I'm glad too. I'll stay close by until he's better."

Estelle sniffed into her handkerchief, searching Rachel's eyes. "But what if he—"

"Don't even talk that way. I'll tell you as you've told me—have a little faith. God knows what's best for him."

"You're right, Rachel. That's just what I needed to hear." They both looked up as Annabelle escorted Curtis inside.

Curtis swept off his sweat-stained hat. "Ma'am," he nodded to Estelle, then smiled at Rachel. "Annabelle told me John's real sick, and I'm as sorry as can be. Me and the boys have rounded up most of the calves to treat them." He hesitated. "But you should know that we found five more calves stricken with the blackleg."

"My goodness! I'm almost glad John can't know. He's too sick to help," Estelle exclaimed.

"Just so you know, you may see or smell smoke, but we

have to burn 'em where they die so as not to contaminate the other pastures. We moved all the rest up to the foothills for now."

"Thank you, Curtis, for handling this for us. Would you like to warm up by the fire or have something hot to drink?"

"No, ma'am, but thank you all the same. I best be going. Lots to do now." He looked at Rachel and smiled, and Estelle noticed his lingering gaze.

"Why don't you walk him out, Rachel?" Estelle saw his face brighten at the suggestion.

※

Once they were out on the porch, Rachel thanked him too for taking over responsibility for John. "I wish I knew how long it might be before he's well."

"So you think he'll get through it?" Curtis asked.

"I'm praying so." She wished he'd hurry up and leave. She wanted to get back to John's bedside.

"He's a fighter, I know that much." He took a step toward her. "Well, does this mean our Sunday afternoon ride is off then?"

"I'm afraid so. Annabelle and I will have to take turns caring for him."

His face fell with disappointment. "I'm shore she is mighty grateful to you. I am too. I admire John a whole lot." Curtis put his hat back on and straightened the brim. "You womenfolk need anything at all, just let me know."

"We'll do that." Rachel glanced at the sky. "At least the rain has stopped."

"Yep, but not before it left us with sick calves." He doffed his hat to her, then trotted to where his horse was tied.

Rachel shivered in the cold morning, then hurried back inside, anxious to check on John's condition.

❋

Lura's lovely face appeared. She looked neither sad nor happy. Her beautiful, long hair framed a pale face that held large, luminous eyes—eyes signifying something more. More sorrow? More life? More to come? When John tried to speak to her, he couldn't form the words and fell back against his pillow. He couldn't seem to think clearly and his upper back held deep aching. A cool hand touched his brow, and he could hear distant voices but was unable to make out what was being said. *Where are Rachel and Grams?* He called out for them, throwing back the covers. With eyes burning deep in their sockets and his head throbbing, he fell asleep.

❋

Rachel and Annabelle shared looks across the bed and Rachel shook her head, then motioned for Annabelle to follow her into the hall. Once they were out of earshot, Annabelle pressed her hands against her apron. "He sure does have a high temperature and his cough sounds terrible. I wish I could heal that boy!"

"We have to keep praying and not give up. His fever will eventually break, and I hope it will be soon. If not—"

"Hush. Don't even breathe a word that he may not get better. Miss Estelle's heart couldn't bear it." Annabelle's eyes filled with tears.

And neither could mine, Rachel admitted to herself. "I won't do that. I wish Estelle could see him, but it's best she waits until he turns the corner."

"I agree. I'll go check on her and prepare a light evening meal so I can help take care of John. Would you like something hot to drink?"

"Yes, I'll come down in a bit. I want to sit with him awhile first."

After Annabelle left and Rachel had returned to John's bedroom, she wiped his face, neck, and arms once more. He began to shiver but didn't wake up. She pulled the cover up to his chin, tucking the blankets around him, and sat back in her chair watching and ruminating.

Rachel felt like she was losing control of things. She was still angry about life in general. Losing her parents, losing Preston—being alone. One day she felt grateful for what she had and the next day she didn't.

Ever since her folks had died, she struggled to see any future for herself. Then they'd lost the ranch and Preston left. He'd died and left her with nothing more than a family Bible. Then there was sweet Estelle with a bad heart. On top of that, John was gravely ill and his cattle stricken with some kind of disease. It just wasn't fair! Part of her wanted to give up. Maybe she should move away . . .

The sound of a light knock at the door pulled her from her grumbling, and she turned around just as Beatrice sashayed through the door. *Good grief. What's she doing here?* Behind her, Annabelle shrugged her shoulders and wore a distinct sour face.

Beatrice marched over to Rachel's side. "You can go now. I'm here to see what I can do for John." She waved a hand in dismissal, tossing her bonnet aside.

29

Rachel clamped her teeth tight, then stood, placing the wash cloth in the bowl before turning to Beatrice. "Your help isn't needed, Beatrice. Annabelle and I have everything under control. Annabelle, could you bring some fresh water up?"

"We'll see about that!" Beatrice replied, and she reached under the covers to pull out John's arm.

What does she think she's doing? Rachel watched as Beatrice looked at her watch fob and held her fingers against John's wrist. He would catch cold.

When she was done, she said, "Mmm." She walked over to the windows to yank the drapes back, letting sunlight fill the room.

"Are you trying to kill him?" Rachel asked.

"You're still here? Rachel, you look tired," she said with a tilt of her head. "Why don't you get some rest?" Her voice held no true sympathy. Then to Annabelle she announced, "*I'm* here now so you can attend to your regular duties, which I assume includes running the McIntyre household."

Annabelle seemed glued to her spot by the door. "Well . . . yes, it does. But in this household we all care deeply about John—"

"I'm sure you do, but you have to admit he doesn't need three nursemaids, and since he's more or less betrothed to me, I feel responsible to share my expertise in nursing." She turned around to check John's fever and said, "Oh, and do please bring up fresh water, towels, and some liniment. Perhaps one with eucalyptus? And an apron for me?" She gave her unyielding orders through a brief smile.

Rachel was speechless, but she and Annabelle retreated to the hallway. While they made their way down the creaking stairs, Rachel asked, "What could she possibly know about nursing?"

Annabelle gave a wry smile. "Some time ago, she fancied studying nursing, but I can't say why she didn't finish nursing school. Maybe when her father died she felt it necessary to return home."

"Really? That surprises me. I hadn't considered that she did more than shop and run after eligible ranchers."

"Human nature can sometimes surprise us. I say, if she knows more than us and it can benefit him, then let her have a go."

Rachel could've said more but clamped her mouth shut. The way in which Beatrice took over stuck in her craw. She couldn't understand why Annabelle let her come upstairs. *Betrothed?*

❧

Later, John tried to open his eyes to focus on the figure in front of him. "Rachel . . . I'm so glad you came. My head . . . hurts something awful."

The woman leaned over him. "Shh . . . you rest and I'll take good care of you." She slipped her hand into his. "You know that I love you."

He smiled and closed his eyes, satisfied that Rachel was near and loved him.

✻

Estelle patted the settee next to her, indicating for Rachel to sit down. "You seem troubled, dear."

Rachel complied. Outside the wind was blowing hard, sending tumbleweeds across the yard, and she knew it would bring in a cold front. She was glad to be indoors with the fire burning brightly in the grate. "I worry about John. He doesn't seem to be better yet."

Estelle nodded her agreement with a long face. "Me too, and it's very hard for me not to charge upstairs and see him for myself."

"Soon you will after the fever breaks. You'll be told immediately. Why did you ask Beatrice to come?" Rachel posed her question with trepidation, not sure how Estelle felt about Beatrice as far as John was concerned.

Estelle jerked back. "Oh goodness! I didn't. I believe she said she heard about the illness from someone in town. Word travels fast, so when she showed up earlier insisting she wanted to help, what was I to say?"

Send her packin'! "I see. She acted as though she had some knowledge of nursing. I have to admit, I didn't like being told to leave," she spat out.

Estelle stared at her a moment. "Beatrice can sometimes be lacking in manners, but I don't believe she meant anything by it. I don't have the right to say this to you, but you and I have become good friends, so I hope you won't take offense to what I'm about to say."

Here it comes, Rachel thought in frustration. *What did*

I do wrong? The fire popped, startling both of them, then Estelle continued.

"I'm not sure, but it seems you have a little resentment in your soul. Correct me if I'm out of line here, but I believe it has to do with losing Preston and the ranch—and now you feel like you're losing John."

Rachel snapped her head around to look directly at Estelle. "I never *had* John."

"Hmm. Maybe so in the truest sense of the word, but I see how you interact with him and he with you. Your eyes soften whenever my grandson is in the same room. But what I wanted to say was this—you must let go of the anger, dear. It will hold you back from true living. Wouldn't you agree you have a tiny dose of it?"

Sighing deeply, Rachel looked down at the rug, studying its intricate patterns. "You're right, and I know it, but I don't know how to do that. I'm not happy with the way things have developed so far in my life."

"Tell me, what do you consider the worst thing that's happened so far?"

Rachel gazed at Estelle, who was visibly concerned. "I guess it was losing Preston. I was not expecting that. We were planning on running a large ranch someday, but the fact that he didn't save one penny while he was gone astonished me. I keep wondering what he did with the gold he'd worked so hard for. I'm angry that he had to die so young and I haven't any family now—or anyone else for that matter."

Estelle touched Rachel's arm. "You have us. We are your family now, but only if you'll let us in. Things happen that we have no control over, whether it's death, a financial loss, or a broken heart. Anger only leads us to separation from others and from God, eventually."

"I hope I'm not doing that." Rachel wasn't sure she agreed with her older friend.

"Think of it like this. Anger causes us to be preoccupied with our own problems rather than with God's will for our lives. One reason is because of what it does to others. Soon I hope you will open the family Bible Preston left you and read Proverbs 30:33, which talks about how anger causes strife in our life. Later, read Galatians 5:22 about having patience. You're young and bright, Rachel, and have so much life to be lived. Live it victoriously!"

Rachel wiped a tear away. "Estelle, you are like another mother."

"And you, dear one, have become like another granddaughter. Let's work together and promise to help each other in our losses." Estelle's voice quivered with emotion.

Rachel picked up Estelle's hand and held it. "I know you've been so hurt by Lura's death, and I'm so sorry. I hope I never made light of any of your problems. I promise to do all I can to lighten your load."

Beatrice waltzed into the room, interrupting their talk, and Rachel frowned at her, which didn't faze Beatrice at all.

"I'm going home since it's getting late. Annabelle has Levi getting my horse and buggy for me," she said from the doorway. "John's fever is not as high as it was, and I gave him a dose of the laudanum for the pain in his upper back he complained about. His pulse is better."

"That's good news, Beatrice, and I'm grateful for anything to further John's recovery." Estelle rose and walked over to where she stood.

"I really think he's going to get better."

Annabelle came into the hallway, removing her apron. "Your carriage is waiting for you, Miss Beatrice."

"Thank you, Annabelle." She handed the apron to her. "I'll be back in the morning, and Rachel, you can return to work tomorrow if you'd like."

"Rest assured, Beatrice, I won't leave unless he's improved," Rachel answered. *How dare she tell me what to do!*

Beatrice stared at her a moment, then said, "As you wish, but John is not your responsibility." She pulled on her coat and gloves. "Good night," she added before Rachel could say anything. She followed Annabelle to the door.

When she was gone, Estelle's face brightened, and she clasped her hands together. "Oh, this sounds like John's improving, if she can be believed."

"I'm going up to check on him, and I'll come back and let you know before I go to bed." Rachel leaned over to kiss the old lady's cheek. "Thank you . . . for everything."

John was sleeping but mumbling something about the trail drive, and Rachel tried to reassure him that Curtis was handling things for him. He began to thrash about, although his forehead didn't feel as hot as before, so she pressed her palms lightly against his shoulders, trying to calm him. "It's okay. Everything's going to be all right. Try not to worry."

"Okay," he murmured, and his eyes fluttered open briefly. "Glad you . . . love me." It seemed to take all his energy to utter the words. Rachel thought the medicine must be confusing him. She hoped Beatrice hadn't overdosed him. She pulled the covers about him, and once his shallow breathing became even she slipped out of the room.

193

30

Significant weather changes swept over Paradise Valley while everyone slept. Rachel awoke later than normal and was surprised to see her breath on the air. She hurried to John's room. Annabelle was already there, building a fire. To Rachel's surprise, John was partially propped up on two pillows, looking haggard and discouraged. His thick hair bushed out at the side and needed a wash and trim at the neck.

"John, you're awake," Rachel exclaimed and hurried over to his bedside. "How are you feeling this morning?" Even as she asked, she touched the inside of her wrist to the front of his forehead. It did feel much cooler.

He gazed at her without a smile. "Better, but my chest hurts from coughing and so does my back." He had his hands and arms on top of the quilt, picking at its knotted threads. "Between you and Annabelle, I'm getting good care. So I'll make it." His eyes flicked down her robe and Rachel was mindful that she hadn't dressed yet.

"We weren't the only ones—"

Suddenly Beatrice appeared in the open doorway, interrupting the conversation with a sweeping hello before she bustled up to John's bedside with all her usual aplomb. The look of surprise on his face said it all, and Rachel had to suppress a giggle.

"Beatrice, what are you doing here?" It seemed to take all of John's strength to speak, his eyes half closed. He began a coughing fit that lasted a moment or two before she answered, fussing over him while she spoke.

"Why, John, I couldn't stay away knowing you were so ill. Since I've had a bit of nurse training, I was able to keep you comfortable and advise Estelle." She checked his pulse and forehead, then lifted one of his eyelids. "You're definitely on the mend."

Rachel noticed Beatrice was dressed in a fetching fall outfit that any woman would envy—right down to her kid leather boots. She looked pretty, capable, and engaging. *And here I am with my hair askew, in a raggedy old robe and worn slippers with barely the sleep washed from my eyes!* Rachel wanted to rush from the room.

"I'll see you after a while, John." Rachel turned to go, and Annabelle looked up from the fireplace with a scowl. Rachel hurried on back to her room and slammed the door.

I may not be a nurse, but it takes more than a nurse to make a person feel better. Instantly she had just the right idea!

Hurrying through her morning ablutions, she threw on her plaid dress with long sleeves, then had a quick breakfast under the watchful eye of Annabelle. Rachel grabbed her coat and warm hat and stepped outside in the cold, making her way over to the barn. She saw Levi with the barn door open saddling his horse, Winchester next to him.

"Morning, Miss Rachel. How's John?" he asked as he tightened the cinch under his horse's belly.

"He's a little better, but seems discouraged. I was wondering if I could persuade Winchester to come lie next to his bed for company."

Winchester's ears perked up at the sound of his name and he made a whining noise, making Rachel laugh. "I think he answered yes, don't you?"

Levi chuckled and leaned against the saddle. "He did for a fact, ma'am. I think it'd cheer John up. When you think he's up to it, let me know, because I'm sure John will want to get the particulars from Curtis about the trail drive. It's obvious that John is in no condition to go with us."

"I think you're exactly right. I believe the doctor might stop in today to check on him."

Levi nodded. "Let me know if there's anything you need."

"Thanks. I will." She looked down at Winchester. "Come on, Winchester. Someone wants to see you." She clapped her hands together near her leg and Winchester trotted over to her, sniffing her and wagging his tail. Rachel waved as the two of them walked back to the house.

As they moved past the parlor, Estelle saw her. "Are you taking Winchester up to see John?"

Rachel paused, holding on to the dog's collar lest he run off to the kitchen to follow the remaining smells of bacon and biscuits. "Yes. I thought it might cheer John up to see his old pal."

Estelle walked to the hallway. "Why didn't I think of that? I think it's a wonderful idea. Is his fever gone yet? I'm dying to see my grandson."

"I'm not certain. Beatrice was checking him over and pretty much pushed me aside."

196

"Rachel, don't give her control. Stand your ground," Estelle said, pursing her lips. "I tell you, if his fever is gone, I will ask her to leave."

"Yes, ma'am." She climbed the stairs with Winchester trailing her.

At the top of the stairs, Winchester knew his way and ran straight into John's room, nearly knocking over Beatrice, who gasped and scolded him. He paid her no mind but hopped directly on top of the bed, happily licking his master's face.

"Who let that mongrel in this room?" Beatrice nearly shouted and whirled around to see Rachel. "You! I should've known. It's not sanitary to have a dog around a very sick person! Get him out of here," she ordered.

Rachel strolled into the room, ignoring her protest, and heard John respond to his faithful dog. He reached out and held Winchester's face in his two hands. "My old friend, I've missed you," he whispered to the dog. Winchester made whining noises and was clearly thrilled to see John.

Beatrice stood with her arms folded across her chest, eyeing the reunion scene in disgust.

"I thought he might perk you up a little," Rachel commented with a look thrown to Beatrice for understanding. "It seems I was right." The dog finally settled down and curled up near John's thigh. Beatrice tried to shoo him off, but he refused to budge though she tried to push him off the bed. Winchester ignored her altogether, which made Rachel smile inwardly.

"Oh, leave him well enough alone," John ordered, his voice stronger than it was the day before. "He's my pal."

Beatrice looked mollified, then stepped aside, reaching for her wrap. "It seems I'm not needed right now. John, I hope you'll send for me when you're well." She threw her wrap about her and stormed out of the room without looking back.

After she closed the door, John looked at Rachel and they both laughed. Winchester raised an eyelid but otherwise didn't move a muscle.

❋

More than a week later, John's temperature finally returned to normal and Estelle climbed the stairs to see him. His color was returning, but the cough still lingered. Rachel was teary-eyed watching the two of them. Estelle hugged and kissed him, sniffing into her handkerchief as she leaned close to him.

"The Lord answered my prayers! I've never been so worried in all my life," she chattered on.

"Grams, I couldn't leave you, don't you know that?"

"Yes, dear, but sometimes we don't have control over issues of our health. Just look at me," she said as she took a seat on his bed. "I'm better now and God's been good to me, but it could've turned out much worse."

John reached for her hand and said, "I'm so glad it didn't for either of us. I only wish I wasn't so weak, but I intend to go downstairs to send the men off on the trail drive." He took several deep breaths, then turned to Rachel. "Do you think Annabelle can send Slim up to give me a shave?"

Estelle laughed, which Rachel decided was a wonderful sound. "I'll be happy to go downstairs and ask." She left so the two of them could spend some time alone to talk. Rachel knew John was discouraged that he wouldn't be able to do the trail drive tomorrow.

John squeezed his grandmother's hand. "Rachel has turned out to be a very competent lady. She's nursed me and cared for your shop in your absence."

Estelle smiled and lowered her voice. "Yes, and you should be grateful that she's taken a shine to you . . . unless you are planning to continue to spark that Beatrice woman."

"Grams, how do you know Rachel is interested in me? She's never indicated that to you, has she?"

"She's waiting on you. Besides, haven't you noticed how attentive she's been to you?"

"Not until she whispered she loved me last week."

Estelle jerked back. "She did? That's wonderful! She hasn't said a word to me."

"She's probably only trying to make me feel better. She already has other proposals to consider, and I'm not sure she's forgiven me totally."

Estelle sighed, looking at him with a steady eye. "John, have you ever considered that your conscience is holding it against her that she danced at the saloon?"

"Grams, she can say whatever she wants me to believe. After all, Wyatt seems to be very familiar with her."

"You can't really believe that. Why, Rachel is a woman of integrity. Why don't you pray that God will help you to trust her?"

"Grams, I'm suddenly tired. Do you mind if I take a nap?" All this talking took a lot of his energy, and he didn't have an answer for her. Not yet.

31

Streaks of sunlight were dancing through the trees in the late afternoon when Rachel embarked on her walk. She was glad John was improving, but today fresh air beckoned, so she started down the side of the house to the pasture, hoping to get a glimpse of Midnight again. She leaned against the fence rail, feeling the cold of the wood through her coat sleeves. Could winter be far away? Most of the colorful leaves had fallen with the recent wind and rain they'd experienced. It surprised her to realize how much she missed working with Molly at the shop, and now that John's crisis was over, she'd go back to work. Estelle was going to stay behind for now.

Out of the corner of her eye she saw Midnight lope near, then pause as if considering whether he wanted a visitor or not. She pretended not to see him and took an apple out of her coat pocket, waiting. Before long he approached, but still stood a ways back from the fence.

"Midnight, I'm so glad you're here. I came to visit and tell you about John." She talked soft and low. His ears perked up at the mention of John's name, and Rachel nearly laughed but didn't want to frighten him away.

"If you come closer, you can have this apple." She stretched out her hand, palm up, holding the apple. "You remember me, don't you?"

Midnight took his time, pausing to look around before walking over to lift the apple from her hand, his velvety muzzle tickling her. Rachel took that moment to stroke his forelock, cooing to him. "One day, I intend to ride you." Midnight looked her in the eyes. "Is that all right with you?"

Midnight snorted his response, then tossed his head. This time Rachel laughed at the horse. "John has been very sick, so don't feel neglected, you hear?" Midnight's ears twitched again.

Rachel noticed Curtis coming toward the corral, bowlegged and wearing chaps. She shielded her eyes from the sun with her hand as he approached her.

"Rachel, I thought I saw you walking this direction." Curtis smiled shyly at her.

"Hello, Curtis. Isn't it a beautiful day?"

"How's John faring?" He squinted at her from beneath his hat brim.

"He's much better, but weak."

"I'm glad he's on the mend. All of us cowpunchers have great respect for him." Curtis propped his arms across the fence railing and looked out at Midnight, who'd trotted off. "Sorry, I won't be able to take you on a Sunday ride now. I'm the trail boss in John's absence." His smile faded as he said it. "But maybe when we return. We can plan something better than an afternoon ride, like—"

Rachel gently placed a hand on Curtis's sleeve. "Curtis, I

have to be honest with you . . . I'm afraid I only feel friend-ship for you," she blurted out.

"Shore, but sometimes when people spend more time to-gether the friendship can grow to love."

Rachel took a deep breath. She truly didn't want to hurt Curtis's feelings, but there was no way to avoid it. "Maybe, but I don't think so between us. I'm not attracted to you in that way. Can you understand?" She watched his crestfallen face. She hated to tell him that right before leaving for the trail drive. However, it wasn't fair to let him think she felt otherwise.

"I see—"

"I'm sorry, Curtis. Truly I am, but I felt I must tell you the truth instead of keeping you dangling with thoughts of us while on the trail drive."

He dropped his arms. "You telling me won't stop me think-ing about you on those lonely nights under the stars. But as you wish." Rachel watched his Adam's apple bob when he swallowed hard. "I won't be bothering you anymore. Heck, just so you know, it was John that told me to spark you in the first place," he said, his jaw working.

Rachel figured that telling her this made *him* feel better about his letdown. "He did, did he?"

"For a fact. I should've known that it wouldn't work." Curtis stalked off, leaving her wondering why in the world John would encourage Curtis to court her.

***

John slowly got dressed the next morning, grateful that his legs felt stronger but wishing he had more energy. Slim's shave made him feel more human, but he wasn't happy with what

Doctor Wilson had to say when he came to check on him. Doc had told him privately that his lungs were permanently compromised and he would never regain the lung capacity he'd had before—meaning he would have to slow down and turn over much of his work to his ranch hands. John was shaken by this news. How could he be a cattle baron if he couldn't do more than his men? No one respected a cripple. He simply couldn't accept this news and would pray the doctor was wrong. Somehow, he'd keep this from Estelle and the others.

Still, he planned to go downstairs to send the men off in the trail drive. His hands were shaky, but he attributed that to not having eaten much lately. When he belted his jeans, he had to slide the notch tighter to hold them up. He didn't have the energy to comb his hair, and though he figured it wouldn't matter to the men anyway, he decided to throw on his hat. Winchester lifted his head from the edge of the bed and hopped down to follow when John opened the bedroom door.

John heard sounds coming from the kitchen and knew Annabelle was already up and had lit the lanterns downstairs. She would be without her man for a while. Slim was a good man. They made a great and loyal couple. Slowly he made his way downstairs, his legs heavy, and then struggled with his coat. Lifting his arms was a chore. Where was his strength? He caught his reflection in the hall mirror and nearly gasped. He hardly recognized the man, gaunt and pale, staring back at him. *Who am I now?*

Once outside, bawling cattle could be heard, so he walked the short distance to the pasture on shaky legs. He paused to take a deep breath, not wanting to appear weak in front of the drovers.

The sun was only beginning to crest above the mountaintops, and they would be moving out soon. Most of the men were saddled and ready or tending to last-minute details, while a couple of cow dogs ran circles excitedly around the cattle. Slim was at the forefront with his chuck wagon and would be leading the drive alongside Curtis.

"Boss, we're nearly ready to head out. Shore wish you were well enough to come along." Curtis tightened the cinch under his horse's belly before turning around with a stony face.

"You and me both. You okay this morning? All the hired men show up?"

Curtis hooked his thumbs in his jeans and his shoulders sagged. "It's nothing like that." He stared over at the remuda being handled by Levi. "More like a certain pretty lady turned me down flat." His lips thinned into a tight line.

John knew he meant Rachel and searched for something to say. "She did? Well, I'll be. I'm sorry." It was all John could think of to say. It surprised him though. He'd thought Curtis and Rachel might make a good team. *That's all they'd make. Why not admit to yourself that you care for the girl?*

John watched as his crew strolled over to say goodbye. "I want all of you to know how much I appreciate everything you do and will encounter to get these steers to rail." He paused to cough, then cleared his throat. "Sorry about that—the cough is sticking with me. I'm very disappointed that I'm not going to be heading out too. I appreciate all of you pitching in to help Curtis out with the blackleg that struck our calves. You men do me proud, now, and stay outta any fracas. Watch out for each other and for trouble along the trail. Take all your orders from Curtis, you hear? No drinking. No arguing. No grumbling. Got it?"

The band of cowboys chuckled, then nodded or mumbled, "Yes, sir."

"Okay. See you when you return, and then we'll have cause to celebrate." Another fit of coughing hit him.

"Take care of yourself, John. And watch out for Annabelle while I'm gone." Slim chortled. Annabelle had come out to give him a farewell hug, and she smiled up at her husband.

"You can count on it, Slim," John said.

John's men and newly hired hands mounted their horses, taking their places as they moved out of the pasture.

John stood a long time, bittersweet, watching the herding of the cattle with an occasional whoop or holler from the cowboys as morning light spread across the meadow. Winchester stood by his side, barking his goodbye. John lifted his hat and waved to them as they left on their way to the Idaho stockyards.

At breakfast, Rachel noticed John ate very little and said little. He had dark shadows under his eyes, and his lean face made him look as though he'd been the one on a long trail drive.

"I'm so glad you felt like eating with us this morning, John," Estelle said, smiling the length of the table at him. "But if you don't try to eat a little more, even Winchester won't recognize you."

"I'm trying, Grams." John glanced down at Rachel and smiled.

"Since you're doing somewhat better, I'm going to work today. But remember doctor's orders not to overdo it. It'll take awhile to regain your strength," Rachel reminded him, then suddenly realized she'd been treating him like a child when she saw him stiffen.

Estelle said, "I'm sure Molly can use your help. Next week, when I feel I can leave John alone, I'll come with you."

Annabelle poured more coffee in John's cup. "I promised the doctor I'd keep my eye on you, too." She grinned at him.

"Please! Stop this! I'm not a little boy." John rose, shoving his chair back hard and looking down at the three of them with his jaw clamped tight. He threw his napkin down and strode from the room.

Estelle blanched, clutching the broach at her throat. His outburst had startled all of them, and Rachel's heartstrings tugged as she watched him go. She wished she could comfort him.

"Now, what was that all about?" Annabelle said.

"I haven't a clue," Estelle answered quietly.

Rachel looked at both of them. "It may have more to do with the fact that he's not leading the trail drive than being treated as helpless."

Estelle pursed her lips together in concern. "The blackleg, the pneumonia, and the trail drive . . . all very bad timing."

32

Rachel hitched up the horse and buggy since most of the men were gone on the trail drive. She was glad her father had taught her many things when she was barely old enough to ride a horse. She smiled fondly, remembering him, and felt fresh longing wash over her to see him. One day she'd see her loved ones—she knew it for a fact—but until then their absence was very hard.

As she was about to climb into the buggy, John waved from across the yard. She clasped her gloved hands and waited, observing the slowness in his gait. She was accustomed to John moving with alacrity. Hopefully, he would soon return to his normal self.

He stood before her, hands on his hips. "I just wanted to say . . . I'm sorry for that outburst at breakfast." He took a deep breath, which caused him to cough.

When his cough quieted down, Rachel assured him, "John, you've had so much on your mind. It's understandable that your feelings are on the surface. Sometimes it's hard to appreciate what we have until bad times come." The wind picked up, and Rachel had to hang on to her bonnet as she looked into his weary, dark eyes.

"And you would know. I guess I tend to forget all the hardships that have come your way in such a short time. All the same, I'm sorry for raising my voice at all of you like that."

"Apology accepted. I must be going if I'm to be home by supper." She turned to put one foot on the step, and he took her arm to help her into the buggy. "Thank you," she said once she was seated. "You need to get out of this cold without your coat. Oops! I guess that was part of the reason you got irritated—we were treating you like a child. I promise not to do that again." She flashed him a broad grin.

"I was being silly. Besides, coming from you, I consider that you're more concerned about my well-being and I . . . well . . . I sort of like that. I can't forget what you said one night. It meant so much to me. Or maybe I was feverish and I thought you said it."

"Said what? John, I'm not sure what you're hinting at."

"You told me you loved me," he said huskily, gazing into her eyes.

Rachel sucked in a sharp breath of surprise. "Either you were delirious or someone else told you that, but I can assure you it wasn't me!"

His face flushed red, and he stepped back from the horse and buggy. "My mistake. It must've been the fever, but I swore it was you because I called out your name. I'm sorry I upset you, Rachel. Have a good day at the shop."

"I surely will," she answered, and felt a flutter in her chest. Did he mean that it was possible he had feelings for her too? *It had to be Beatrice who said that and didn't let on that she wasn't me. How could she do that?* With a light tap of her whip, she set off down the lane to town, with a new dawning gently unfurling within.

❧

"I've never been so happy to see your face," Molly said when Rachel entered the shop.

Rachel untied her bonnet and removed her coat, taking time to give Molly a brief hug. "And I can't tell you how good it is to see you, Molly. I feel as though I've been gone forever." She hung up her belongings and walked to the front counter.

"The shop's been slow the last few days, but that gives me time to work on our newest creations."

"I can't wait to see them."

"Not until you tell me how John is." She propped her elbow on the counter, cradling her chin, her large eyes questioning.

"He's so much better. He has a lingering cough and very little energy, but we were afraid we'd lose him to the pneumonia."

"So you were able to take care of him and soothe his brow, feed him and all that kind of stuff? Rather romantic, I'd say."

"You've been reading too many novels! Yes, matter of fact I did do all those things. Of course, Annabelle was pitching in as well."

Molly rolled her eyes and smiled. "I get the feeling that you enjoyed playing nursemaid."

"I forgot to tell you that Beatrice came too, bossing everyone around."

"Honestly? John must've loved all the attention."

"I doubt it. He had a high fever most of the time and slept a lot. But . . ."

"But what? Tell me. What are you leaving out?" Molly straightened.

"This morning as I was leaving, he said that one night I told him that I loved him. I can assure you, I did not!"

"But you wanted to." Molly stared at her squarely.

How does this young girl who has never been in love know how I feel? "Molly, *really*," she chided. "I don't know how I feel. Don't forget, he is courting Beatrice." The truth was she'd thought about their conversation all the way into town.

Molly moved away from the counter. "I'm sorry. I didn't mean to pry."

"I don't mind, but there's nothing between John and me. Why don't you show me what you've been working on while we have some free time?"

"Follow me to the workroom. We'll be able to hear the bell over the door ring."

Rachel followed Molly to where a hat form stood on an old wooden table. Deep burgundy material and various ribbons and feathers lay about the area. Molly was forming the small hat that required more wire in the newer fanchon style rather than the usual spoon bonnet. Upon further inspection, Rachel could see that the little black straw hat had a wide band of horsehair edging and straw in a basket weave design.

"Oh my, Molly. This is simply exquisite! I believe you have a natural talent for creating. Estelle believes so as well." Rachel pressed the burgundy satin ribbon between her fingers. "Lovely," she said.

"Thank you. I've been working on it for more than a week. I hope by the time I add the velvet ribbons to trail down the back, it will fetch a nice price."

"I'm sure you won't have a bit of trouble, and Estelle will

love it. I'd buy it myself, but you already know I'm trying to save every penny I earn." The bell over the front door sounded, so Rachel urged Molly to continue working on the hat and hurried to greet their customer.

The patron was none other than Sue, and Rachel gave her a warm smile and grasped her cold hands. "Sue, I'm so happy to see you. Where are your gloves?"

Sue shyly looked at her. "I believe one of the girls stole them, but don't worry about me. I'm inside now where it's warm."

"What can I help you find today?" Rachel let go of her hands and stepped back, surveying her friend's slim frame.

Sue glanced around, then said, "Er . . . I didn't come to shop. Was wondering if I could talk to you, when you are free."

Sensing Sue's need to talk with her alone, Rachel answered cheerily, "Of course, Sue. Why don't we have a cup of tea now? Molly's working on a new hat and we've not had a customer this morning, so it's a good time."

"But—I can't come before your customers—"

Rachel took her arm, trying to calm the worried look on Sue's tired face. "No need to worry. Molly will attend to them. I'll tell her, then let me put the teakettle on so we can chat." She directed Sue to the small table she and Molly used for breaks or when they had customers who perused their fabric swatches. "We won't be disturbing her in this corner. Take your coat off, and I'll be right back with our tea," she said, noticing the threadbare coat two sizes too large for Sue's slight frame.

Rachel returned moments later with a tray of steaming tea and some tea cakes she'd found. Sue looked as though she could use a lot more than a few tea cakes. She was thinner than when Rachel had worked at the saloon and her blue eyes held a haunted look. Rachel poured their tea and added sugar, waiting for Sue to speak.

"I'm not sure I should've come, perhaps I'd better leave." Sue started to stand but Rachel stayed her.

"You can talk to me, no matter what has brought you here, Sue. You know that."

"I'll come right out and say it then. I want to leave the Wild Horse," she leaned over and whispered.

"What's holding you back?"

"I have nowhere to go, no job, and very little money. Not even enough to catch a stage back to Kansas."

"Sue, I can loan you the stage fare if you want to leave. Do you have anyone back in Kansas? Family?"

"Only my father, who's ill and poor. I left home because we were penniless with barely enough to eat." Sue stared down at her hands in shame. "My brothers disowned me when they found out what I did to survive." A lone tear trailed down her painted cheek. "Even God won't forgive me for what I've done—stealing and then . . . well, you know."

Rachel pulled out her handkerchief and handed it to her. "Sue, that's not true."

"Yes, it is. You never did anything but dance, nothing like me or Fannie did." She dabbed her eyes.

"You're right, but if I'd stayed, I may have."

"No, not you. Never." Sue shook her head adamantly. "I'm a bad person and no man will ever want to marry me now."

"You can start your life afresh, Sue. No one is perfect, not even me," she added when Sue gave her a startled look. "The ground around the foot of the cross is level—we are all the same there. God can forgive anything, but you must trust Him and ask Him to forgive you. He'll be with you and show you the way. I know He will." Rachel paused to let that penetrate Sue's mind.

"You really think so?" Sue finally asked. "I'm not sure they'll let me leave."

"I know so. I've never told anyone this before, but three weeks after I became a dance hall girl, I began praying for a way out. I had nowhere to go and Preston had left town. Then look what happened. But you have family! Go to them and explain how you wound up here. They'll forgive you. I know they will. This is a chance for you to make a new life, and I'll happily advance you money to get out of the saloon."

Sue bit her bottom lip, then took a long sip of her tea. "How? When can I get away? Someone will come looking for me."

"Not if we get you on the five o'clock stage tonight. There's no time like the present."

"*Tonight?* But I can't go dressed like this," she said, spreading her fingers against her satin outfit.

"Mmm . . . that's very true. Let's go talk to Molly. I'll bet you she can whip up a simple skirt or finish one she's already started and have it completed by the time you leave tonight."

"But I'm scared someone will come looking for me." A look of fear shadowed Sue's face.

"Let 'em. You can stay in the back of the shop until we are ready to get you on that stage tonight."

"I can't thank you enough." Sue reached over and squeezed Rachel's hand.

"You can—just have that talk with the Lord. That's thanks enough." She rose from her chair. "Come on and follow me, and we can get started before I have customers." Rachel was tickled to see Sue's face suddenly brighten, even with her timidity, as she gathered her coat to follow.

"I'll take that," Rachel said, indicating Sue's coat.

"What—"

"You can wear my coat. You'll freeze to death on the stagecoach in this thing."

33

Adrenaline coursed through Rachel as she and Molly worked feverishly between customers on a suitable travel outfit for Sue. When it was finished, Sue twirled around, showing off the plain homespun brown plaid skirt with its shirred crème shirtwaist blouse. Rachel winked conspiratorially at Molly.

"I honestly don't know why you both are being so good to me. I don't deserve it." Sue stopped admiring the outfit and her reflection in the mirror long enough to convey her thanks.

"Stop that, now! Thank goodness Molly is skillful and fast with a needle," Rachel commented with a pat on Molly's shoulder.

"Aww, I'm glad I could help you, Sue. Just think how neat I can sew when I'm not under pressure! I hope the seams hold together."

They all laughed, and Rachel felt like they were all three partners in crime as they whisked Sue to the depot, her face void of makeup, a plain chignon under the simple spoon bonnet that hid her face, and wearing Rachel's heavier coat.

"Shh . . . we mustn't giggle or we'll be found out," Rachel

admonished as they neared the stage depot where other travelers stood waiting for the departure. "I'll get your ticket and you two stay here."

After the stage arrived, emptied its passengers, and changed to a fresh team of horses, Rachel and Molly began their goodbyes.

"Dear sister, it was a pleasure to have you visit. Please don't wait so long to do so again," Rachel said loud enough for folks standing around to hear. "God go with you, my friend," she whispered in Sue's ear. Sue nodded, her eyes filling with tears.

"Yes, sis, and please write to us about home," Molly added to their ruse.

Sue took on proper English. "Oh, dear sisters, I shall indeed. It's been wonderful to see you both." She gave them both a quick hug, then stepped up to the stagecoach ready to be handed inside by the rugged but handsome driver who smiled broadly at her, tipping his hat. Sue shrugged her shoulders at her friends on the boardwalk. Rachel stifled a laugh as Molly grabbed her hand with a squeeze. They waved to Sue, who was peering out the window, and both of them fought back tears as the stage left in a cloud of dust.

As the two of them turned to leave, a familiar voice behind them called out. "Rachel, I didn't know you had a sister," Beatrice said with a wry little smile as she approached them. She looked fresh as a Montana meadowlark in her deep yellow dress with a plunging V at the throat and an accompanying black caplet.

Somehow, Beatrice continually irritated Rachel's good nature. "Hello, Beatrice. My sister? Oh, yes—"

"That was . . . *my* sister," Molly interjected, thankfully

covering for Rachel. "Rachel thinks of her as the sister she never had, and she treats me the same way. It's a wonderful virtue to have."

"I see. How nice. I don't believe I ever saw her in town while she was here," Beatrice pressed.

"Well, we can't know everyone's whereabouts, now can we?" Rachel muttered through tight lips while doing her best to remain friendly.

Ignoring Rachel's comment, Beatrice asked, "And John. Is he still doing well? I'm sure my nursing did quite a bit to speed his return to health." She batted her eyes at them.

"He's doing very well." Rachel wasn't about to tell her much of anything. Let her find out for herself.

"Please give him my regards, and I'll try to make it over to see him this weekend."

"I'll be sure to tell him, Beatrice. Now, if you'll excuse us, we must be going." Rachel nudged Molly and they started down the boardwalk, leaving Beatrice to stare after them.

As they were nearing the shop, Rachel paused. "Don't forget, Molly, you're to come to dinner after church."

"I can't wait, and since we've already locked up, I'll run on home. Oh, and Rachel, today was a fun day after all, wasn't it?" Her smile widened.

"It was, and thank you, Molly, for jumping right in to help Sue. I hope her life will improve and her brothers are willing to forgive."

❧

John sat at his desk trying to make sense of his ledgers, but he had a difficult time concentrating and his eyes burned. He was mildly surprised how fatigued he still felt, even though the doctor had warned him. How in the world was he going to adjust? *With My help*, a voice inside his head reminded him. *Then, Lord, I need Your help to face it*, he prayed, resting his head in his hand. What was the true measure of a man, anyway? He used to think it was having one of the largest herds around, with folks looking up to him in respect for what he'd acquired. Deep in his heart today, he admitted that was no longer the truth at all. After a few minutes pouring his heart out to his Maker, he sat back and closed the ledger, feeling better somehow.

Between his grandmother's health and then his illness, Rachel's promise to help out with the books hadn't materialized yet. Maybe he would ask her again this weekend.

⁂

Estelle always looked forward to the end of the day when Rachel returned from work, so she sat near the window watching the wind tip the top of the spruce trees in the distance. She was glad that John had come to her apologizing for making a scene at breakfast, but she told him she was worried about him.

He'd answered with his own concern. "Don't be spending time ruminating over me. I'm certainly more concerned about your health than mine. But I have to say, you look the picture of perfect health now."

"And I do feel well. The only thing I've noticed is that I tire sooner than I did before. But I'm getting my rest and plan to go check out the shop next week. I've been so bored that I want to ask a few folks over for dinner after church, if you're feeling up to it."

"I'm up to it if you are," he answered with a challenging smile, and she noticed the twinkle had returned to her grandson's eyes.

"Good! We could both use some cheering up, and the place seems so dreary without the cowboys around." She paused then added, "I'm so sorry you weren't well enough to go on the trail drive. I know how disappointed you are."

"It's like you always say—there's a reason for everything. I intend to throw the cowboys a nice celebration when they return. In fact, Grams, I've been thinking about all this property and how hard all of it is to manage. So, I want to do something real special for my men."

"Don't you think a celebration party is enough? What did you have in mind?"

"I'm going to give each of them some land to start their own homestead. If they don't want to start one and would rather move on or stay like they are—then I'm for that too. Later, they may have an opportunity to buy more."

Estelle's heart warmed knowing John had a generous spirit for a change. "John, that's the most wonderful thing you could do! But what if they all decide to homestead?"

He smiled, then looked serious for a moment. "I wager I can handle it. After losing the calves to blackleg and seeing how hard my men worked for me when I couldn't, I wanted to give them something back. So your lessons about greed didn't go unheeded," he teased with a chuckle. "It's not like I have anyone to leave it all to." He sighed. "I'll go wash up for supper," he added and left.

Estelle closed her eyes, thanking God for seeing them both through the hard times of late and for all of the blessings that were theirs. When she looked up, she saw Rachel drive into the yard and hop down. She glanced up at the grandfather clock and saw that Rachel was later than normal. She hoped nothing had gone wrong at the shop. Whose coat was she wearing?

She didn't have long to wait. Rachel burst through the door, her face shining with excitement. She whipped off her coat and tossed it into a chair before hurrying over to where Estelle sat in the sun.

"I've had the most unusual but fulfilling day!" She knelt by Estelle's chair to give her a brief hug. "How are you? And how was your day?"

Estelle chuckled. "I'm fine, but I would much rather hear about your day as you seem very excited about it."

"I made a spur-of-the-moment decision today, and I'm not usually impulsive, but I think it will turn out to be one of the best ones I've ever made." Rachel stood, then took a chair opposite her.

Estelle thought Rachel looked lovely with her bright eyes snapping as she talked. She wished John was in the room. "You have me hooked, so tell me all about it. Does it have something to do with making a decision for the shop in my absence?"

"No. Nothing like that at all. Do you remember Sue?"

Estelle nodded. "How could I forget her and Fannie?" She laughed, remembering how they'd showed up at Preston's memorial service.

Rachel hurriedly recited the day's events to get Sue to the last stagecoach leaving Cottonwood with Molly's help. "The shop had only a few customers today, so I hope you don't mind that I didn't spend time tidying up. Instead, between customers, Molly and I worked on a simple outfit for Sue and got her ready for her new adventure."

"My goodness! So you gave your coat to Sue. I think it's

great that you used the time so wisely. Getting Sue out of the Wild Horse was the kindest thing you could do. I'm very proud of you."

"I was hoping you would say that. After we pretended to be sisters, guess who showed up?"

Estelle shook her head. "I have no idea. Someone from the saloon to take her back?"

"Beatrice. Of course she asked me about my sister, and thankfully Molly said it was *her* sister. Later, Molly felt bad that she fibbed."

"I'm sure the good Lord will forgive her if she asks. I'll make a point to pray for Sue and that her brothers will accept her back into the fold. We all make mistakes."

"Yes, and I made mine by earning quick money at the saloon." Rachel looked out the window and sighed. "No matter what others think, the only thing I did was dance."

Estelle reached over to pat the top of Rachel's knee. "You did the best you could at the time. You've told me before, and I believe you, Rachel. Don't listen to gossip or worry about what others may think about you. The only one that matters is the good Lord who looks at the motivations of our hearts."

Rachel laid her hand on top of Estelle's. "I hope someday I'm as wise as you."

"Whenever you need to unburden or need someone to talk to, you know I'll be right here."

John stepped lightly away from the parlor door after he'd come upon their conversation, stifling the cough that tickled his throat. He hadn't meant to eavesdrop but hadn't wanted to interrupt them either. He could see Rachel's happy face through the crack between the door and molding. He wasn't surprised at Rachel's generosity toward Sue, but was stunned that she said she'd made a mistake working at the saloon. But he was glad that she was never the "soiled dove" he'd thought she was. He knew what he'd have to do—and soon.

❦

Rachel smoothed her hair back, placing the heavy mass into a silky black snood at the back of her head before she went downstairs to supper. It had been a good week—John was better, and Sue was off to a better life, she hoped. The smells from below made her stomach growl, so she swung her door open wide and it banged hard against John.

He steadied her with his hand to her elbow, and for a brief moment neither of them moved, his dark eyes penetrating hers. He smelled freshly shaven and his thick hair was combed neatly into place. She'd like him to hold her in the crook of his arm again like he'd done when she received the news about Preston.

"I'm sorry, John. I didn't see you in my haste to get down to supper."

"You must be starving by the way you swung that door into my nose." He rubbed his nose, pretending to be hurt.

She stepped up to have a closer look. "Oh my! Your nose is red. I'm so sorry. Does it hurt?" She touched her fingertip to the end of his nose with a gentle rub.

"Not when you're touching it. You must have healing powers," he teased with a grin. "I'll give you all day to stop that."

Rachel laughed. "What a joker you are. I see no damage, so why don't we go have supper?" She held her arm out for him.

"I'd be mighty pleased to escort you down to dinner." He bowed with much aplomb, then hooked her arm into his elbow at his side. A fit of coughing seized him as they started down the stairs.

"John, maybe you should have the doctor check your lungs again since you have that lingering cough," she said when they reached the bottom of the stairs.

He gave her a funny stare and bent close with a whisper, his breath tickling her ear. "There's no need. The doctor told me my lungs have been permanently damaged—"

"What?" She looked at him, disbelieving what she'd heard, but he placed a finger to his lips to silence her as Estelle walked into the foyer on her way to the dining room. "We'll talk later."

34

The sounds of the night wind and a lone wolf's mournful howl kept Rachel wide awake—or at least she told herself that was the reason. In truth, she kept going over her encounter with John before supper and the feeling his nearness gave her—a giddy sensation like she'd never experienced before. From the look in his eyes gazing down at her, he felt the same. Didn't he?

It saddened her to know that John's lungs would not be healthy as before, but she would pray for his healing—that he would gain strength. He looked healthy, and except for the lingering cough no one would know any different. Maybe she'd get a chance to talk with him tomorrow.

She got up and pulled the drapes back at the windows that overlooked the pasture. Big, fluffy snowflakes were just beginning to fall, the moonlight creating a softening light across the pasture that was too beautiful for words. Before long, the ranch hands would return and Thanksgiving would be celebrated. The cold floor beneath her bare feet forced her back to the warmth of her bed.

She burrowed beneath the heavy quilts, praying that Sue was safely on her way home. Other concerns flittered through her mind—paying Wyatt for the hotel room, Curtis's obvious hurt at their conversation. This made her consider talking soon to Jeffrey and Wyatt. Friendship with them suited her best, but would she be doing herself a disfavor? She may never have another chance at marriage. But she didn't want to marry for convenience even if it meant she would be alone. John had not given any true indication that he wanted their relationship to be more than it was. If Preston were here, he'd tell her that she was simply being too romantic.

Sighing, she rolled to her side and punched her pillow, willing her eyes to close. Her mother always said sufficient unto the day is the evil thereof—or not to borrow trouble. The verse reminded her of the family Bible Preston had left behind for her. Perhaps tomorrow she'd take time to read it. Knowing her mother and father had held it in their hands many times drew a large lump in her throat.

❧

The millinery shop was not busy because of the cold and light snow, although it only amounted to a couple of inches. Rachel was sweeping the fluffy white stuff from the sidewalk in front of the shop's door when she looked up and saw Wyatt approaching. He looked handsome in his heavy duster, black cowboy hat, and gloves, and his boots rang out against the boardwalk.

"You're just the person I wanted to see," he said.

Rachel paused. "Well, here I am. I've been hoping to see you so I can pay you for the hotel room."

"I told you it wasn't necessary." His eyes stared into hers.

She leaned the broom against the door, saying, "Let's go inside where it's warmer and we can talk." Wyatt followed her inside.

Molly lifted her head and smiled at them as they entered, then went back to adding her receipts for the week. Rachel gestured toward the small table, removing her coat while Wyatt surveyed the shop and its contents.

"Guess I've never stepped foot in a female shop before."

Rachel laughed. "Then you're missing out. We also have gloves for men, walking canes, and other haberdashery. You may want to take a look around."

"Mmm . . . I never knew. I normally buy what I need when I travel," he said, taking a seat.

"What was it you wanted to see me about?" Rachel asked, sensing Molly watching the two of them.

"I wanted to tell you that Estelle has invited me to dinner at the ranch after church."

"How nice. She told me she was having a few friends over. I think it's been a little too dull for her since she got sick."

"Maybe you and I can find a moment alone Sunday afternoon?" He flashed an engaging smile and she wondered briefly why she couldn't manage to work up an attraction toward him. He was good-looking, had a large spread, employed servants, and wanted to marry her. What more could she ask for? *Love, that's what. True, blinding, catch your breath kind of love.* "Wyatt—"

"Now, don't go saying no yet. You might grow to care for me if you give me half a chance." He was sincere and his jovial smile disappeared as he reached for her hand.

"Wait here. I'll only be a moment," she said as she withdrew her hand. Rachel dashed off to the back, found her reticule, and removed the money she owed him. Returning to the table, she held the money out and insisted he take it. "Thank you for coming to my rescue that rainy night. I truly did appreciate it and the company." She took a deep breath. "But Wyatt, you must listen to me. I want to be your friend, but that's all. I hope you understand. You'll find the right person for you, I'm sure."

He froze for a moment. "I see. It's not what I'd hoped to hear, but I'll honor your request and try to think of you as a friend. It may be hard to do but I'll work at it. Do you have someone else on your heart?"

Rachel's heart pounded, and when she didn't answer, Wyatt stood. "I think I know the answer to my question. I'll be on my way now. Guess I'll see you Sunday then. Give my regards to John." He tipped his hat, and with a solemn face turned and strode out of the shop.

Molly gave Rachel a sharp look. "What was all that about?"

"He doesn't want to give up on marriage with me, so I tried to make him understand that it can't be." Rachel sighed.

"Are you sure? It would make your life easier, and he seems to be a very nice man." Molly cocked her head at Rachel.

"Yes, I'm sure. Now, let's have our lunch before a customer comes. It won't be long before we close for the day."

"I have a feeling there's something or someone you're not telling me about," Molly teased.

The shop door opened and Fannie marched in, her silken fancy dress peeking out at the bottom of her coat. She sported a matching hat with a large peacock feather and went straight to where Rachel stood by the counter.

"Morning, Fannie—"

"Rachel, I'll get straight to the point. Where is Sue?" she said in a clipped tone.

"How would I know? I don't work at the saloon." Rachel stiffened. She wouldn't lie, but the truth was she didn't know where in Kansas Sue went or if indeed she had made it there.

"You're not fooling me a'tall. I know Sue liked you and always listened to you. If she were in trouble, you'd be the first one she'd come to." Fannie snickered.

Rachel looked at Molly who excused herself and went to the back for their lunch. Rachel knew it would be easy for Molly to open her mouth.

"Fannie, all I can say is that she wasn't happy at the saloon—"

"Well, neither are a lot of us, but that's our lot in life!"

"It doesn't have to be, Fannie." Rachel observed the woman who was probably close to her age but looked far older. Her slack red lips, drawn face with wrinkles, and dark circles under her eyes spoke of aging before her time. Gone was her usual jovial disposition.

"What would you know? You had a man sweep you off your feet and whisk you away. Why, you don't even have to work, so why the devil do you?" Fannie's tone was harsh.

"It's not like that at all and you know it, Fannie. Why don't you have lunch with us and we can talk. Maybe help you find somewhere more suitable to work."

"Ha! Ain't nobody going to want me, and for your information, I have a brain and don't need none of your advice!" She harrumphed, turned away with her head held high, then paused at the door. "You know, Sue was the only true friend I had." She slammed the door behind her before Rachel could utter another word.

Molly came back with a tray laden with two soup bowls and nodded toward the door. "I heard everything she said. I don't think I care for that woman," she said, carrying the bowls to the small table.

Rachel shrugged. "She's a poor soul that needs someone to love her and show her the way. I just wish I could help her. She probably didn't start out to be what she became."

"That's what I like about you, Rachel . . . your kindness to everyone, even when they don't deserve it."

Rachel smiled. "I wish that was always true, but it's not—but I do try to be fair most of the time. Don't forget you're coming to dinner on Sunday."

Molly grinned. "I wouldn't dare miss it."

❧

John found himself watching the clock for the time when Rachel returned from work every day. The house was dull except for chatter between Annabelle and his grandmother, who'd been planning the Sunday dinner menu. Nothing formal, but she told him she planned to invite folks after church. Ones who could come on such short notice. He had to admit, impromptu gatherings seemed to work out best for her, but he missed the drovers. He hoped everything was going along well for them.

His health had improved much in the days since the cowboys had left, and he wondered if he could've made the trip despite what the doctor said. Yet even though he didn't want to believe it, he got winded when he walked out to the pasture and down to the other corrals. *Maybe more walking would make my lungs stronger?* He could only hope so. He'd do whatever it took. He couldn't envision a sedentary life.

He was napping in his easy chair while his grandmother worked on a crochet piece when he heard Rachel arrive. He hurriedly sat up, smoothed back his hair, and tried to look alert.

A few minutes later Rachel poked her head inside the parlor and he motioned for her to come in. Her pale lavender paisley wool dress had a matching jacket—just right for a business woman but also the perfect touch of femininity. He was glad that now she usually dropped the formality she used to have around him and his grandmother.

"I'll go out and unhitch Sal," John said and started to rise.

"No need. I've already done that. But I'm glad a hired hand is helping you out with the small chores while the cowboys are away."

"I can handle some of it, but that handyman sure does help." *I can't get enough of looking at her. Does she know how she affects me?*

"How was your day, Rachel?" Grams asked as she laid aside her crocheting.

Rachel took a seat on the settee before answering. "*Eventful* would be a good word for it."

"Oh. Want to tell us about it?" His grandmother cocked a brow, and John knew if she had her way, she'd dig it out of Rachel.

"Well, I had a visit from Fannie, who'd decided that I knew Sue's whereabouts. She was upset and I tried to reason with her, but she wouldn't listen. I know she could change her life like Sue if she really wanted to."

"That's too bad. I know you have a heart to help those ladies," Grams said.

"Well, that could've been me. I guess I owe John my appreciation. He came along before that did happen to me." She gazed at him, and John's throat felt dry as the dust on the top of his boots.

"No need to thank me—it was Preston's letter that got me involved. But I'm glad you're here and not there . . . the Wild Horse, I mean," he choked out. When he took more time to study her, he found she had a pure beauty, and when her eyes caught his, he suddenly knew what kind of woman she'd become—one of strength and tenderness wrapped with courage. In her gaze, he could see her faithful heart. No wonder Wyatt, Curtis, and Jeffrey were smitten with her.

"John John, did you hear me?" Rachel asked.

"I'm sorry, what were you saying?" He tried to focus on the conversation.

"I was saying you look better today. I see more color in your face."

"Oh, yes, well . . . I feel a little stronger every day." *So she's interested enough in me to notice.* He felt a strange sensation in his stomach.

"I agree with you, Rachel. Before long you won't find my grandson sitting inside the house, I'll wager."

"I'm going to freshen up before supper. Oh, by the way, Wyatt says to give you his regards and he'll see us Sunday," Rachel called over her shoulder. John's heart froze. So Wyatt was coming. Suddenly, John's spirit deflated.

35

Rachel enjoyed getting to know more of the hardworking church folk of Paradise Valley when they stood about chatting before the service began. She found most to be very friendly and willing to lend a hand when needed. In the beginning, a few had thumbed their noses at her because they'd heard she used to be a dance hall girl, but apparently Estelle had put a stop to that, and they accepted her now, thankfully.

Sunday's crisp weather energized the church members, and Pastor Jeffrey preached a good sermon about tithing, making direct eye contact with Rachel at least once. She would have to find a time to speak to him alone soon.

John sat between Rachel and Estelle while Annabelle sat with her friends. Rachel studied the backs of John's hands while he held his hymnal, trying to squash the feelings that surfaced with him seated so close. He caught her eye and smiled, turning the page as his rich baritone filled the small space around them on the last song of the service. She finally found her voice and was surprised at how their voices blended so well. Estelle looked over at them and whispered, "You two sound like you should be in the choir. They need you."

Rachel glanced at John who nodded with a cough. Maybe they should join the choir when his breathing was stronger. Now, if they *were* a couple, she could envision going to practice together, singing a duet, raising their voices in grateful praise. Estelle was right. The choir consisted of only four women and could desperately use some male voices.

When the service concluded, everyone filed outside after talking a moment to Pastor Jeffrey, who waited at the door. It was proving to be a cold, clear day with blinding sunlight. John held his grandmother's arm as they greeted Jeffrey, then proceeded down the stairs to their waiting buggy. Jeffrey touched Rachel's sleeve to speak to her as she passed.

"I think it's great that Estelle is having a few friends over for dinner, and I'm looking forward to spending some time with you." His eyes softened as he gazed down at her. *Oh dear.*

She agreed. "Yes, she is very gracious—more than a little bored with all the quiet around the ranch. Not being able to go to the millinery shop because of her health hasn't helped."

Jeffrey's smile broadened. "All very understandable. She seems well enough, though."

"She is. I'm holding up others waiting to greet you, Jeffrey. And John and Estelle are waiting for me." Over Jeffrey's shoulder Rachel could see John craning his neck around, hands on the horse's reins, looking for her.

"To be sure. Well, I'll see you soon, then." He reluctantly turned to the next couple behind her.

I should have said something! But how could she with members lined up to speak to him? She'd just have to make it a point to speak with him this afternoon before he declared his affection for her, if indeed that was his intention. Never in her life did she think *three* men would suddenly show such interest in her, and she wasn't certain that she'd choose any of them. At least she felt certain she really couldn't—not as long as her heart threatened to strangle her whenever she caught a glimpse of John's eyes latched on her.

John guided the buggy around and Rachel bustled down the stairs, waiting for him to stop. He hopped down, jaw clenched as he assisted her before spreading a fur across her lap for the ride back home. What was bothering him? When they were singing in church, he'd seemed cheerful.

As soon as John pulled up in front of the house, Annabelle stepped from the buggy without waiting for assistance. Rachel called out that she'd be glad to help and was surprised when Annabelle agreed.

"I'd like that very much, Rachel. I'm looking forward to seeing folks today. It's been awhile since we had a crowd over to eat with us." Annabelle looked down the driveway with a frown. "We'd better hurry, they're nearly here."

Rachel directed her gaze down the lane and saw buggies in the distance, with Jeffrey astride his horse bringing up the rear. John came around to her side and she placed her gloved hand in his while she stepped down from the carriage. Her sleeve brushed against his fine wool coat as her feet found the ground, and their eyes locked in a deep gaze. Painfully aware that Estelle was watching their interaction, Rachel shyly whispered a thank-you, then whirled around to follow Annabelle as John turned to help his grandmother.

"Take your time, Annabelle. Our guests can all chat for a few moments until the food is set out."

Annabelle nodded. "I'm glad it's a nice day since you wanted buffet style."

"Yes. I thought that way our guests can mingle and become better acquainted and can be inside or out on the porch, whichever suits them." Estelle held John's arm as they all walked into the house.

"I'll let you women do whatever it is you do in the kitchen, and I'll go unhitch the horses and greet everyone," John said, helping his grandmother with her cape. "I can hardly wait for a hot meal."

Annabelle let out a hearty laugh. "Today it's cold fried chicken, I'm afraid."

John chortled. "Now, Annabelle, you know that's always been a favorite of mine." He tweaked her cheek, then strode back outside.

Watching the two of them interact always brought a warm feeling to Rachel's heart. They were like mother and son, leaving no doubt Annabelle would fight for him if need be. From the door, Rachel watched him with the horses. He still moved slower than what was usual for him, but he didn't cough as often. Estelle seemed unaware of his slower pace.

"Rachel, are you coming?" Annabelle quirked an eyebrow at her, touching Rachel's arm.

Rachel quickly closed the door. "Oh, yes, of course." Annabelle moved toward the kitchen.

"It's okay to watch the man you love. I remember when I could not take my eyes off Slim when he was in the corral wranglin' a horse or in the field ropin' a steer. He was a sight for sore eyes!"

"You miss him, don't you?"

"For a fact, I do. Slim can't return soon enough for me!"

They entered the kitchen, where edibles seemed to cover every available surface. Rachel decided Annabelle must've been up at the crack of daylight getting so much food cooked. "Why don't you move the chairs away from the dining table in there, set up the plates and such on one end of the table, and then I'll start setting the food out."

"Okay. Annabelle, do you have an extra apron to cover my church dress? I'd hate to get something on it."

"Right here," Annabelle answered, snagging an apron off the peg by the kitchen door for her. "Here's a clean one for you," she said, tossing it to Rachel.

In less than fifteen minutes, the table was laden with fried chicken, potato salad, pickled beets, green beans, and two huckleberry pies with thick cream for topping.

John ushered Jeffrey, Molly, and Wyatt toward the dining room when Rachel called everyone in to eat. From the hallway, he noticed Beatrice and her mother arrive, so he walked out to assist them.

Vera greeted him warmly. "John, Beatrice told me how sick you were, but I'm so happy to see you up and about . . . a little thinner, but better." Before he could reply, she jabbered on, "I know Beatrice's nursing skills had a lot to do with your recovery." She continued to talk as they went inside, barely giving him a chance to say hello to Beatrice.

"If you ladies will head to the dining room, you'll find the food is served buffet style today. Grams didn't want anything formal, just friends getting together." John pointed them in the direction where everyone was already talking with light banter, joking about how much they could put on their plates.

Beatrice took his arm, though he hadn't offered it, smiling up at him in her coquettish way. Inwardly he groaned. "Darling, you're looking a little pale. Are you getting enough rest and eating properly?"

"Yes, I am. Don't be worried about me."

"I hope so because we have lots of things to plan for the long winter while we keep company." Her sparkling blue eyes were fetching and should have made his pulse race, but they didn't. His mouth was dry from the dratted cough that tickled the back of his throat, and he politely covered his mouth. Suddenly, John was one hundred percent certain Beatrice wasn't the one for him. He kindly removed her hand to give her a plate, motioning for her to go ahead of him.

He couldn't help but look down the table as Rachel tipped her head up to smile his way, but when she saw Beatrice next to him the smile faded. The Sunday dress she wore was a pretty blue that showed off her figure, and he caught himself staring while she helped Annabelle replenish the serving dishes. He loved watching her pale pink lips tilt upwards in a bright smile, amused as Jeffrey and Wyatt seemed determined to outdo each other in vying for her attention. *I should muster up enough gumption to ask her outright if she is considering them as future husband possibilities.* Then he decided that it was not his place to ask such a personal thing of her.

"John, are you even listening to me?" Beatrice fumed. "I declare, I think that pneumonia did something to your head. I asked if you'd get me something to drink."

John snapped his head away from Rachel's sweet face to Beatrice's pinched one. "Sure. What would you like?" *I've got to get away from this woman . . . I can't breathe.*

237

❧

Rachel and Annabelle were the last to fill their plates, and Rachel noticed that everyone had found a seat. The luncheon had been a good idea—she noticed Estelle was unusually cheerful. Rachel walked to the parlor to find Molly and was mildly surprised to see her sitting by the window balancing her plate with Jeffrey sitting opposite her. When she saw Rachel, Molly gave her a shy smile.

Sooo . . . maybe I won't have to have that talk with Jeffrey after all. Feeling relieved, she decided to carry her plate to the porch where it was sunny. John was leaning against the porch railing eating, while Beatrice was picking at the food on her plate in a nearby rocker. Wyatt offered Rachel his chair when he saw her.

"I'm finished, so you can have my seat. I must tell Annabelle everything was delicious," he said, rising from his chair. "A full stomach and the sun beating down can make a fella sleepy."

Rachel took his seat, thanking him. "Yes, Annabelle spoils us with her cooking."

"I don't suppose you know how to cook, Rachel?" Beatrice asked in a clipped tone.

"I can get by, but I'm not sure anyone would be standing in line to dine on my cuisine." Rachel chuckled. She knew Beatrice was trying to bait her. "But I make up for that with my skills at ranching and helping to run the millinery shop for Estelle."

"And a fine job you're doing, too," John added.

Rachel smiled at him, then turned to Beatrice. "So besides the nursing course you didn't complete, just what *is* it that you do best?"

Beatrice shifted in the rocker. "Well . . . it's true I didn't get my degree, but I learned enough to help out when needed, like in John's recent illness."

"But what is it that you spend time *doing* is what I believe Rachel meant by her question." John quirked an eyebrow, then swallowed his last forkful of food. He reached for Wyatt's plate, stacking it with his.

"I'm involved in many community affairs. I stay knowledgeable of the goings-on in town." Beatrice handed John her half-empty plate.

Wyatt chuckled. "I didn't realize that Cottonwood had many things going on, Beatrice. Perhaps you and I could take a walk and discuss some new ideas I have for the town."

"Why, that would be nice," she said, rising from her chair and tucking her arm in the crook of his. Wyatt's surprise was evident as they descended the porch steps into the yard.

"We'll be back for dessert, Rachel. You don't mind, do you?" Wyatt looked back, a bit befuddled—either from Beatrice's acquiescence or the fact that he'd asked her.

"Well of course she doesn't mind," Beatrice said, shooting him a saucy smile.

"No, no. Not at all," Rachel said with a small smile. She was just a bit hurt that Wyatt had gotten over her so quickly. Their laughter floated back as they strolled out into the yard.

"Guess it's just you and me, Rachel," John said. "How about we go cut the pies for dessert and give Annabelle a break?"

Gathering the plates, she answered, "Yes, we should. She's been up since before daylight." *And I'll get to spend some time alone with you.*

36

"You slice the pie and I'll put it all on a tray," John said after they shooed Annabelle out, forcing her to take a break.

"It's a deal." Rachel smiled back at him, then went to retrieve a knife and dessert plates. John was in good spirits and had a little more zip in his steps, and she hoped it meant that he was getting stronger. "You appear to be feeling better," she stated.

He grinned. "I believe I am. Must be all the prayers." He cleared his throat. "Now that we are away from the crowd, I have to ask you—are you and Wyatt courting? And if I may be so bold to inquire—what about Jeffrey? It appeared to me that he and Molly were having a good time talking together in the parlor, so I'm trying to figure out who's courting who."

Rachel paused for a moment from slicing the huckleberry pie and looked up at him with a grin. "You are nosy, Mr. McIntyre. Jeffrey and I are friends, nothing more. And as for Wyatt, he understands how I feel but continues to pursue me—that is, until today. It's like he suddenly has eyes only for Beatrice. Which brings me to ask, how do *you* feel about that?"

"I think it's obvious that Beatrice has bigger fish to fry than me, which suits me fine. She was more aggressive than I like in a woman. There's no love lost." John paused, then continued on, "I thought for certain you and Wyatt were growing closer. He did offer you marriage, remember?"

A boyish look crossed his suntanned face, and it reminded her of grammar school when a boy had asked her if she liked him. But this time it was a grown-up man who wanted answers to his questions.

Rachel chuckled, then continued cutting pie slices and adding them to the plates. "I remember quite well, but I'll bet you didn't know that I turned him down." She glanced up, handing him a plate as a look of relief washed over his face. He took the dish, catching a drip from its edge and licking his fingers.

"No, I didn't know that. But am I allowed to say I'm relieved? Wyatt's a good man though—he could have shown you the world and treated you like a queen."

"Maybe I don't feel the need for that." She searched his eyes until he swallowed and reached for a tray.

"Then how do you want to be treated?" he said, placing the pie on the tray.

"Mmm, let's see . . . Like a cherished loved one that her spouse can't be without—that shares her dreams with him and he doesn't laugh at her foibles. Someone who can be trusted with the promises made to her."

John took a step closer. "That's not all that hard to do with someone like you, Rachel." His voice was husky, his eyes narrowing. He reached for the knife in her hand and laid it aside.

For a moment she thought he was going to kiss her, and he might have if Annabelle hadn't barged through the kitchen door. John moved swiftly, putting space between them. Rachel's heart was fluttering and she was sure her face was flushed, but she knew Annabelle was gracious enough not to say anything.

"Land sakes, you two! Our guests are waiting for the dessert. I'll put the coffee on if you will serve the pie." She shook her head at them, then lumbered over to the stove.

"We'll get right to it," Rachel said. The two of them hurried out of the kitchen to serve dessert, with John chuckling all the way down the hallway to the parlor. She liked the rich timbre of his voice when he laughed.

"I wanted to ask if you'd take a look at my ledgers and do some posting for me. I'm so behind, especially since I got sick. I'm not sure if I can begin to make sense of it. As soon as the drovers are back with the cash for the cattle, I'd like to be caught up to see where I stand."

"I can do that tomorrow if you'd like."

"That'd be great. Now, let's give these folks a taste of heaven with Annabelle's huckleberry pie."

Monday night, after a day at the shop and dinner with Estelle and John, Rachel began to organize the books. She didn't realize how tired she was until she'd finished entering receipts into John's ledger. With the house quiet, she reflected back on the day before.

It'd been a good time visiting with everyone, and even Beatrice's countenance changed for the better with Wyatt hovering nearby. But Rachel was more surprised when Molly pulled her to the side and told her Jeffrey was going to take her back to town.

"That's wonderful," Rachel had told her.

"Are you sure?"

"I'm more than sure," she affirmed. "I told you before, he and I are only friends." It was good to see Molly look excited for a change, and Rachel thought they'd make a very good match. So the afternoon had turned out better than she ever thought it would, with everyone leaving in high spirits.

Rachel leaned back in the chair and yawned. The late afternoon sun had disappeared behind snow-laden clouds that soon began dropping tiny flecks. Rachel knew these could turn into heavy flakes throughout the night. John had lost some money from the calves that died and had spent a lot of money purchasing land, but he definitely wasn't in debt. Then again, he wasn't rich either. However, he had large equity in his property. Since he and Estelle had retired for the evening, she took the time before going upstairs to write a note and leave it on top of his notebook, explaining that all was in order.

Once she was in her nightgown and in bed, Rachel realized she wasn't sleepy. She kept seeing John's sometimes teasing, sometimes serious looks yesterday when they were alone. She was certain he was going to kiss her, and she lay there almost feeling his lips against hers. Would he ever make a real move and declare his love? She knew only that her feelings for him were growing stronger every day.

She flipped onto one side and her eyes rested on her family's Bible, drawing her. "Oh, all right, Preston! You win." She got up and lifted the heavy Bible, carried it to the bed, and lit a candle to read by. Where should she start? She liked to read in the book of Hebrews and began to thumb through when something stiff in the center of the Bible stopped her. *What in the world? An envelope?* Who had put that in here? It wasn't there before. Or had it been there, and in her anger she hadn't seen it?

Her hands shaking slightly, Rachel opened the envelope and unfolded the letter inside. A wad of bills fell onto her lap, and she gasped in surprise and delight. Looking down at the bottom, she saw Preston's scrawling signature.

> *Dear Rachel,*
>
> *If you're reading this, you've figured out the secret box that I sent and the secret compartment that held a key to the safe in Bozeman and have made the trip to the bank. You can see by the amount of money here why I decided to send it to the bank for safekeeping. I'm pretty sure it is close enough to buy our ranch back. I only wish I were going to live long enough to be with you again and see this become a reality, but it's not in the cards for me.*
>
> *Forgive me, if you feel like I failed you by not returning sooner or writing. I love you, brave sister.*
>
> *Have a wonderful life,*
>
> *Preston*

Rachel stifled a sob with her fist to keep from waking anyone, clutching the letter to her chest. *How silly I've been, blaming Preston for everything! Why didn't I open the Bible?*

She gathered the money without counting it, stuffing it back inside the Bible before putting both in her bureau drawer.

Grabbing her dressing gown, she slid her feet inside her mules and headed downstairs, tears blinding her. Reaching the door with a heavy heart, she donned her coat and hat, unmindful of the falling snow. She set out to the cemetery, where Estelle had had a marker made in Preston's memory and erected it next to where her parents were laid to rest.

※

John listened to the wind and watched the swirling fat flakes of their first major snow, thinking about his men who should be returning next week after a hard trail drive. He was glad he could count on them, especially now.

He crawled back to bed, wondering if Rachel was fast asleep. Was she thinking about him? He could still feel her gentle hand on his brow and hear her soft voice when he'd thrashed about with fever. What a turn there'd been in the events of his life since receiving the letter from Preston. John had had no thoughts of marriage on his mind then, but if he was honest with himself, he'd never had them for bossy Beatrice. From the very beginning he was intrigued by Rachel—her wit, laughter, and pure gumption to face anything.

He wanted to tell her how he felt about her, but he was afraid and unsure. He wasn't strong physically anymore, might never be again. What if she rejected him? And yet something told him she wouldn't. He'd left her tonight at his desk wading through the stack of receipts and bills that needed paying. If she didn't feel about him the way he felt about her—well, he'd consider handing her ranch back to her, free and clear. It seemed the right thing to do. He'd changed. There was a time when he wouldn't have been so generous, but after nearly facing death certain things were clearer to him. He realized what was really important—people he loved, like his grandmother and Rachel.

He pulled the quilt up to his chin, staring up at the ceiling, when he thought he heard the front door slam. He jumped out of bed and listened, and sure enough, he heard a noise from downstairs. Swiftly, he threw on his jeans over his long-handles. As he passed Rachel's room, he saw the door open and a candle still burning on her nightstand. He tiptoed just inside the door.

"Rachel?" he whispered. Again, "Rachel?" There was no answer. He moved into the room and saw the bed empty.

A sound behind him startled him. "Annabelle, you scared the wits out of me. What are you doing up?"

Annabelle held her candle up higher. "Trying to find out where the noise was coming from when I heard you in the hallway. Where's Rachel?" she asked.

"That's what I'd like to know. I was about to go downstairs," he answered.

"Shh . . . you'll wake your grandmother. I'm coming with you then."

Downstairs, the front door was swinging on its squeaky hinges and snow was blowing inside the foyer. John quickly stepped to the doorway and looked around, then quietly shut the door. "I don't see anything, but that was the noise we heard."

"Mmm . . . Rachel's coat and hat are gone from the rack. John, where would she go in this weather? You don't think she was sleepwalkin', do you?"

"As crazy as that sounds, I wonder. Go get the broom and let's sweep the snow back out. We're going to have quite a few inches by morning from the looks of it."

Annabelle leaned down to pick something up off the floor. "Well, would you look at this! It's a letter from Preston." She scanned it, then handed it to him. "I'm not sure what this means."

"When did she get this letter?" John read the brief message, not understanding what it meant.

"I haven't seen any post delivered, so I don't know. But something's amiss, John, I feel it in my bones." Annabelle shivered. "Whew . . . a letter from the dead. Somethin' ain't quite right."

"I think you're right." He kept his voice lowered as he reached down and pulled his winter boots on.

"Where are you going?" Annabelle's face was full of concern.

"I'm not sure, but it's not safe for Rachel to be out, so I'll go have a look around," he answered, donning his long duster, hat, and gloves. "You may need to lock the door so it'll stay closed against the wind. I'll worry about the hinges later."

"I'll get a fire going in the kitchen . . . and pray . . . and make coffee. It may be a long night."

John hurried on to the barn, and the first thing he noticed was Midnight's stall was empty. Drat! Rachel must've taken him, but his saddle was still right where it always was. Quickly he threw a saddle on Cutter, then a bridle. Winchester trotted over from his warm bed of straw, wagging his tail. "You can come too, old man. You may be of help." He reached down and scooped him up to share a seat on the saddle with him.

The snow was coming down heavily now, and with the wind it created drifts against the corral posts and barn. He said a silent prayer for Rachel's safety and mounted Cutter—hoping for signs of Midnight's tracks. But they were lost in the snow.

❧

Biting cold and snow stung Rachel's face as she made her way the two miles to the graveyard by the church, but she didn't care. Midnight's hide began to chafe her legs and she was mindful that she should've thrown a blanket over him along with the bridle, but he was fast and took right to her when she'd approached him.

The snow was getting heavier now and it was harder to see, but she must reach Preston's marker. There was a pain in her heart weighing her very soul down. She'd blamed him for everything after he left—her job at the saloon, losing the ranch, and his death. How silly that she blamed him for his own death! God knew the number of hairs on one's head, and He knew their future. Preston did what he hoped would bring back the ranch. She cried the entire ride until she felt her tears freeze on her cheeks.

She sighed as she slid off Midnight's back. *What a fool I've been.* She walked through the tombstones until she found Preston's and knelt beside it in the snow, sobbing her heart out as she talked to him.

"If you can hear me from heaven, I ask for forgiveness for the terrible thoughts and feelings I had against you, dear brother. In my own blind way of thinking, I thought you didn't care and were never coming back. I'm so sorry. My heart and very being hurts from missing you and not being with you when you died. As for the money you saved, I will think of some way to honor you—somehow the ranch doesn't seem that important anymore. I know what's important, and that's the people you love and every beautiful day the sun rises and sets and the one more day of life. I love you." She felt a tremendous burden lift. She was ready to put the past behind and move forward with her life.

The snow began to penetrate her coat at her knees, so she rose and stood for a while, unmindful of the blowing snow until her teeth began to chatter. Grateful that Midnight stood waiting, she grabbed his mane, pulled herself astride his broad back, and picked up the reins. Suddenly, she couldn't see the wrought iron fence that surrounded the graveyard. The snow was thick, so she headed for where she thought the road lay. In other whiteouts she had been safe and warm inside her parents' cabin. She leaned over and whispered to the horse. "Midnight, I need you to lead me home, please." Midnight tossed his head in a commanding way, and she hoped she could trust him.

Rachel couldn't see anything at all with the thick, swirling snow. Foolishly, she hadn't worn her boots, and now her toes were going numb, as were her fingers. Neither had she planned to be gone this long, but the fast-moving weather changed her plans. Wind rose through the trees with a mournful, lonely sound and she shivered, but worse, she was losing her bearings. Midnight was struggling in the deep snow and snorted his disagreement, his nostrils flaring and his breath floating across the vastness of white.

Shouldn't I be back at the ranch by now? Or have I been riding in circles? Fear struck with a strange tingle down her spine. She was *lost*! She tried to pray aloud, but her lips were numb and wouldn't move, so she prayed silently for help. She yawned, sleep trying to overtake her, and struggled to keep her eyes open. Snow-crusted eyelashes made it more difficult to see. All she wanted to do was lie down, but Midnight decided to stop in the shelter of snow-laden trees. *Concentrate on staying alive!* she told herself. Maybe if she concentrated hard enough, John would somehow know she was in trouble.

37

The snow was deeper now as John rode into the valley, not sure which way Rachel could've headed. If his cowboys were here they could spread out to search. Was she in trouble? Where would she go? His logic told him she was upset and it had something to do with her brother and the letter—and the ranch. Something clicked in his head—maybe she went to the cemetery, however crazy it seemed to him. He saw the towering ponderosa pines and turned at the fork in the road, pulling his neckerchief over his face and nose for protection while Cutter plodded through the snow drifts. It was a true whiteout, and the sooner he found Rachel, the better.

Soon, he and Cutter made it to the cemetery, and he called out to her but there was no answer. *She's lost, I'm sure of it.* John headed in another direction, calling out her name. She could freeze in this weather if he didn't find her. *Please, Lord, help me find Rachel. She means the world to me.*

The cold permeated John's coat and his horse was breathing hard when suddenly Winchester's ears perked up and he whined. John let him down and followed him as he sloughed through the snow. Apparently Winchester had spotted something in the distance, because he barked and looked back to see if his master was following. Cutter forged ahead through the whiteness all around. John caught a glimpse of Rachel's red coat and his heart twisted in his chest.

John could hear Winchester barking at Midnight, who was standing underneath the shelter of a stand of trees. His head was bowed against the elements, and Rachel was swaying on his back, barely hanging on to his mane.

"RACHEL!" John yelled. "I'm coming. Hold on!" he croaked, as he and Cutter launched through the deep snow to get to where she was. Her eyes blinked briefly, her lips blue under her bonnet, a cap of frozen whiteness.

She muttered something, but it made no sense at all to him. John slid off Cutter's back, moved toward Rachel, and peeled her stiff fingers from Midnight's mane. He gently lifted her limp form, folding her against his chest. Finally, he pulled back to look at her. "Rachel, thank God . . . I was so afraid I might not be able to find you! I couldn't bear to live without you." He leaned forward, kissing her blue lips. When her eyes fluttered wide open she gave him a lopsided smile as he continued to shower her face with kisses that he'd held back for far too long.

There was no time to lose so he placed her on his horse, then slung Winchester on Midnight's back to follow him from behind.

"Good ole boy, Winchester. You have saved a life today!" He noticed the dog's paws half-frozen as he mounted Cutter, and felt sympathy for his old friend. He shielded Rachel with his warm body pressed against hers until she slumped against him.

Annabelle was waiting as promised with a crackling fire in the kitchen and steaming coffee when John made it back after what seemed hours to him.

"Mercy me! Bless her heart. Put her right there by the fire," she ordered as he carried Rachel, her head lolling against his shoulder. "I'll get those wet clothes off her and cover her with blankets." He allowed Winchester to follow him inside, where the dog immediately plopped down by the hearth and began licking his paws. John would see to him later.

"I'll get the horses back in the barn and be back as quick as I can. Try to get her to wake up, but keep her still. You don't want to warm her too quickly. That can be dangerous."

Annabelle waved her hands at him. "Shoo! I'll take it from here. There's hot coffee waitin' when you return."

Rachel struggled against Annabelle. "What are you—?" she mumbled.

"We've got to get you outta these wet clothes. Glad to see you're awake." Annabelle slipped off Rachel's damp gown and pulled a fresh one over her head, then covered her with a pile of blankets.

Annabelle gasped when she removed the mules from Rachel's feet. "Land sakes, Rachel, your feet are mighty red." She placed her warm hands over them, rubbing slowly and gently.

After a while, Rachel tried to bring Annabelle into focus. "How did I get here? I got lost," she added, taking a deep breath.

"Thankfully John can find a prairie dog in a whiteout, that's how." Annabelle chuckled. "You're lucky. It could've turned out worse. I'll get you some hot coffee to drink now."

"What's all the commotion in here?" Estelle stood in the

252

doorway, and seeing them, her hand flew to her chest. "Rachel!" She hurried to her side and took Rachel's icy hand, rubbing it between her own while glancing over at Annabelle for answers. Rachel's head seemed fuzzy as she listened.

Annabelle brought a cup of steaming coffee to Rachel's lips as she told Estelle the story of how the wind woke her and John and they discovered Rachel missing. "Have you looked outside? We had a whiteout—first time that's happened so early in a long time."

"No, I haven't. I'll take your word for it," Estelle answered as she continued to warm Rachel's hands. "Rachel, why in the world were you out in this storm?"

"I had to talk . . . to Preston . . . let him know I was sorry." A sob leapt to Rachel's throat again. "But I had no idea the weather could change so fast. I got lost and kept going in different directions. I'm so tired . . ." Her teeth chattered.

The back door swung open and John strode in, stopping in front of her.

"John, I was so afraid . . ."

"You can thank ole Winchester here for finding you. You sit right there and get warmed up now. No more going out in a snowstorm alone," he said, gazing at her with a soft look. "Promise?"

"I promise," she answered.

Estelle commented, "Looks like you're getting color back in your hands and feet. What a scare you've given me. I guess my old ticker works better than I thought." She laughed, then looked over at John. "And from the looks of it, John was very worried too!"

John shifted on his boot heels. "You got that right!"

Rachel blushed, remembering his kisses earlier, and her

heart warmed at all the love and attention from those she considered her new family. "I guess this snow means the shop will be closed?"

"Oh, Molly may be able to open it late since she lives in town. Folks will be shoveling the sidewalks—that's if the snow ends before morning," John said.

"Well, thanks to all three of you—and you too, Winchester. It's good to be in a warm house by the fire with people I care about."

"Okay, now you can tell us what was so important that you had to venture out on a cold night," Annabelle said. "You said you had to go talk to Preston?"

Rachel took a deep breath. "All this time Preston had saved the money for the ranch. It was in the Bible that he left, but I never opened it because I was so angry with him for not coming back, not communicating, and then dying." She paused, looking down at her pink hand in her lap. "I wanted him to forgive me."

"Aww, baby, he knows." Annabelle wiped a tear from her eye while John folded his arms across his chest, watching her.

"I suppose he wanted you to buy the ranch back from me? Well, you won't have to. It's yours," John said softly.

"No, John. You paid all the back taxes—you're the rightful owner now. I don't have the means to stock the cattle or hire help. I know now that I can't handle a ranch alone," she answered in a ragged breath. "That was wishful thinking."

Estelle placed her hands on her hips, staring down at Rachel. "Let's talk about all this another time. You need to rest."

Rachel smiled, but felt exhausted and fuzzy in her head. She was beginning to feel her fingers and toes. Rest was definitely in order, and she didn't protest when John carried her off to bed. Even in her state of mind, with his strong arms about her, she worried about his strength since he'd been so sick before. He was breathing hard by the time they were halfway up the stairs, so she insisted that he put her down, though she'd rather have stayed against the warmth of his chest, feeling his heart beating.

"Oh, all right, but hold on to my arm for support."

She gladly took it, making her way to the top of the stairs before turning toward her room. Annabelle was right behind them, eager to help Rachel get settled.

"Well, I reckon that's enough excitement for one day!" Annabelle said.

Estelle slowly made her way up the staircase, then stopped John at his bedroom door. "John, are you all right? I couldn't help but notice how winded you became on the stairs. That's not like you at all."

He tweaked his grandmother's cheek. "I'm going to be fine. It's just the lingering cough has me run down. That's all."

She wasn't sure she could believe him but left it at that. "John, I'm so proud of you—going after Rachel like that."

"I had to find her. It could've turned out much worse if that front door hadn't remained open. It was the banging that alerted me." He ran his hands through his disheveled hair.

"I know she means a lot to you," Estelle whispered, watching the change in John's face as she said it. Proof enough to her that it was as she suspected—John was in love. But did he know it yet?

"More than you know, Grams."

He didn't say more, so Estelle bid him good night. Back in her bed, she prayed the two of them would see they were

255

A Sweet Misfortune

meant for each other. Nothing would please her more than to see John settled with a family. She sighed, grateful to be tucked inside against the snowstorm, and hoped her neighbors were safe and sound as well.

When John tromped to the kitchen for his morning coffee, Annabelle was standing over the stove stirring oatmeal.

She shot him a look, then asked, "Rough night?"

"Maybe . . . I had a little trouble falling asleep. I reckon I was worried." He walked over to the window and wasn't surprised at the amount of snow. He loved how the sun made it sparkle like diamonds on a queen's crown. He was glad he'd decided to let Winchester sleep in the kitchen. His dog was getting old, and it was his way of thanking him for being a faithful companion.

She continued her cooking and lifted a pan of hot biscuits from the oven. "No need to be. I checked on Rachel a couple of times before morning. She seems fine."

"Who's talking about me?" Rachel shot them a sassy smile as she breezed through the kitchen door, looking fit.

John jerked around as she took a seat at the table, dressed in a simple wool dress with a fringed shawl about her shoulders. Even the pretty housedress couldn't steal her beauty, and it took a few seconds before his heart began to pump normally again.

"I'm so glad that you're up and walking around. Do you feel all right?" he asked.

"Yes, I do." She smiled, showing her small, even teeth. "Perhaps I should attempt to drive to town."

He was beginning to believe there was nothing imperfect

256

about her. How hadn't he noticed before? "Not today, you won't. Have you looked outside?"

"Yes, but—"

"Don't even think about it, Rachel," Annabelle added. "Estelle wouldn't hear of it. How about some coffee, oatmeal, and a biscuit?"

"Sounds divine. I woke up hungry."

Winchester loped over to her chair and sniffed around. Rachel reached down to stroke his head. "I'll be forever grateful to you, sweet dog. And to you, John," she said, giving him a sheepish look. "This morning I realized how fortunate I am to have all of you looking out for me. That's what Preston used to do. I've been thinking . . . I want to do something to honor him. I'm not sure what, though."

"That's what I like about you, Rachel. You're always thinking about others," John said, looking at her over the rim of his cup. "I'm beginning to learn a few things from being around you."

"Me?" Rachel's laughter floated across the room. "Please don't look to me for your example. Best to look at Annabelle or your grandmother. I have so much to learn yet."

Annabelle beamed at the two of them, and John took the two bowls of oatmeal from her and set one in front of Rachel. "Eat up." He took a chair before sprinkling sugar and pouring milk on the top of his oatmeal. "I'll be out most of the day, clearing a pathway to the barn to take care of our milk cow."

"I can help, John." Rachel grabbed a biscuit and began buttering it.

"Naw, why don't you stay in and keep Grams company today? I think she'd really like that. I'm sure she'll be down in a few minutes."

"I will then, but I do know how to milk a cow, you know, and I'm not above shoveling."

"I'm sure you could, and if I feel the need for you, I'll holler." *Which for me could be any minute.* He smiled back at her, letting his gaze linger as her cheeks took on a rosy hue.

"Same goes for me," Annabelle said, taking a seat at the table.

John chortled. "Nope, I need you right here fixin' up a good pot of beef stew and cornbread. I'll bring more firewood in for the kitchen and parlor, then we can shut off the extra rooms today. I doubt we'll get above zero from the looks of it." Taking his last bite of biscuit, then washing it down with coffee, John decided he could get used to this domestic scene in the kitchen.

"I can do that, and perhaps you could peel the potatoes and carrots for me, Rachel."

"It would be my pleasure, Annabelle."

"Wonderful! I'm going to go check on Estelle and see if she needs anything." Annabelle lumbered out of the room.

They were alone at last. John reached across the table, covering Rachel's hand with his. "Rachel, I meant what I said last night." He coughed nervously this time. She looked up at him with a furrowed brow. Did she not remember? He hurried on. "About how deeply I care for you—love you, in fact." There! He'd finally choked it out. "And I need to confess—I believe you were not like those other gals at the saloon. I'm sorry I doubted you."

Her eyes flew wide open. "John." Rachel said his name so softly it sounded like a caress coming from those pink upturned lips. "I'm so happy to hear you say that. Last night I thought maybe I'd been dreaming."

"It was no dream, Rachel. Do you think you feel anything for me?"

Rachel's face softened and her eyes misted. She seemed to struggle to speak. "I feel the same way about you, John."

"You do?" He couldn't believe his ears. He swallowed hard. "Regardless of my health?"

Rachel rolled her eyes at him. "But of course! Your health has nothing to do with how I feel for you. Besides, I loved you before you contracted pneumonia, truth be known."

"My dearest Rachel, you've made me happier than I deserve. Do you think we could seal it with a kiss?" She nodded, tilting her head toward him as he leaned across the table. Before he knew it, he was touching those sweet lips he'd ached to taste, and a fire singed him clear down to his boot tops.

38

Rachel and Estelle watched from the parlor window as John created a pathway through the snow to the barn. The snow had stopped and it was cozy inside.

"I declare, Rachel. There's something about you this afternoon that I can't quite put my finger on." Estelle studied her with a keen eye. "Has something happened or are you merely happy you didn't freeze to death?"

Rachel laughed and dropped her arm about the older lady's shoulder, giving her a brief squeeze. "It shows?"

Estelle leaned back with a chuckle. "Then something has happened! Anything you'd like to share with me? I'll understand if you'd rather not."

Rachel guided Estelle to her chair and sat down across from her. "I was hoping John might take the time to talk to you, but then he's been very busy today."

"Yes, well—what is it then?"

"John has told me that he cares for me deeply . . . that he loves me," Rachel whispered shyly as if there was a roomful of people. Her breath caught in her throat with excitement.

Estelle sat up straight. "Oh, please tell me that you feel the same way too!"

"Matter of fact, I do, Estelle—care deeply for him, I mean."

Estelle clapped her hands together with sudden joy. "Rachel, I couldn't be happier—for you, for John, and selfishly, for myself."

Looking at Estelle's wrinkled, beaming face brought tears to Rachel's eyes. "I'm not sure if John is considering marriage now. It was only a declaration of love."

"Are you sure?"

Rachel paused a moment to think. "He did tell me that he didn't want to live without me when he found me in the snow."

"Trust me. John has never declared his love for any of the women he's courted, including Beatrice."

"Well, we'll have to wait and see, won't we? But if you're wondering, yes, I'd love to be your granddaughter-in-law, if he asks."

Estelle rose from her chair and bent over Rachel, kissing the top of her head. "You have my blessing, dear."

"Thank you. Your acceptance is very important to me."

"Say, why don't we go talk Annabelle into making some cinnamon cookies? If the weather permits, tomorrow I'll ride into town with you, and I can visit the store for the first time in a long time."

"Do you think that's possible with the snow?"

Estelle tweaked her cheek. "Dear girl, I've been in much worse conditions in my many years. I've seen snow drifts as high as the house and times when we had to climb to the rooftop to knock it down for fear it would cause the roof to cave. I think we can manage, but we can wait until the sun starts to melt it off and we can have John drive us."

Rachel looped her arm through Estelle's. "Then I say Molly will be grateful for a batch of Annabelle's cookies."

Annabelle walked into the parlor. "I heard something about cookies, and I agree with you. Let's go whip us up a batch or two. Oh, and I plumb forgot with all the commotion last night." She fished inside her apron pocket and took out a letter. "Rachel, this came for you yesterday. Looks like it's from Sue." She craned her neck around to get a look when Rachel took the letter.

"Thank you, Annabelle. It must be from Sue because it's postmarked Kansas, which means she arrived." She walked over to the window seat before running her finger under the envelope flap and pulling out a single sheet of paper. The other two ladies waited anxiously while she read, hoping to hear good news.

Rachel put the letter back in the envelope, then said, "Sue arrived safely, and her family was very surprised but happy to see her. She asks for prayer as she tries to mend relationships and thanks us again for getting her out of a bad situation. I'm just thrilled that she's out of harm's way now."

"That's good news. I'm so glad you decided to help her," Estelle said.

Annabelle poked Rachel. "See, Rachel. John was right about you putting others ahead of yourself."

The rest of the afternoon was spent baking, chatting, and swapping stories as the three of them sampled the cookies while the delicious smell wafted through the house. Rachel couldn't remember when she had been this happy.

※

The bright sun began to melt the snow as the temperatures quickly rose the next morning. John insisted they not leave until mid-morning for Cottonwood. Annabelle decided to ride along to pick up supplies from the general store. As the wheels crunched over the snow-packed road to town, Rachel sat next to John with a blanket tucked tightly around them both.

When they entered Cottonwood, the town was bustling with wagons and people going to and fro. Many businesses had their sidewalks shoveled and had opened for the day. "I'll drive you to the front door of the shop, Grams," John said over his shoulder. "Then I'll return later to pick you up."

Estelle marveled at how immaculate the millinery shop was when she and Rachel entered the store. Molly scurried up to give them hugs and take their coats.

"I got here early to build a fire in the stove so the shop wouldn't be so cold. I didn't expect you to make it in today, Rachel, but I'm glad to see you both."

"Who shoveled the snow from our storefront?" Estelle asked.

"Oh, I did. It was nothing. Besides, I haven't had but two customers today so far. Everyone is still thawing out, I suppose." Molly's head of curls bobbed as she talked.

"Then, I'm very proud of you. Please tell me you weren't here yesterday."

"Oh no, ma'am. I confess, I thought about it but figured you'd understand. The streets in town were empty anyway."

"Smart girl." Estelle walked around the tiny shop giving everything a brief scrutiny and was satisfied with Molly's work. "I don't know what I did before I had you two girls running the place."

"It's our pleasure," Rachel answered for both of them.

Estelle walked over to the mannequin with the beautiful hat that Molly designed and inspected the workmanship, fingering the satin ribbon. "Molly, Rachel told me about this hat. My, but it's exquisite!"

Molly flushed. "You really think so?"

"I do indeed. I knew you had the creative bent to your nature when I hired you."

Molly's brow quirked. "How did you know?"

Estelle laughed. "It's what I do best—analyze people."

Both Molly and Rachel giggled.

"In fact, I've been giving this a lot of thought—I want to make both of you partners of Estelle's."

"What?" Molly's jaw dropped and Rachel shot her a look of complete surprise.

"You're serious, aren't you?" Rachel asked.

"I am indeed. I don't make jokes, as you know." Estelle loved taking folks by surprise, and it made her very happy to be about this venture with two ladies she cared about.

"But I don't have money to invest in a business," Molly sputtered.

"Well, neither do I," Rachel added.

Estelle continued. "I have that all figured out. Consider your share in the business as a gift. Later, when I'm ready to retire—and that won't be too long—you can buy me out . . . that's if you're interested at all in my plans."

Molly squealed with delight, grasping Rachel's hand, and Rachel stood staring at Estelle in disbelief. Estelle's heart felt full at their reaction. "So . . . what do you think?" she asked.

"I'm so honored that you would even consider doing such a thing, Estelle," Rachel choked out. "But why?"

Estelle strolled to stand behind the counter facing them. "Because I want to do something good before I die, and I've chosen you wonderful girls because you've been loyal and faithful to run the shop for me in my absence. I hope you'll say yes."

"I, for one, don't have to give your generous offer another thought. I'm accepting with gratitude," Molly declared.

"I'll agree," Rachel said, and Estelle saw tears in her eyes.

"Then it's settled. I'll have my attorney see to the particulars, then draw up the contracts for your protection and mine. Why don't we celebrate with lunch later?"

The two nodded in agreement. "Good! Now, let's see how the books are coming along in my absence."

The shop door swung open and in marched Vera. "Brrr, it's cold out. I see all three of you made it in today. I came by yesterday and was very displeased to see that you were closed." Vera huffed out her ample chest as though she'd encountered an altercation.

"You did?" Molly asked. "I'm sorry, but I saw no need to open the shop with the heavy snow that was bearing down on us."

Vera looked sharply at the young woman. "Since when did you begin making decisions about Estelle's?"

"Since she and Rachel became co-owners, that's when." Estelle knew it was a bit of a stretch in truth, but saw no need to explain to Vera the dangers of being out in the snow yesterday or the fact that nearly everyone had closed for the day.

"Humph! Have you lost your senses, Estelle?" Vera snapped.

"Hardly! Is there something we can help you with?" Estelle asked, trying to change the subject.

Vera fingered the tight collar at her throat. "Yes. I ordered some nice winter gloves for myself and Beatrice. I was assured they'd arrive yesterday." She glared at Rachel and Molly.

Estelle looked through the received orders that were stacked on the end of the counter. "Mmm . . . I don't see anything with your name on it, Vera. Perhaps the freight stage didn't arrive with the bad weather."

"I'm sure that's what it is," Molly added.

"In that case, I'll be back tomorrow in spite of the inconvenience. Those gloves would've come in handy with this sudden cold snap."

Estelle looked at Vera's hands. "It's good you have on a decent pair of leather gloves for now."

Vera acted as though she hadn't heard her.

"I'll be most happy to drop them by when they arrive," Rachel told her.

Vera seemed placated and gave Rachel a forced smile. "That will do nicely. I must be going. Beatrice and Wyatt are having dinner together, and I want to make sure everything is perfect."

Estelle pretended interest knowing that Vera made sure they all knew about Beatrice and Wyatt, but she only replied, "That's nice, Vera. See you soon and watch out for the slippery sidewalk."

Vera nodded as she left, and the three of them let out loud sighs when the door finally shut.

"Why is she always such a hard-to-handle customer?" Molly asked while she opened the received packages.

Estelle shook her head. "Some folks think they are the only people who matter. Sadly, she raised Beatrice to think the same way."

Molly turned to Rachel. "Speaking of which, what happened with you and Wyatt? And I thought Beatrice and John were courting."

Estelle smiled and listened as Rachel filled Molly in on everything—the letter from Preston, getting lost, and John's rescue. Despite all the trouble it caused, it was very romantic from Estelle's point of view.

"Oh, I almost forgot to tell you, Molly. I got a letter from Sue and she made it to Kansas."

"Oh, good. That wasn't easy for her."

Soon customers arrived who were happy to see Estelle, and it felt good to know she'd been missed. Life was good. *Thank you, Lord!*

When John came to pick up Estelle, Rachel saw the look of surprise on his face when all three of them followed him out. Rachel flipped the sign over to "Back in an hour" while Molly turned the key in the lock and John assisted his grandmother.

"Will someone tell me what's going on?" John asked Estelle, who had settled in the front seat.

"Remember the secret I shared with you about my business the other night?"

John nodded.

"Both of them agreed to become my partners," Estelle announced proudly. "So we are going to have lunch together and you are welcome to join us. Then you can drive me back home."

"That *is* good news," he said, turning around to smile at Rachel and Molly. "Let me help both of you. We only have to drive one street over, but your dresses would get soggy and wet if you walked." He handed Molly and then Rachel into the seat behind Estelle.

"We were very surprised but honored that she would even dream of asking us," Rachel said. Estelle noticed his hand lingered on Rachel's a moment longer than needed.

"That's my Grams—always up to something. Congratulations to both of you. I think you'll both be glad that you accepted. Now, on to lunch." He hopped up to the driver's seat and they took off down the snow-filled streets, following the ruts other wagons had carved.

39

A few days later, the only reminder of the storm was puddles of melted snow. As Rachel remembered her night in the whiteout, she silently thanked God for John and Winchester's perseverance. The mere thought of John's arms around her that night gave rise to bubbling happiness within. Even through tragedy and Rachel's unwise choices, good had prevailed. *I know the plans I have for you, that's why*, a still small voice reminded her. She marveled at God's faithfulness to see her through each day.

On her way home from work today, she was going to stop by the church with an idea she had. She hoped Jeffrey would be there. Molly told her he would. Molly seemed to know his every move these days. Rachel told her she'd make a wonderful, caring wife for a pastor, which seemed to please Molly.

It wasn't long before she reached the church. She set the brake on the buggy and looped the reins over the hitching post in front of the building, then scampered inside calling out his name. She knew Jeffrey's office, hardly bigger than a closet, was at the back.

Jeffrey's face poked out from his office door and he waved her on back. "I'm surprised to see you today. It's not Sunday you know," he teased. "Please come in."

Rachel laughed. "I wanted to have a word with you, if I may." His office was neat and tidy, with a worn wooden desk supplied by the church, two chairs, and a bookcase.

"If it's about me and you . . . well, I hope you know that Molly—"

Rachel stopped him. "It's not about that at all. In fact, I'm very pleased that the two of you have found each other."

"Oh, I see. I did have feelings for you, you know, but after meeting Molly, I felt an immediate connection with her."

Rachel nodded. "Believe me, I do understand exactly what you mean. But I came by with a gift—and a request." She opened her reticule and handed him a wad of bills. Jeffrey's mouth dropped open. "I want to finance a bell for the church's bell tower."

"I don't know what to say," Jeffrey gasped. "Rachel, are you sure?"

"I wanted a way to honor my brother Preston's memory, and I like to think that every time I hear the bell, I'll remember him—and that God is my true inheritance."

"Rachel, I don't mean to pry, but how can you part with all this money?"

"It's actually Preston's money that he saved while he was gold mining. I've recently inherited it. If it's more than the cost of the bell, then please use the rest as my tithe."

Jeffrey was overcome and suddenly reached over to give her a quick hug, nearly knocking Rachel off her feet with his reaction. "Oh, I'm sorry." He released her quickly. "Thank you. I can hardly wait to announce this to the members."

"I'll be on my way now so I can make it back to the ranch by suppertime." Rachel turned to leave, and he followed her through the church and out to her buggy.

"Molly tells me wedding bells may soon need to be ringing for you and John, so I'll place my order soon."

"Molly told you that? Oh my goodness . . . John hasn't asked me yet, but that is a lovely thought." Rachel climbed up into the buggy and Jeffrey handed her the reins. She looked down at his kind face. "Maybe we'll be ringing them for you and Molly soon."

"I certainly hope so. Have a wonderful evening, and again, I can't thank you enough for your generosity."

"It has been my pleasure to do this. You take care of our Molly now. She deserves the very best."

"Yes, she does. Goodbye."

"Goodbye, Jeffrey." Rachel clattered down the lane in the direction of the ranch, hoping to be back before darkness settled in. It felt good to do something nice for the church. Anyway, God had planted the idea and she'd acted on it. She decided she would strive to be aware when things came to mind like this, to help someone in need or just do an act of unexpected kindness, like Estelle had done.

Lately, Rachel had noticed that John was nowhere about before she left for work or when she returned. Some days he barely made it back in time for supper. He never said where he'd been all day, but Rachel suspected that it had much to do with trying to keep chores done while all the ranch hands were away. However tired he was, he seemed to always be in good spirits and when he could, tried to steal a kiss in the hallway if they were alone, which unfortunately wasn't often. Not under the watchful eyes of Estelle and Annabelle, she mused.

After supper, Rachel sometimes worked on the books for John or read to Estelle while they shared the evening by the fire. Often Annabelle, who was lonely for Slim, would join them, falling asleep next to the warm fire after a long day's work. Rachel had observed Annabelle helping John and knew she was splitting her time between her own chores and his. If Rachel wasn't working in town, she'd gladly pitch in, but because of the time she and Molly closed for the day, it was dusk before she arrived back at the ranch.

One time in town, Rachel had spotted Wyatt and Beatrice walking arm in arm down the street together. She was glad they'd found each other, but she pitied Wyatt when Beatrice's true personality became evident. But then again, Beatrice might be herself around him. She hoped so for Wyatt's sake— she wished him no harm and was glad that everything had worked out the way it did during Estelle's Sunday dinner.

Jeffrey told her the steeple bell had been ordered and would take two weeks to arrive. He proudly told the congregation after Sunday's sermon, and everyone was mildly surprised but pleased, each one taking time to greet her personally after the service.

"I'm going up to bed now, ladies. How about you?" Estelle whispered softly, waking Annabelle.

"I'm sorry. Did you say something? I believe I must've dozed off." Annabelle straightened in the overstuffed chair.

"I was saying that I'm going to bed, and looks like you need to, Annabelle. You look plumb tuckered out."

"I am, so I'll see you in the morning. Good night."

Rachel closed her book with a yawn. "I'm going too." A

sound on the porch steps meant John had returned and she stood waiting for him.

"Everyone off to bed?" John asked as he stepped inside the parlor.

"Yes, we are. Where have you been so late?" Rachel queried.

John tossed a look between Estelle and Annabelle. "Well . . . I reckon I didn't notice how long I was in the tack room in the barn—trying to clean up and mend things before the ranch hands return," he said with a grin that showed off his even white teeth.

His answer seemed odd to Rachel and she caught the look he threw Estelle and Annabelle. "Doesn't Slim do that?" she asked.

Annabelle pressed her hands down the front of her apron before answering. "Er . . . he usually does when he's here. But someone's got to do it when he's gone." She hurried off to the room she used while Slim was away.

Estelle was already at the stairs, seemingly unconcerned that her grandson still recovering from his illness was spending hours in the tack room. Rachel didn't know what to make of it, so she shyly told him good night, wishing he hadn't waited so late to come inside.

"Rachel, can I talk to you a few minutes before you retire?" John asked as he removed his coat and tossed it on the settee.

Rachel looked up at him. He was so tall, still a bit thin but very handsome. His skin stretched tightly over his angular face and lines around his eyes crinkled when he smiled at her.

"I guess so. I was about to go to bed too. It's been a long day."

He stood still, lacing his long fingers together before cracking his knuckles.

She winced.

He swallowed hard.

"Well?"

"Can we sit down for a moment?"

Rachel strolled over to the settee again, picking up his coat and studying him as he sat down next to her. "What's wrong? Are you feeling ill?"

He laughed softly. "No. I'm feeling very well." He reached over, taking her hands in his, and turned to face her on the settee. "I'm going to get right to it. Rachel, will you marry me?" His gaze was steady and deep and unmoving as he waited for a response.

Rachel sighed with relief and her shoulders slumped. She hadn't realized how taut they were.

"I know it may seem soon, but I love you. I probably could've picked a better way to ask you, but I couldn't help myself, and I couldn't sleep tonight until I asked."

"John." Rachel lifted her hand to stroke the smooth jaw of the man she loved with all her heart. "I thought you'd never ask . . . and my answer is yes! Yes, of course."

———

John immediately pulled her to his chest, breathing in the very scent of her as his senses reeled. "Rachel, I'm a happy man to have a woman like you promise to be my wife!" He pulled back slightly and showered her misting eyes, forehead, and the cute little dimple in her cheek with kisses. The best part—besides her answer—was how fervently she returned his kisses with her own until they both pulled apart, breathless.

John leaned back and laughed. "Words cannot express how I feel at this moment. We need to make plans to marry soon, because I can't wait to hold you in my arms forever and call you my wife!"

"Shh . . . settle down, John." Rachel giggled quietly.

"I don't care who hears. I want to shout it from the rooftops that you said yes!"

"Thanksgiving is coming. Maybe we can celebrate with thanks and a small ceremony."

"That suits me just fine, Rachel." He kissed her again, tasting the sweetness of her lips mingled with her tears. For the first time in a long time, John knew he'd be able to sleep the whole night through.

※

Upstairs, Rachel paused outside Estelle's bedroom door. "Estelle?" she whispered.

"Rachel? I'm awake. Come on in," Rachel heard her reply. She turned the knob and entered the bedroom. Estelle was propped in bed, quilts pulled up to her chin, with a frilly cotton nightcap on her gray head. She held a tablet and pencil in her hand.

"I was afraid you were trying to sleep."

The older lady smiled. "I was, but I decided to make a list of things I need to do and a list of items Annabelle will need for Thanksgiving. We always invite all the ranch hands to dine with us that day."

Rachel chewed her bottom lip, thinking.

"Is something the matter? You do like Thanksgiving, don't you?" Estelle peered over her notebook at her.

"Of course. It's . . . well . . . I came to tell you that John proposed."

Estelle bolted upright, setting aside her notebook. "And you said . . . ?"

"Yes!" Rachel blurted out.

"Congratulations!" Smiling from ear to ear, she patted the bed next to her. "Come sit down and tell me all about it."

Rachel took a seat on the bed and told her how he'd proposed. "We want to marry at Thanksgiving, but if that's a problem—"

Estelle took her hand and squeezed it. "I think that's a wonderful idea. It'll give us plenty to be thankful for."

"It won't mess up your plans?"

"No, of course not. Everyone will already be here anyway, and you can invite even more. It'll be a great time!"

"Then you can add that to your list." Rachel laughed softly.

"I will, and you can count on me and Annabelle to help." Estelle smiled through teary eyes.

Rachel frowned. "Annabelle has been so busy lately with the hands gone that I hesitate to ask her to do more. I know she's been helping John."

"We both—" Estelle stopped and cleared her throat. "What I meant to say was, the men will be back from the trail drive by then, so that won't be a problem."

"Estelle, how can I ever thank you for all that you have done for me?" Rachel felt a lump in her throat, gazing at the sweet lady that she considered her grandmother.

"You are already doing that by marrying my grandson and making him very happy. I have no doubt of that."

"I certainly will try to do my very best. I promise."

"By the way, I've been worried about John since he was ill. He has less stamina and energy. I'm thinking of asking

275

him to go see the doctor for an evaluation." The older lady pursed her lips in concern.

"It takes awhile to get over pneumonia. I'm sure it's nothing to worry about," Rachel said quickly, looking down at the design on the heavy quilt.

"Rachel, is there something I should know that John's not telling me?"

Rachel bit the inside of her jaw. She'd promised John not to say anything.

Estelle pushed a bit more. "Rachel? I'm his grandmother and I should know. I sense you know something."

"I told John I wouldn't tell you. He doesn't want to worry you with your health and all."

"I promise I won't say you told me, and I figure he'll eventually tell me. But let's face it—I figured this much out on my own just watching him and Annabelle working on—never mind . . . I know something is amiss."

Rachel released a sigh and told her that John's lungs would never be the same. "They were compromised from the pneumonia. He doesn't think folks will look at him the same way if they know he'll never be as strong as before, so he didn't want to share this." She watched Estelle's face blanch.

"Oh, dear me. I can certainly understand his feelings. My precious boy! I know he doesn't want pity and we won't do that to him, but he'll have to make concessions on what he can and can't do around here."

Rachel rose from the bed and walked to the door. "That's true, but it's best to let him make those decisions himself or he'll feel less than a man."

"That's wise coming from one so young, but I believe you are right. I guess we can both be thankful that John pulled through at all. Most people die if they get pneumonia. Yes, this Thanksgiving we'll have much to be thankful for. Good night, my dearest. I'm so glad that you came into our lives suddenly."

"Me too. Good night." With deep affection in her heart for Estelle and a flooding of peace filling her heart, Rachel knew she'd be able to sleep without tossing and turning tonight.

40

John had just ridden home from Wyatt's one late October afternoon when he spied his band of ranch hands, minus the cattle, cantering up the dusty road to the house. He waved his hat in a greeting that was returned by Curtis.

The tired, small group rode into the yard, and John stepped off Cutter, glad that they'd returned. Curtis had a full beard and his tanned face resembled a worn leather saddle. He looked a few pounds lighter. The rest of the men had fared pretty much the same, with worn-out faces that said a hot bath, a homemade meal, and a nice bed inside were needed.

"Welcome home, boys. It's been like Death Valley around here without all of you."

"Howdee, boss." Curtis removed a leather glove and clasped John's hand in his grip. "It's mighty good to be back."

The other hands dismounted, all talking at once about the trip, the dangers, and the weather.

"We had our own snowstorm too, but it only lasted a day or so." John walked among them, making sure he shook everyone's hand.

"Annabelle in the house?" Slim asked, clearly eager to find his wife.

"She is—go on in. You'll find her in the kitchen, I'm sure," John told him. He didn't have to say it more than once. Slim crossed the yard before anyone could say skedaddle.

Curtis reached into his saddlebags and handed John a drawstring bag. "Boss, here's the money for the sale of the cattle. We did well, all things considered."

John grinned. "You men served me well. I'll count it and then hand out your part if you'll stay put for now. Congratulations on a job well done!"

A whoop and a holler came from the house and they all laughed. Annabelle had greeted her man, no doubt. John thought about it and smiled. One day he hoped Rachel would be that happy to see him, and if she meant what she'd told him when he asked her to marry him, then it would happen. He was incredibly happy and could hardly wait for Thanksgiving when she would become his wife. Now if he could just keep his secret.

❧

A few days after the ranch hands returned, Annabelle told Rachel that Estelle wanted to see her after breakfast. Speculating that Estelle wanted to talk to her about the wedding ceremony, Rachel hurried to the parlor without delay.

Estelle smiled warmly at her when she walked in. "I want to talk to you for a minute before you leave for work, if I may. Please sit down."

Rachel took a seat. "What do you want to talk about—the wedding?"

"More specifically, a wedding dress for your ceremony. I assume you don't have your mother's wedding gown?"

"Heavens no. They were married by the justice of the peace. But I have been wondering if Molly and I could whip something up from one of the fine pieces of satin in the shop. Of course, you can take it out of my salary."

Estelle laughed and leaned forward. "Dear Rachel, you are part owner now. I wouldn't think of charging you for a few yards of satin. But I want to propose something to you."

"All right. I'm open to any ideas you may have."

Estelle tilted her head, thoughtfully looking at Rachel. "I hope it's one you'll like. My granddaughter was close to the same size as you before . . . well . . . you know the story. Lura ordered a wedding dress from England for her trousseau in preparation for a certain young cowboy she thought would marry her." Estelle's eyes misted. She composed herself and continued. "I'm not trying to interfere, but I was wondering if you'd like to be the recipient of a beautiful gown that was never worn. I'll understand perfectly if you don't. I know how women want to have their own gown made or use their mother's, but because the wedding is so soon I thought . . ."

"What a generous offer. I'd love to see it, and if there's anything to alter, perhaps Molly will help me." Like most girls, Rachel had always dreamed of a beautiful wedding gown even as a child.

"Absolutely! To my way of thinking it solves the problem for you. No time like the present to show it to you. Then, if you want to use it, you can take it with you to the shop and Molly can alter it."

Before Rachel could say a word, Estelle called out Annabelle's name and she appeared suddenly as if she'd been standing by the door all along, waiting with the gown in her hands. Rachel knew they were both excited about planning the event, and she was only too happy to allow them to help.

Rachel stood while Annabelle spread the full length of the dress across the settee. She fingered the patterned silk gown, which featured a long-waisted, form-fitting bodice with narrow sleeves and a modest neckline. She admired the long sleeves and skirt, both trimmed with gathered tulle, strips of braid, and decorative silk buttons. The cream silk fabric was unlike anything Rachel had ever seen or dreamed about, with its figured flower baskets, stripes, and floral sprays. Lace elbow flounce spilled over fitted sleeves and across the neckline in delicate fashion.

All of it took her breath away. Clapping her hand to her chest, Rachel exclaimed, "It's absolutely exquisite! Your granddaughter had excellent taste. But this is far more elegant than anything I could ever have hoped to wear." She continued to marvel at the gown's beauty.

Estelle waved a hand. "Oh, pish-posh. Of course you can, because it will look lovely on you."

"She's right, Rachel. It's almost as if the gown was in Lura's chest just waiting for you," Annabelle added, smoothing the folds of the dress. "Shall I wrap it in a sheet so you can take it to the shop for alterations?"

Rachel glanced over at Estelle, who was waiting for her answer. "If you're sure it's all right, Estelle."

Estelle answered quickly, "I assure you that it is. Besides, there's no one else here who'd protest and John has agreed, though he's never seen it."

"Which is good, because you want him to be bowled over the moment he sees you on your wedding day." Annabelle nodded.

Rachel's heart raced at the thought of wearing such a beautiful wedding gown. "Then I'm going to say yes! I will be honored to wear it in Lura's memory. Thank you, Estelle."

Estelle shook her head. "No. Thank you for agreeing to wear it and marrying my grandson. You're going to fill his heart with joy." She dabbed her eyes with her handkerchief. "Now go ahead, Annabelle, and wrap this up. She can try it on at the shop and Molly can adjust it if needed."

Rachel's heart was soaring as she traveled the short distance to town. Cottonwood trees stood naked in contrast to the conifers dotting the mountainside as winter began to settle over Paradise Valley. Filled with anticipation for Thanksgiving and what it would mean for the rest of her life, Rachel could hardly wait to get to the millinery shop to show Molly the gown.

After Rachel arrived and unwrapped the wedding dress, Molly clapped her hands together in delight. "For goodness sake! This is the prettiest gown I've ever seen. How fortunate for you. And how sad for Lura that she never got to wear it."

Rachel frowned. "So you don't think I should? Wear it, I mean?"

"Of course you should. It would be a pity for it to stay in a cedar chest unused forever. Let's go in the back so you can slip it on, then I'll pin it for any adjustments that may be needed."

They scooted to the back of the shop while all was quiet. Rachel removed her blouse and skirt, and Molly helped her slip into the dress. After they hooked the back together, Rachel swung around and looked in the mirror, amazed at her transformation in the cream wedding dress. She turned this way and that, admiring what she saw.

"Land sakes! You're going to be the most beautiful bride in all of Montana!"

"I don't know about that, but I do feel beautiful in this gown."

Molly reached up and lifted Rachel's hair off her neck. "We'll pull your hair up, leaving some curls, and add some pearl pins to complete your look. You'll take John's breath away for sure."

Rachel giggled. "I hope you're right." The shop's bell rang out and Molly scurried to the front, saying over her shoulder, "Stay right there and I'll be back to pin the waist and bodice in a little tighter."

"Oh, it's you, Fannie," Rachel heard Molly say.

"Don't act so pleased to see me, Molly," Fannie said sarcastically. "I'm not here shopping but stopped in to see Rachel if she's here."

"Oh, she's here, but she's busy at the moment."

"Doing what? I thought she was to wait on customers?"

"But I thought you just said you were here to see her, which would indicate you aren't buying anything."

Fannie shook her head and was about to retort just as Rachel came to the doorway. Smiling, she held back the curtain that separated the shop from the back room. "You came to see me, Fannie?" Rachel asked. "Come on back. It's okay, Molly." As another customer walked in, she added, "You see to our customer first."

Fannie drew in a shocked breath. "Jumpin' jackrabbits! You're about the most beautiful thing Cottonwood has seen since Sue left." She went behind the curtain and Rachel let it drop back into place.

"That's a sweet thing to say, Fannie. Now, what can I do for you?"

"You heard from Sue? I've been thinkin' a lot about her."

Rachel stood stiffly in the gown and concentrated on Fannie's dull expression that mirrored lack of sleep. Gone was her jovial attitude, and her wrinkled face belied the youth she tried so desperately to convey. "She wrote me and told me that she's very happy in Kansas. Do you want me to ask her to write you?"

A tear appeared at the corner of one eye and Fannie hurriedly brushed it away. "Humph! You think she'd do that without being told after all we've been through together."

"I'm sure she has a lot on her mind right now. She only wrote me because Molly and I helped her escape life at the Wild Horse." Rachel licked her lips, considering saying something to Fannie about her situation.

"It's not so bad, you know. I have a roof that don't leak, and food in my belly for now," Fannie said wryly. "That's a lot more'n some women who show up out here in this godforsaken hole." Fannie looked away.

"It doesn't have to be that way, Fannie. You have the power to change your life. Sue did. I doubt this is the life God chose for you." Rachel lowered her voice so customers couldn't hear.

"God? What in tarnation does He have to do with my life?"

"He wants to—"

"I'll tell you. Nothing. Absolutely nothing. Where was He when my mama died having me and I was given to a couple that beat me? Nowhere!"

Rachel's heart twisted. "I'm so sorry, Fannie. I didn't know—"

"Yeah, well there's plenty you don't know, so don't go tellin' me God has a plan for me."

"But He does. What happened to you was terrible, but you can't blame God for what man did to you. There's evil people all around, but there's good folks too that want to help you. Don't you see that?"

Fannie shrugged. "I doubt that. You go on ahead and live those dreams in your head, girlie, but they're not true for everyone. If they were, God would have stopped the awful things that I had to bear."

"And things you still bear," whispered Rachel. "There's a way to fill your heart with joy—but you have to be willing to let God do surgery on your heart. And that hurts, I won't lie."

Fannie shot her a skeptical look. "How would you know? You ain't lived the kind of life I was forced into."

Rachel sighed, trying hard to get through to her. "Maybe not, but tragedy occurs in many different ways and evil takes on many different forms. Let me pray with you."

Fannie straightened her shoulders back proudly and through painted lips pronounced, "No thank you, ma'am! If it's all the same to you, I'm not in need of your prayers." She turned to leave and Rachel touched her arm, aching to help her.

"Fannie, I'll be here for you anytime day or night if you need me." Rachel didn't give up easily, but what else could she say to Fannie to convince her that God was good?

"Don't fret yourself, Rachel. I won't be needin' you or anybody else, I'm afraid—especially someone I can't even see." Fannie tried to hide her pain but Rachel could see right through her act.

Fannie pulled the curtain aside to leave. "Who's the lucky fella?"

"John McIntyre."

"Well, boy howdee! He's a catch. I do wish you well."

"Then come to the wedding, Fannie. It's on Thanksgiving Day at the ranch, and dinner will be served. You could use a home-cooked family meal, right?"

Fannie paused, chewing her bottom lip. "I'm sure I'm scheduled to work, but thanks for inviting me."

"I understand, but think about it, Fannie. It's only part of one day." Rachel watched her, with her head held high in all her satin finery, walk past the customers Molly was waiting on, out the door, and down the sidewalk. *I guess I handled that entirely wrong. But I'll be praying, Fannie. You can count on that!*

41

Rachel found Estelle writing letters at the desk when she returned from work. She hated to interrupt but needed her wise counsel. "I'm sorry to intrude, Estelle, but if you have a moment, I'd like to ask you about something."

Estelle looked up with a smile and laid her glasses and pen aside. "Rachel, you can interrupt me anytime you need to. Is it something to do with the wedding?"

"In a way, but I'll get to that in a minute." She dragged up a straight-back chair by the door and plopped down. "It's about Fannie."

"Oh?" Estelle turned in her chair to face Rachel. "I'm listening."

Rachel told her about the conversation she'd had with Fannie. "I feel like I've failed her in some way. She doesn't want anything to do with God. I don't know how to help her."

Estelle took Rachel's hands. "Rachel, listen to me. You are not responsible for someone else's salvation. The Holy Spirit draws someone to Himself. You planted the seed in Fannie's mind, and she must decide what she'll do with it. Remember the sower in Scripture? Some seed fell on hard ground and withered away from lack of moisture. Some fell among the thorns and the thorns choked it. Some fell on good ground and bore much fruit. So it is when we share our faith. God's Word is the seed. Some will receive it and believe and others will not."

"Yes, that makes sense, Estelle. But I won't stop praying for her heart to soften."

"Nor should you. I'll pray for her too, but let her be and observe." Estelle let go of Rachel's hands.

"I guess I should tell you that I asked her to the wedding. I know I should've asked you first, but I sort of blurted it out, without thinking."

"And you should, because she's your friend."

"But what will others think?"

"It doesn't matter. Remember, it's your wedding." Estelle looked at her watch. "We'd better get ready for supper."

Rachel leaned over and planted a kiss on her cheek. "You're so dear to me. Oh, I forgot to mention this. Molly is going to take in the bodice and waist a little for me on the gown."

Estelle rose from her chair. "I'm so glad you decided to wear Lura's dress. It suits you well." She smiled. "Let's go eat. I'm sure John will show up late as usual."

Estelle was correct. They were nearly finished with supper when John strode in, pulled out a chair, and sat down to eat. "Sorry. I didn't notice the time."

Annabelle rushed in, nearly out of breath, with his dinner plate teetering in her hands. He winked conspiratorially at her.

Estelle nodded with a smile then laid her napkin aside without a word about his tardiness.

Rachel stared down the table at him. "I would've thought with the ranch hands back, you'd have more time to yourself—not less."

If he was bothered by her remark, he didn't let on. Instead he continued to throw down his food with a hearty appetite. He paused and wiped his mouth with his napkin, grinning at her. "How was our fair town doing today?"

"Thriving since the snow, but I didn't have a lot of time to notice, really. We were busy in the shop in between Molly altering Lura's wedding gown for me."

He gave her a smoldering look. "I know you will look beautiful in it," he said with a husky voice. His Adam's apple bobbed at his throat when he swallowed hard.

Rachel was struck once again by how handsome he was— high cheek bones, tanned face, deep-set eyes. Her heart skipped a beat when she considered that he was soon to be her husband. Her gaze skittered away as she murmured, "Thank you. I hope so. By the way, before I forget . . . I asked Fannie to the wedding, although I doubt she'll show up."

John's eyebrows knitted together. "You did?"

"John, she really needs a friend now that Sue is gone. She had a difficult time growing up, and it's no wonder—without guidance—she became, uh . . . a soiled dove," Rachel replied.

"I'm sorry to hear that. Maybe being around you, some good will wear off. Don't worry. It's okay with me. Since we're discussing the wedding, I need to ask you and Grams . . . You both know I plan to give my men some land to start their own homesteads."

Estelle glanced at him. "Yes, dear, and I'm so proud that you want to do this."

John set his fork down. "It's not as though I'm going to

miss a few measly acres. And they're a hardworking bunch, taking over for me like they did when I was sick."

"I think they'll be quite surprised at your generous gesture, John," Rachel added. "But what is your question?"

"I don't know if it's a good idea to give them the land at our wedding. I don't want to overshadow our day, Rachel. Perhaps I should wait. What do you two ladies think?"

Estelle looked at Rachel for an answer. "Since it's also Thanksgiving, I think it's a wonderful thing to do, and it's certainly not going to overshadow our nuptials. Estelle, do you agree?" Rachel asked. She was pretty sure what the older lady would say.

Estelle nodded. "It's your wedding, but if you want my opinion, then I'll say it fits right in with giving thanks to God for His blessing upon both of you."

"Good! Then that's what I'll do since we're all in agreement."

Annabelle poked her head around the dining room door. "John, uh . . . there's someone at the kitchen door to see you."

"Oh? I'll be right there," he answered. Turning to Rachel and Estelle, he said, "If you'll excuse me." He scraped his chair back.

Rachel thought he'd exited the dining room unusually hastily. And it seemed rather late for someone to be stopping by.

———

"It's Mason from Cottonwood. He's waiting on the back porch," Annabelle said, nearly shoving him to the back door. "I thought you'd taken care of the furniture order, but it seems there's a mix-up."

"I'll take care of it. Not to worry. Did you get the fabric from Molly while Rachel was at the post office like we planned?"

Annabelle chuckled. "Yep! Molly was a big help, and I'm working on that now. Estelle is taking care of the rest of the list, but there's still plenty to be done. I'd better get back to clearing the dishes or Rachel is going to get curious."

As she whirled around, John caught her apron strings, stopping her. "How am I ever going to thank you?"

Annabelle beamed at him. "Oh, I promise I'll think of something."

John roared with laughter. "I just bet you will." He went out to the porch to speak with Mason, who'd driven all the way from town about his delivery. John couldn't help but be excited and was praying everything would work out as planned. He was determined to make sure Rachel was the happiest bride in Montana.

After he'd settled things with Mason, John went looking for Rachel and found her sitting by the fire with his grandmother. She looked up at him, melting his heart with her golden eyes that softened while the glow from the fire reflected in the light brown hair that fell about her shoulders. He stopped before her. "How about a short evening stroll before bedtime? If that's okay with you, Grams. Or was I interrupting wedding plans?"

"We were just enjoying the fire, and I am contemplating my warm bed that awaits me." Estelle yawned.

"A walk sounds nice," Rachel murmured.

"I'll get your coat and gloves then. We won't be out long. I can't have you getting sick before we exchange our vows." John's eyes latched on to Rachel's as he took her hand.

"No, that wouldn't do, would it?" Rachel bid Estelle good night and followed John to the foyer.

He held her coat while she thrust her arms through the

sleeves, handed her gloves and a hat, then ordered her to wear her rubber boots. He laughed. "You look like a bundled-up papoose now, but adorable."

She blushed prettily, answering, "It's hard to move when I'm dressed this way. I have a feeling this is going to be a very short walk."

Outdoors, the air was indeed cold. Dusk turned into night, with stars filling the inky black sky while they strolled in no particular direction arm in arm. Their breaths filled the frosty air. John's heart soared as they laughed and talked. He told her he'd asked Jeffrey to perform the ceremony at the church. Plans were falling into place.

Finally, they stopped to face one another and he took her gloved hands in his, holding them tightly against his chest. "Rachel, I know you'll be missing your brother and parents when we speak our vows, and I'll be thinking of mine too, although they've been gone much longer than yours." Even in the full moon's bright light, John could see Rachel's eyes suddenly fill with tears. "I'm sorry. I didn't intend to make you sad."

She sniffed. "You're right. I'll think of them, but I plan to focus on my future with you, dear husband-to-be. And to think, I gain a grandmother. I couldn't have prayed for a better ending to our most unusual meeting months ago," she teased, pulling her hands free to pat his chest. "One day I'm going to pay you back for the disgraceful way you threw me over your shoulder like I was a sack of feed." The dimple in her cheek deepened with her infectious smile.

He couldn't help himself. He pulled her to him, bracketing her face between his hands. "You little nymph! I don't doubt you'll find a way somehow, and I'll be looking forward to it." He laughed, then planted a kiss on her cold lips, holding her there until she pulled back. His heart pounded thick and heavy. He liked this playful side of her and wondered at all the fun they were going to have together after they were married.

"I'll race you back, John. My face is freezing!" She whirled around and took off running toward the house, but he overtook her in two long strides and swept her into his arms to spin her about. She giggled as large snowflakes fell, covering them like a white blanket.

※

"I have something for you, Rachel." Molly held out a box.

Rachel shot her a quizzical look. "For me? Molly, you shouldn't have." Nevertheless, she eagerly tore off the wrapping and lifted the lid. "Ooh . . ." Rachel drew in a sharp breath and stared down at a bridal veil of tulle. "Where did you get this?"

"Take it out." Molly beamed proudly. "I made it myself."

"You did? Molly, it's too beautiful for words." Rachel held up the veil, admiring the tiny stitches and frothy tulle attached to a satin-covered hair comb.

"Thank you. I hoped you'd like it. Let's put it on so you can see what you look like. The shop is quiet." Molly placed the veil on Rachel's head, securing the comb in her hair and fluffing out the layers of tulle. She stood back to consider her handiwork, tapping her finger to her chin.

"I must say, I did a fairly good job for my first bridal veil. See what you think." Molly twisted Rachel around to see in the mirror.

Rachel stared at her reflection with a huge lump forming in her throat. She hardly recognized herself. "It's pure loveliness," she said, fingering the delicate tulle touching her shoulder and trailing down her back.

"Just think how gorgeous you will look with the entire wedding outfit!"

Rachel burst into tears as she reached for her friend and hugged her tightly. "Thank you, Molly. I'm so touched, words don't seem enough. You are definitely a worthy partner for Estelle's millinery shop. But you'd better watch out. I think you'll be asked to create more of these when the ladies see it." She drew back and Molly's face blushed with pride. Rachel was so glad they'd become good friends. She brushed her tears away with a hanky. "I guess I'm a little more emotional these days."

"It wasn't that hard once I set my mind to it, and it thrills me to see something I created on you."

"And I insist when it's your turn to marry that you will wear it too."

"That I will proudly do. How about we eat our sandwiches now? My oatmeal left me long ago."

"Good idea. And we can make a list of things to order before Christmas for the shop."

42

As her wedding drew near, Rachel found herself thinking more and more about her parents. Would they have given their blessing on her marriage? She hoped and prayed it was so. While her heart was so full of love for John and the life they were planning, she was somewhat melancholy about the wedding day itself.

Today she felt like taking the long way home, past her family's ranch. From her vantage point on the ridge road, she stopped Sal and twisted in her seat to gaze below. Memories of her childhood flooded her mind and heaviness settled over her. The ranch looked peaceful—and lonely. Though not a big house, it was still charming with a homey look to it. For a moment, she thought she saw a flash of blue in one of the front windows, but she decided she must be mistaken. She stared intently again to be sure, and when the window stayed dark, she shook her head. Maybe it was the memory of her mother in her blue dress. But it was just a memory, nothing more.

Rachel sighed, then picked up the reins—and once again

saw a blue dress out of the corner of her eye. Surely she was mistaken. The place was deserted. She could ride down there, but it would be dark soon, and what if someone *was* there? Best to tell John and let him investigate. *If there's anything but my mind that needs investigating.* She chuckled to herself.

As soon as she drove up to the McIntyre ranch, Levi appeared at the barn door. "I was wondering when you'd drive up. You're later than usual, especially in this cold," he chided, helping her down. "Why, I had to break the ice in the trough today to water the livestock!"

"Sorry to keep you waiting. I took a little detour by my family's ranch. I know Slim probably has supper on the table for you by now. By the way, you wouldn't happen to know if John has rented out my family's—I mean, the ranch—do you?"

Levi pushed his hat back, scratching his forehead where his hat band left its imprint. "Naw, don't know nuthin' about that, but John don't tell me everything. Why do you ask?"

Rachel opened her mouth to explain but changed her mind, lest he think she was a little touched in the head. "Oh, no reason. I was just curious, that's all." She gave him a wave, then scampered across the distance to the house in search of John.

John was in the parlor with Estelle, stoking the fire in the grate, but he turned around when he heard her come in and flashed her one of his big grins. "I was beginning to get worried about you."

She got right to the point. "John, I drove past my family's ranch on the way home. I believe I saw someone in the house—or at least I thought I did."

"What? There's no one living there. I haven't rented it." He glanced over at Estelle, who shrugged and seemed surprised, then bent back down to lay another log on the fire.

"Perhaps a vagabond passing through for the winter? What if they start a fire or something?"

John straightened and placed the poker back in the stand on the hearth, regarding her. Placing his hands on his hips, he said, "Tell you what, I'll ride over now before supper and see if everything's as it should be."

"I'll ride with you in case—" Rachel began.

"No, dear. I need you to address some envelopes for me." Estelle looked around at the desk that was closed up.

"Can't that wait until after supper?"

"Well, no. You see—"

"I won't be long, and you don't need to be out in the cold again. We don't want you getting sick before the wedding. So stay put, my sweet." John gave her a brief peck on the cheek, then strode to the foyer. She followed, wondering if she was leading him on a wild goose chase. He threw on his coat and hat, but it seemed to Rachel that he wasn't the least bit concerned.

"All right." She reluctantly nodded in agreement. "Be careful."

⁂

He almost felt guilty, but he didn't even bother riding over to the ranch. He knew what Rachel had spotted, and it was not a figment of her imagination. He ambled along the lane away from the house, thinking they'd have to be more careful. He wanted everything to work out perfectly, but how was he to know she'd take the long way home today of all days? He shook his head and his chuckle floated on the frosty air.

One thing was for certain, life wouldn't be dull whenever Rachel was around. But somehow, he had to keep her away from the ranch house.

He turned back after a few minutes, not wanting to miss supper, when he saw Clay wearing a blue shirt and walking toward the bunkhouse.

"Clay!" John called out, and he turned around and stopped.

"Boss, I just returned from the ranch and did what you told me to do. Is there a problem? 'Cause if there's not, I'm downright starving."

"I won't keep you, but no. Not a problem really, but I think Rachel may have spotted you at the ranch house late today."

"She did? I tried to be real careful and took my horse out back by the trees."

"Seems she was missing her parents and rode by on the way home from work. It's nothing that could've been foreseen, so don't worry. Just tell the rest they need to be as inconspicuous as possible."

Clay thumbed his finger to his hat. "Got it."

"I sure appreciate what you men are doing for me, Clay."

"Glad we can be of help. We all have our own unique hidden talent." He chortled, then with a wave, sprinted off to the cookhouse.

Moments later, Rachel met him at the door. "Well? Was I seeing things? Or did you find a vagrant holed up there?"

He removed his coat and hat and looked down at her sweet, earnest face. He wanted to kiss the worry away from her brow. Instead he shook his head.

"Nope! Didn't find a thing there." He didn't feel too badly about his answer. There wasn't anything there. He tried to keep a straight face.

"Whew! That's a relief. I reckon it was only my daydreaming about the past. My mama wore a pretty blue dress." She hooked her arm in his as they strolled to supper.

"Seems a waste to let it sit, but I can always rent the ranch."

Rachel smiled up at him, her small, even teeth peeking out from a pink mouth. Staring too long at her would make it hard not to steal a kiss, so he changed the subject.

"Did Molly finish altering your gown?"

"Yes, and she did a wonderful job." They entered the dining room where his grandmother was already waiting.

"I was just about to ask you that. I'm glad she was able to do it," Grams said.

John pulled out Rachel's chair, then took his seat. "It was a good decision you made, Grams, making those two talented ladies your business partners."

"Oh, I almost forgot. Molly made me a beautiful bridal veil to wear," Rachel exclaimed.

"How very thoughtful. You two will be lifelong friends, I'm sure. I can't wait to see it, but of course we mustn't let John." She smiled, then turned John's direction and asked, "Will you say our blessing?"

John blessed the food, adding a few things of his own. "Lord, thank You for all You have favored me with and for my wonderful Rachel. I'm grateful for Grams's good health and for mine. I pray Your continued blessing on our family, and may we pour it back into others' lives. Amen." When John finished, both his grandmother and Rachel were sniffing into their napkins.

☙❧

Mouthwatering smells of cinnamon and other spices wafted up the stairs, filling the house, and Rachel smiled to herself. Annabelle had been cooking the last couple of days in preparation for the wedding and Thanksgiving. Excitement crackled in the air, and Rachel had taken half of her Saturday off from work to spend the afternoon deciding what things to pack for the short trip they would take after they were married, less than a week away. John had told her he wanted them to be alone for a few days before starting their life at the ranch. She had no idea where they would go—maybe Bozeman—but anyplace with him would be glorious. A pleasant tingle shot through her spine at the thought.

She folded the delicate white linen gown and robe Estelle had given her, then made certain her two best dresses were neatly folded before laying them in her suitcase. She'd never taken a real trip before and was surprised at how much she was looking forward to it. *Who knows, maybe one day we'll travel to Europe.* She hoped so. It would be exciting to see the places she'd read about in books.

When Rachel finished packing, she decided a cup of hot cocoa by the fire would be good. Downstairs was strangely quiet. Neither Estelle nor Annabelle were anywhere to be found, so she strolled into the kitchen to make the cocoa herself. She heated water, milk, and sugar together, then when it was hot, poured the mixture over cocoa powder. She was about to carry it to the parlor when she heard laughter, then Annabelle and Estelle talking in low voices as they swept through the kitchen's back door.

Their chatter immediately stopped when they saw Rachel. "There you two are! I was just about to sit by the fire with my cocoa. Would you care to join me?"

Estelle looked at Annabelle, who twittered something back to her, but Rachel couldn't hear what she said.

"Give us a moment and we'll meet you in the parlor. Annabelle can make a cup for us. You go on ahead and enjoy yours while it's hot."

Rachel hesitated. "Okay. I think I will if you don't mind."

"We insist," Estelle said without removing her coat. "We'll be along directly."

Rachel shrugged, then went through the door and down the hall to the parlor, wondering what the two of them were up to. Something about the way they were acting was strange, but she decided if they wanted her to know, they'd tell her.

She set her cocoa next to the wingback chair by the hearth, then stoked the fire before settling down in her chair. Sipping the cocoa by the warmth of the crackling fire, she felt altogether content. It was an opportunity to catch her breath and reflect on all the planning of the past few weeks for their small wedding. Rachel could hardly believe she would soon become Mrs. McIntyre! Would people think more highly of her now? Could she make John happy for the rest of his life? Would she be enough for him forever? *That's a lot of years to work at keeping one person happy and in love.* Did love always last a lifetime? For her parents it had.

Sudden doubt filled her head, gripping her heart in fear. She and John hadn't known each other all that long—even though they knew each other as children. What if she was wrong about him? She shook herself, banishing those thoughts while she finished her cocoa. It was simply too hard to think about the far-off future. She must concentrate on where she was today and let God handle the rest, because she was certain He had brought them together—when she'd been lonely, afraid, and without any hope for the future.

Rachel heard Annabelle and Estelle coming, and their talking filled her heart like warm sunshine on this cold afternoon. Soon all three were enjoying the cozy afternoon, and they were still chatting away when John joined them.

"Shall I make you a cup of cocoa?" Annabelle rose from her chair.

"I hate to interrupt. You all look like you're having such a nice time chatting."

Annabelle walked over and pinched his cheek, red from the cold. "It's never an inconvenience to do something for you. Sit down, and I'll be back before you can rub your hands warm over the fire."

"Yes, ma'am!" he answered, and she scurried off.

Estelle beamed at her grandson and then Rachel. "This is such a treat. It's nice to get things done today in time to relax by the warm fire."

John leaned toward the flames with his hands outstretched, warming them. "I got to thinking earlier . . . did you invite Vera and Beatrice to the wedding?" he asked, glancing over at Rachel.

"I did. I hope that's all right with you. If it makes you uncomfortable—"

He shook his head. "Heavens no, as long as *you're* not uncomfortable, Rachel. I was hoping you would. They're our neighbors, and Beatrice seems to have found her future with Wyatt."

"Me? No, not at all. I hold no ill will toward Beatrice."

John stepped over to her chair and reached down to squeeze her hand as Annabelle returned with his cocoa.

Estelle said, "I invited some young ladies from church. That will give the cowboys someone to dance with, or perhaps they'll get to know each other better. It's a lonely life for a cowboy, you know."

John chuckled. "Grams, I know. That's part of the reason I wanted to give the hands some land. It's an incentive to begin thinking about their futures while they're young. You're never too young to plan." He sipped his cocoa, looking thoughtfully over the rim of his cup at Rachel and smiling.

She smiled back. "Why don't you sit down here in my chair and I'll move to the settee, John, so you can get warm?"

"I am warm, but I have a better idea. How about you and I sit together on the settee and let Annabelle enjoy a few moments by the fire before she begins what I know will be a delicious dinner?"

Annabelle laughed but gladly took Rachel's seat while they moved over to sit on the settee. "I want to take a minute to tell all of you how much I appreciate the way you've always treated me as part of the family in your home. I'll continue to be the cook when you're married, John, unless Rachel wants to take over. It won't hurt my feelin's none and I'll understand. Either way, it's okay with Slim."

"Rachel, this is totally up to you. As the new head of the household when you marry John, and rightfully so, you will be making the decisions. I'm only the grandmother." Estelle gave a nod to Rachel.

"Me? Well, I can't assume to take your place, Estelle, but neither do I want you to leave, Annabelle. It's not my desire to change that. Besides, I have a job." Rachel shook her head, then looked at John for approval. He smiled warmly.

"I want whatever makes you happy, Rachel," John said.

"You won't be taking my place, Rachel," Estelle added, her face softening. "It's your rightful place, but I'll still be grandmother as long as you and John will have me, or I can move into town."

"Don't do that! We want you here, don't we, John?" Rachel protested.

"Of course we do," he answered with a gleam in his eye directed at Estelle.

"Then it's settled! Annabelle and I will continue on as before," the older lady affirmed.

Rachel pondered being the head of the household—with John. She'd never thought of herself in that way, but yes, she would be making decisions she'd never made before plus maintaining a partnership in business. *Can I do it all?* Rachel prayed she was up for the challenge until children came, and determined to do her best to make John and Estelle proud that she'd entered the McIntyre family.

43

"Everything's been taken care of. So quit worrying," Estelle told her grandson when she saw the creases in his forehead. "Jeffrey even told me that the bell he ordered will be hung in the church tower just in the nick of time."

John stuck his thumbs in his jeans pockets, rocking back and forth. "I want the bell to ring before and after the wedding. Did you remind him of that?"

"Yes, I did. Annabelle and Molly will decorate the altar with candles and ribbons. It's going to be lovely and so is your surprise." She paused, watching his face relax. "Have I told you how delighted I am that you are going to marry Rachel? I knew from the first time she was at our dinner table that you were perfect for each other. She's very bright, energetic, and capable, but the best thing is she loves the Lord. As your grandmother, I couldn't ask for more."

He laughed. "Is that so? I can't argue with you there. You were always the wise one in the McIntyre family."

"And so I am . . . which leads me to another thought altogether. I've been worried about your health ever since you had that bout of pneumonia. You seem to have less energy than before. Are you holding something back from me?"

A strange look crossed his face at her question. Though he tried to recover, she knew he was surprised by her question. "No . . . ," he began to answer quietly.

"John, please humor me," she pressed, taking a step closer. "I need to know. You know my secrets—now I need to know yours."

He shifted on his feet, folding his arms across his chest. "It's only a small thing, honestly, although I was worried that Rachel might not want to marry me."

Estelle clutched her handkerchief to her mouth in pretend surprise. "What?"

"The doctor told me that my lungs were badly compromised and I'll never regain full strength again." He sighed. "But I'm hoping to prove him wrong. I feel my strength gaining more each day, and I'm going to do what I can to build it up and get better."

Estelle, tiny as she was, grabbed her grandson about the waist and hugged him as hard as she was able while he patted her on the back soothingly. "Oh, I'm so sorry, John. I do know Rachel will love you no matter what—as do I." Then she leaned her head back to look up at his handsome face. "We also have the mighty power of prayer. Sometimes bad things happen to the best of people and we won't ever understand God's purposes this side of heaven." She released him and stepped back. "But we must never stop praying, never stop believing God is in control and He is sovereign. Don't forget that."

"I won't, Grams. I can promise you that. Now, you promise me that you'll stay around a long time."

She chuckled. "I'll do what I can."

❧

Thanksgiving dawned cold and cloudy with a definite threat of snow to come. Rachel tried to help Annabelle in the kitchen, but she wouldn't hear of it, so instead she helped Estelle set the tables with their best silverware, tablecloths, and silver candlesticks. With Levi's help, Slim removed most of the parlor furniture and set up several smaller tables for their guests along with the dining room table as the head table. It was a little cramped, but that way everyone could be in one room for dinner. The kitchen table was then placed in the dining room and covered with a pretty tablecloth to hold all the food.

John stuck his head inside the doorway of the parlor and perused the changes. "It's a transformed dining room now and looks fit for a king."

Rachel and Estelle both turned around when they heard him, and Rachel sashayed over to him to greet him with a quick kiss. "And queen, I might add," she teased. "It was Estelle's idea so we could all be in the same room together for the celebration."

"I stand corrected." He put one arm around her shoulders and squeezed. "Leave it to Grams to know exactly what to do and how to do it." Looking to Estelle, he said, "Is there anything you need me to do?"

Estelle walked over and looked across the parlor with satisfaction. "Mmm . . . I think we're about done here. Soon it'll be time to clean up and get ready for the wedding." She beamed with enthusiasm. "We mustn't be late."

"The snow has accumulated quickly, but we should have no trouble getting to the church," John assured them.

"I think I'll go upstairs now. Please send Molly up to help me with my dress as soon as she arrives." Rachel pulled away from John, blowing him a kiss.

"See you soon, my sweet," he said in a husky voice before blowing a kiss back to her that made Rachel's heart skip a beat.

❦

Rachel felt like a princess the moment Molly helped her into the gown and added the beautiful veil over her face. She wondered briefly if John would think she was beautiful. She got her answer when she started down the staircase to meet her groom at the bottom and glimpsed his eyes widen and jaw drop.

They barely said a word as they all left together for the church, and then Rachel heard the church bell pealing in the distance. She remembered Preston, and the bell helped it seem as though he were here with her today. He would've been so pleased with her choosing his best friend as her husband.

❦

It was a wedding and Thanksgiving Rachel was certain she would never forget. Full of friendships, gratefulness, best wishes, and delicious food. Even Vera and Beatrice minded their manners. Rachel was blessed indeed, and from the happy look on John's face, she could tell he felt the same way. As John shot her a conspiratorial wink then stood tapping his water glass for quiet, Rachel noticed Estelle watching her grandson with pride. Another thing to be grateful for—Estelle's continued good health.

"Today has been a very special one for me and Rachel, and also a time of thanksgiving for how we have all been blessed throughout the year." He paused, pulling envelopes from his coat pocket. "The good Lord saw me through a difficult time, and it allowed me time to reflect on many things. One of them was how ungrateful I had grown." He choked on his words.

"Anyway, this year I decided to do something very different to express my gratitude to my group of ranch hands. So I'll make this short. Curtis, Slim, Nash, Levi, Clay, and Billy— I debated with myself on whether to do this publicly but decided I wanted everyone to know what fine, loyal drovers you are. No crew works harder for their wages than all of you young men."

Laughter spilled across the room as the drovers pointed in the direction of Slim, the oldest one of the group, but he took it all in good stride and laughed with them.

John continued, "This is in no way to brag on what God has blessed me with. It's for you men. Will you please stand where you are?" He waited until the cowboys stood, as quizzical looks passed from one to the other.

"I want to give each of you men twenty-five acres of land to homestead."

A sharp intake of breath swept the parlor as the stunned cowboys stood wide-eyed in surprise and a buzz of chatter began. John waited until everyone settled down, then handed each one of them a deed. When he'd finished he said, "You're under no obligation to homestead, but take this for what it's meant—a gift. For the moment, I hope that you'll continue to work the cattle for me—then someday, do what you will. Build a cabin, homestead, grow a garden or raise a family. It's entirely up to you. If you don't intend to stay on here, you can move on. All I ask is that if you decide to do that, you will sell your land to another well-deserving man."

Curtis was the first to speak. "John, I'm mighty honored that you think this highly of us, and I'll gladly stay on and accept your gift. I've been hankering to settle down for a long time."

"Me too," Levi murmured, and the rest nodded their agreement and added their thanks to Curtis's.

"Let's celebrate then!" The men surrounded John with handshakes and slaps on the back in exactly the kind of camaraderie one would expect a rancher to have with his ranch hands, Rachel thought. She was deeply proud of her new husband, and suddenly thought back to the day he'd kidnapped her. All had turned out for the best in the end, and she had Preston to thank for that. How she missed him this day.

"Rachel." Fannie had been sitting next to Molly and Jeffrey, and got up from her chair to speak with her.

"Fannie, I'm so glad you could make it." Rachel beamed up at her.

"I reckon I got mighty curious to see this here wedding with the most eligible rancher around, so I decided to see for myself."

"And? What did you think?" Rachel almost laughed. Fannie had toned down her rouge and bright lipstick and must've borrowed the dress she wore. But it didn't matter what Fannie wore—only that she'd come.

"It was a right nice ceremony and this here is a purty good shindig. I feel somewhat out of place, but Molly and Jeffrey seem right friendly."

"I'm glad you approve."

Fannie nodded. "By the way, I finally got a short letter from Sue. Guess what?"

"I have no idea, Fannie. What did she have to say?"

"She wants me to come see her in a few weeks." Fannie bit her lip. "I'd like to, but—"

"If it's a financial burden, I can loan you the money for the trip."

She shook her head. "No, Rachel. I have some money saved." Fannie licked her lips nervously. "I'm scared to leave even for a short time. Bad things have happened to some of the gals. That's why I was so afraid for Sue. She's like a younger sister to me."

Rachel squeezed her friend's hand. "There's always a way, if you have the perseverance. We'll figure something out. I promise."

John returned to his seat next to Rachel, acknowledging Fannie, but she scooted away without a response. "Odd woman."

"Not really. Just one who's lost her way, and I hope I can help her."

"Oh no, here we go again." He rolled his eyes. "How can I help?"

Rachel smiled. "I was hoping you'd say that. I'll let you know, but not yet. This is our time."

"Right you are, my love." He tapped her nose with the end of his finger. "Let's go cut our cake."

※

It all passed too quickly—the vows, good wishes, and guests throwing rice while the church bell rang out in the distance. John settled Rachel underneath a thick robe for warmth in a beautiful red sleigh decorated with fresh greens, pinecones, and ribbons. He hopped in next to her, picking up the reins as they both waved goodbye to the smiling crowd.

311

Their new life began as the heavy sleigh surrendered to the horse's pull with a jingle of sleigh bells.

Rachel held tightly to John's arm and leaned into him for warmth, grateful she could openly do so now as his wife. Thick snow swirled and she thought it seemed magical. She could hardly wait to get to town to catch a stage to somewhere wonderful. But where she thought he'd turn off the road toward Bozeman, John veered a different direction.

"Mr. McIntyre, where might you be taking me?" she asked, leaning close to his ear so he could hear.

"You'll soon see, my dear, and I hope you'll be pleased." It was the only answer she could get, which only intrigued her more.

A mile farther, he stopped the sleigh on top of the ridge. She couldn't imagine why until she looked down into the valley and saw her parents' ranch home aglow with lights at every window and smoke coming from the chimney stack.

"John . . ." She was confused. The house hadn't been lived in for nearly two years but now looked welcoming in the swirling white snow.

With a click of his tongue and a tap of the harness, John set off wearing a broad smile, his sleigh sliding down the lane to the ranch. He stopped at the front of the house and leapt out of the sleigh. Scooping Rachel into his arms, he trooped up the wooden steps and pushed the front door open. The door flung backward, and John paused to look down at her while he held her.

"Welcome home, Mrs. McIntyre!" he said with a raspy voice. Their eyes locked and her heart pounded against her rib cage. He carried her over the threshold and let her slide out of his arms to stand gaping at the transformed house.

Gone were the cobwebs, peeling paint, broken glass, and musty smells. The home smelled of lemon oil and fresh evergreen boughs. The staircase had been rubbed with linseed until it shone in the candlelight. Thick new Oriental rugs adorned a new hardwood floor while a fire burned brightly in the parlor. In place of her parents' old furniture, new chintz-covered wingbacks sat on either side of the fireplace, and a solid deep-blue couch was flanked by walnut tables with heavy lamps atop them.

A tea cart waited as though recently prepared, complete with warm scones, hot tea, and thick clotted cream. Rachel squealed in delight as her eyes fell over every detail of the room, and John hooted at her reaction.

"I take it you are pleased?" His eyes danced with merriment.

"My, oh my. I don't know what to say." Rachel held her hand against her heart while tears burned her eyes. "It's beautiful, John. How in the world did you do all this?"

He walked over and drew her to him. "I had lots of help. The hardest part was trying to keep the surprise from you."

"Now it becomes clear—all the whispers between Annabelle and Estelle and your long hours away from the ranch."

"You're not disappointed that we won't be taking a trip out of town, are you? Or that I've changed everything here?"

Rachel stood on tiptoe and kissed him, taking her time before answering. When she heard him release a loud breath from his lungs, she stepped back. "Does that answer your question?"

"It'll do for starters." He grinned down at her.

"I think what you've done with my parents' home is wonderful."

"Then you're not mad at all the changes? I thought new furniture would make it feel like your own."

"No, I'm not mad. I'm delighted. Is this going to be our home instead of your ranch now?"

"Well, that all depends on you, but I thought for a few days we could cocoon here and not be bothered by anyone while we get to . . . uh . . . know each other better." His voice was thick and his eyes smoldering.

She threw her arms around his neck, interlocking her fingers. "I'm thinking you have a very creative side to you and I'm beginning to like it, Mr. McIntyre." He lowered his head down toward hers, his eyes full of desire while he kissed her—causing every nerve within her to come alive.

He released her finally and a slow smile spread across his face. "Let's have our tea and scones before I show you our bedroom. Sit there by the fire."

Rachel's gown made a rustling sound in the quiet as she took a seat and watched him wheel the tea cart close. She poured the tea while he sat down and stretched his legs in front of him. Flickering firelight danced across his face, and both of them appeared momentarily content to be right where they were—alone, without words, enjoying the stillness, the silent falling snow, and the crackling fire. After a few moments, she leaned over and, giggling, placed a tiny piece of scone in his mouth. A smile twitched at the edge of John's mouth and all thoughts of hunger disappeared.

Their eyes met.

His gaze softened.

Her breath caught.

His eyes swept over her.

She moistened her dry lips.

"I'd love to show you the rest now . . ." He loosened his tie, then waited.

"I'm ready. More than ready," she whispered with her heart beating wildly.

He stood then, closing the distance between them and tenderly reaching for her, allowing his fingers to trail the outline of her face, then down to where her pulse beat fast at her throat.

She took in a quick breath, staring at him with unabashed shyness as she placed her hand in his and allowed him to help her to her feet. He led her to their bedroom, where candles burned in the windows, above the mantel, and in every corner of the room—giving off a pleasant, sweet smell of beeswax with their glow. A bowl of oranges was placed on the nightstand next to a Queen Anne mahogany bed piled high with a fluffy white comforter and fine linens embroidered with the McIntyre initials, folded back in an invitation. A fire burned in the grate, casting a romantic glow across the room.

"Oh my . . . John, our bedroom is so beautiful," she whispered in awe, then noticed her nightgown ensemble lying across the foot of the bed and her slippers on the floor. "You've thought of everything. But how did you get my nightgown? I thought I packed it."

"You did, but Annabelle retrieved it," he answered with a twinkle in his eyes.

Rachel walked over to the bed and picked up her nightgown, then stopped when she saw a piece of paper flutter to the floor. John reached down and handed it to her, and she frowned with curiosity. "John—what is this?" she asked as she opened the thick paper.

"It's the deed to your parents' ranch. I want you to have it. It's in your name now."

Her eyes filled with tears and she flung herself into his arms. "But it's ours. Not mine. We're married now."

"No. I want you to do whatever you want with it. Rent it out, run it with some hired help—or we can live here for a while to begin our new life. Whatever you want."

She wiped her tears with the back of her hand. "I love you, John McIntyre!" She kissed him soundly and would've let go, but he crushed her to his chest, nipping at her lips, kissing her face and eyebrows until all she heard was his heavy breathing. John gasped for air, his hands trembling. His eyes burned and narrowed into slits gazing into hers.

"I love you too, Rachel. You've made me the happiest rancher alive today!" His hands pressed against her back, sliding up and down with caresses. "Turn around and let me help you with your dress," he rasped in her ear.

Rachel murmured her assent, her eyes drifted shut, and she was unable to speak. But this time, no words were needed. She would belong to John in the true sense of the word—body and soul—and all timidity began to melt away in the warmth of his embrace.

KEEP READING FOR A
SNEAK PEEK OF BOOK 3 IN

Virtues
AND **VICES**
OF THE **OLD WEST**

1

Love is patient, love is kind and is not jealous;
love does not brag and is not arrogant.

Gallatin Valley
Montana Territory
Spring 1866

Grace Bidwell pushed her way through the busy mercantile store in the bustling town of Bozeman, certain that it would be the most beneficial place to post a "Hired Help" sign for everyone to see. She had no choice in the matter—if Bidwell Farms was to remain in operation, then she must have help or they'd lose the small potato farm. As she looked for Eli, the store owner, several men moved aside to allow her room, grinning at her like young schoolboys. She felt her face burn from their obvious stares and tipping of their hats, mindful that other ladies in the store also turned to look at her. She marched on past, giving a brief nod to the ladies, most of whom she didn't really know. Grace hadn't had much time to entertain or be involved with the ladies' sewing circle—or anything else, for that matter—since her pa had fallen ill.

The mercantile was filled with everything anyone could need—farm implements, pots and pans, ready-to-wear clothing, and fabric, as well as household staples. Grace enjoyed the mingling smells of the various items neatly stacked or in barrels, and the wood-burning stove that was always burning—sometimes a roaring fire in the winter or a low-burning one during early spring to keep the chill at bay.

On her way to the front counter, she couldn't help but spy three grubby children standing near the glass case, peering at the delectable candy displayed inside. They looked to be ranging from ages four to eleven if she had to guess, but having no children of her own—a huge void that pained her sorely but God hadn't seen fit to fill—she wasn't the best judge of ages. The smallest one, a petite girl, wore a faded plaid dress, dirty in some places, and her hair was a mat of tangled golden curls.

Grace couldn't help but linger, watching the children while holding tight to her reticule and the notice she'd written. The middle child, also a girl, didn't look much better in her worn dress, which barely covered her calves. Her shoes were run-down with cracked leather and mud at the edges.

The boy, maybe the girls' oldest brother, yanked on their arms in frustration while holding a package beneath his own thin arm. "Come on! We've got to leave now." His dark hair covered most of his eyes and was in bad need of a trim. His pants, supported by suspenders, were extremely short, and he wore no socks with his brogans.

"Please, can't we get at least one peppermint stick to share?" the littlest one whined.

The older girl shrugged her thin shoulders. "Sarah, you already know that we don't have any money left, unless you intend to stay and sweep the floor for the owner of this place," she said, pulling her arm from her brother's grip.

"Maybe next time, Sarah, I promise you, but not today." The boy clamped his jaw tight.

"You have your package now, so you kids run along," a clerk said, shooing them in the direction of the door, right past shopping customers. They nearly pushed Grace to the side, and she rocked on her heels.

Grace quickly steadied herself, then was compelled to step in. "Please, let me buy the children each a stick of peppermint."

The children stood motionless, staring at her with large, disbelieving eyes.

The clerk paused, turning toward her. "Miss Bidwell. I, uh, didn't see you there. I'm sorry."

His weak apology was completely dismissed by Grace as she reached into her reticule and handed him a few coins. Turning, she smiled at the children.

"We can't let you do that," the young lad protested through narrowed eyes. From his shoulder bones poking up through his shirt, it looked as though he could stand to gain some weight, though adolescents were usually thin and gangly. Still . . .

"Why not?" the youngest one asked innocently.

He looked over at her. "Because we don't take money from strangers."

"Well then." Grace drew in a quick breath. "My name is Grace Bidwell, so now we're not strangers anymore. It's only

321

a small gift for you to enjoy this sparkling spring day. Tell your mama that I meant no harm."

"We ain't got no mama," he huffed, casting his expressionless eyes away from Grace's.

Grace nearly took it upon herself to correct the lad's grammar but thought better of it.

The clerk returned, handing them each a stick of candy, then, with a nod to Grace, went back to his work.

Grace frowned, noticing the older girl watching her closely. "I'm sorry." She was about to ask them their names when the lad turned to gather his sisters close, and all three of them clomped down the steps in an obvious hurry, disappearing from Grace's view.

Grace stared after them.

Eli strode over and tapped her on the shoulder. "Is there anything wrong, Grace?"

Grace turned around and looked into Eli's kindly older face. "Oh, no. Not at all. I was wondering about those children just now. I don't believe I've seen them around."

"Seems like I've seen the boy before, but then we have such an influx of folks in Bozeman, a man my age can barely keep up." He chuckled.

Grace waved a gloved hand. "Oh fiddlesticks! You're not old and still have plenty of vigor. I wish my pop did." Tears misted her vision, but she pulled her shoulders back and took a shaky breath.

"I'm really sorry about your pop," Eli said, his face softening. "What can I help you with today? Did you get your field ready for planting?"

She shook her head. "I'm afraid I haven't, and that's exactly why I'm here." She handed him the piece of paper. "I've written a notice to hire a helper with the farm. It's just getting to be too much for me after waiting on my pop and all." Grace thought about how her back ached from helping her father in and out of bed, and the thought of bending in the field all day made her wince, but she didn't mention it. "Do you know of someone needing work, or could I post this on your bulletin board? I'd be glad to pay you a fee."

Eli slapped his thigh. "I don't charge a thing for my board. I consider it a service to the community until we get a newspaper going." He smiled, his hands on his hips. "I can't think of a soul at the moment, but let's go nail it up right now and see what happens. There's always drifters or the like passing through."

"Well, as long as they're reliable. I need someone who's not afraid to work."

"Or someone who *has* to work and will work hard." Eli grunted.

"That's true. You are so kind, Eli, to me and Pa. Please stop over to see him soon. He misses you but hasn't felt well enough to take the ride into town like he used to. It's not easy for him," she said, following him to where the bulletin board hung next to the service counter.

"I'll be sure and ride over with the missus soon." He pinned the paper at eye level where it was noticeable. "Is there anything else today?"

"No, Eli. I appreciate this, but I'd better be getting back to the farm."

"You can repay me with some of that delicious huckleberry pie you make when I stop over." He grinned down at her.

"I certainly shall. See you soon, and thanks again." Grace waved to the clerk as she left, hope springing in her heart.

Before returning to the farm, she decided to stop by and say hello to her friend Ginny. Avoiding the deep ruts in the road, she crossed the street in her buggy, took a left at the corner, and stopped. She hopped out and looped the horse's reins around the gatepost, then stepped through the wrought-iron gate to ring the bell. As she waited, Grace admired the potted plants on the sprawling porch and the wicker furniture where she and Ginny had enjoyed much conversation and tea. Virginia, a Southern transplant after the Civil War, had married well—to a successful attorney, Frank—but she was down-to-earth with all her Southern charm, and once she and Grace had met at church, a fast friendship ensued. She insisted that Grace call her Ginny.

The door swung open and Ginny's smiling face greeted her. "Grace, I'm so glad to see you. Please come in," she drawled, then moved aside to let her enter.

"Are you sure? Is this a bad time?"

Ginny laughed. "It's never a bad time to see my friend." She led the way to the parlor, which was beautifully furnished in colorful tapestries with heavy Persians rugs and comfortable chairs flanking the fireplace.

Grace took a seat on the brocade settee and Ginny asked, "Shall I ask Nell to make us some tea?"

Grace shook her head. "I can't stay long. I needed to see another human face besides my father's or I shall go mad! I get so lonely sometimes." She stared at the fire in the hearth.

"My dear friend, I wish you'd come to dinner soon and meet Warren, Frank's new business partner."

"I know you mean well, Ginny, but I've seen him at church and I don't think he has any interest in knowing a widow."

Ginny nodded. "He does seem to have a flock of ladies around him, I'll agree, but he doesn't know what he's missing."

Grace laughed. "You are so biased, Ginny! But I love you for it. Now let's change the subject, if you don't mind. What have you been doing since I last saw you?"

Ginny frowned at her. "I'm on to you, Grace. You must put the widow weeds behind you now. Life is too short to spend all your time only taking care of your father. He can stay alone for a few hours. You simply must find a way to do something for yourself, and that should include eligible men, because you *could* marry again."

Grace chewed her lip and looked into her friend's eyes filled with genuine concern. "Maybe. I'm not sure I could ever love again. Losing Victor was the hardest thing I've experienced in my life."

Ginny reached over, patting her hand briefly. "I know, and I'm very sorry, but as your friend I feel like you trust me, so you need to get out a bit more—"

The sound of voices in the hallway floated within hearing. Ginny turned in the direction of the doorway. "Looks like you'll get to meet Warren after all."

Grace started to reply but Ginny put a finger to her lips. "Shh . . . here they come."

Grace's protest caught in her throat as the footsteps drew closer. She should've gone on home instead of stopping after leaving the mercantile. She wasn't in the mood to meet a man of Ginny's or anyone else's choosing. But to be truthful, she wasn't sure what she wanted.

Ginny rose from her chair as her husband approached. "My dear Frank, you're home early. Hello, Warren," she said to the gentleman next to her husband. He nodded hello and gallantly bent to kiss her hand, and she gave a slight giggle.

"You're spoiling my wife, and she's going to expect more

attention from me." Frank chuckled, then kissed his wife's brow. "Grace," he said, suddenly spotting her on the settee. "It's good to see you. You must meet Warren Sullivan, my new business partner." He turned to Warren. "This is Grace Bidwell."

"It's very nice to meet you," he said and stepped over to where Grace stood. His dark hair, shiny from applied pomade, fell across his forehead as he bowed, and a whiff of spicy aftershave hung in the air. He wore an impeccable and stylish pin-striped suit.

Grace murmured hello with a slight tilt of her head, mindful of his piercing dark eyes that held a hint of mystery as they swept over her. She wasn't sure if he was giving her a look of appraisal.

"I've heard lots about you—all good." He grinned.

"I was just telling her that we should all get together. How about dinner Saturday? Are you free?" Ginny asked.

"Great idea," Frank said, touching his wife's arm.

Warren turned to smile at Ginny. "Why, yes, I believe I am, but maybe you should ask Grace first."

Grace felt put on the spot. "Well, I'm not certain. I'll have to let you know, Ginny." She rose, clutching her reticule. "I really must be going now. I can't leave my father for too long."

"I'll walk you to the door," Ginny said, flashing her a conspiratorial smile.

Author's Note

Having been to Montana several times and having a brother who worked as deputy superintendent at West Glacier National Park, I'm drawn to Montana's history.

Contrary to popular belief, dance hall or saloon girls were not prostitutes. The term *saloon* alone may conjure up swinging doors, polished wooden bars, and dancing women. However, many of the saloon girls were women who had fallen on hard times and found dancing easy work, earning as much as ten dollars a week. Some were widows or needy women with good morals who were forced to earn a living when there were few options in the era of the Old West. They would sing and dance for the lonely men to brighten their evenings in the Western towns, where men outnumbered the women at least three to one. Most of them were considered good women by the men they danced and talked with. Despite what we see in the movies, most saloons didn't have swinging café doors, and those that did had another set of doors that could be locked. There were a few that had no doors at all since they never closed.

Paradise Valley was the original entrance to Yellowstone National Park and is separated by the Gallatin Range on the west and the Absaroka Range on the east. It seemed the perfect spot for my hero's cattle ranch, with its lush valley, bubbling creeks, and warm waters that keep the grasses green and abundant for cattle grazing. The Yellowstone River flows through the valley, which was a landmark for trappers and fur traders.

Because of Montana's unobstructed skyline that seems to overwhelm the landscape and its sparse population, its nickname, "Big Sky Country," was given by Alfred Bertram Guthrie Jr., a highway department employee, from his book *The Big Sky*. The slogan appeared on Montana license plates in 1967.

The town of Cottonwood is the second-oldest town in Montana but changed its name to Deer Lodge in 1864. Estelle's millinery shop was modeled after shops in the 1800s that were almost always owned by women. Milliners made hats, cloaks, hoods, shifts, and trims for gowns, and were skilled in sewing and fittings for their clientele. They were businesswomen in every sense of the word. Many times a milliner would advertise her imports, such as hosiery and shoes, in the latest haberdashery.

The cattle industry in Montana started in the mid-1850s. The blackleg disease John's cattle contracted resulted from mold spores in the ground after heavy rains. The disease causes lameness, fever, and loss of appetite, though it is not contagious. Animals usually died within forty-eight hours of contracting it.

The earliest account for treatment of blackleg—nitre every week in food—was in 1866, and if the animal survived, it would likely be permanently deformed. Since my novel takes place in 1862, I'm taking some liberty to say nitre was used. Nowadays, penicillin is the preferred drug, and in general calves are vaccinated at the age of three months, then two more times later on. Research shows that inactive mold spores can be in the soil for years and return to an infectious state after livestock graze.

Acknowledgments

I hope you'll indulge me once again while I thank my Revell editorial, marketing, and publicity team—Andrea Doering, Jessica English, Cheryl Van Andel, Lindsay Davis, Lynette Haskins, Claudia Marsh, Twila Bennett, and Erin Bartels. All who work behind the scenes to bring my stories to life—thank you all!

To Natasha Kern, my agent, and her insightful advice and knowledge of the publishing industry.

To my family, who are dearest to my heart and my reason for breathing.

To my forever friends, Connie, Linda, and Kelly.

To Him who lays on my heart the stories I write. Any talent I admit is from the Lord.

To my readers—it's for you that I write!

Maggie Brendan is a CBA bestselling author of the Heart of the West and the Blue Willow Brides series. Winner of the 2014 Book Buyers Best Award (OCC/RWA) for inspirational fiction and the 2013 Laurel Wreath Award, she was a finalist for the 2013 Published Maggie Award of Excellence and the 2013 Heart of Excellence Readers' Choice Award. She is married, lives in Georgia, and loves all things Western. She has two grown children and four grandchildren. When she's not writing, she enjoys reading, researching her next novel, and being with her family.

Maggie invites you to connect with her at www.MaggieBrendan.com or www.southernbellewriter.blogspot.com. You can also contact her on Facebook: www.facebook.com/maggiebrendan

Twitter: @MaggieBrendan

Pinterest: https://www.pinterest.com/maggiebrendan

Goodreads: https://www.goodreads.com/author/show/1682579.Maggie_Brendan

Instagram: https://instagram.com/maggiebrendan

Connect with

Maggie Brendan

★ ★ ★

MaggieBrendan.com

"Brendan delivers a charmingly quirky and endearing romance."
—*Library Journal*

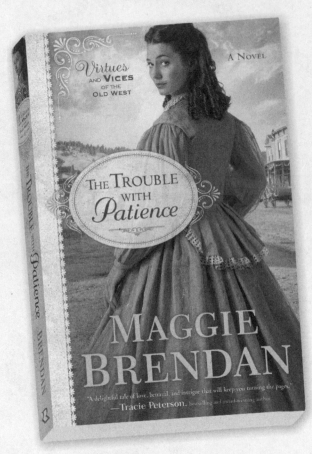

After inheriting a dilapidated boardinghouse in 1866 Montana, young Patience Cavanaugh negotiates an arrangement with the rugged sheriff to make repairs—and gets more than she bargained for.

Life on the American Frontier Is Full of Adventure, Romance, and the Indomitable Human Spirit

Heartwarming Tales of Mishaps, Hope, and True Love

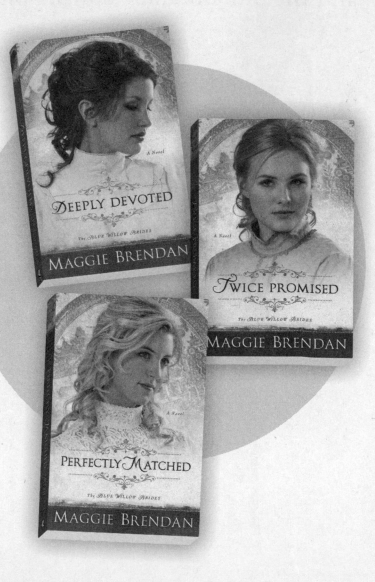